Praise for the Books

"Andi Grace is adorable, resilient, and has a doggedly curious need to solve a murder. A pleasure to read."

—C. Hope Clark, award-winning author of *Edisto Tidings*

"Completely charming—and exactly what a cozy mystery should be. Amateur sleuth (and dog whisperer) Andi Grace Scott is wonderfully endearing, and her devotion to her pooches—and to justice—will have you rooting for her from the absolutely irresistible page one. Bow *wow*—What a terrific debut!"

—Hank Phillippi Ryan, nationally best-selling and award-winning author of *The Murder List*

"I promptly fell head over heels for this cast of characters, and the dogs burrowed quickly into my heart. The plot of *Bite the Dust* was intriguing and complex, with plenty of surprising twists and turns. What impressed me the most, though, was the warm tone of the author's writing voice . . . you just want to snuggle in and keep reading."

—MeezCarrie

Books by Jackie Layton

Low Country Dog Walker Mysteries

Bite the Dust
Dog-Gone Dead
Bag of Bones
Caught and Collared

Caught and Collared

A Low Country Dog Walker Mystery

Jackie Layton

BEYOND THE PAGE
PUBLISHING

Caught and Collared
Jackie Layton
Copyright © 2022 by Jackie Layton
Cover design and illustration by Dar Albert, Wicked Smart Designs

Beyond the Page Books
are published by
Beyond the Page Publishing
www.beyondthepagepub.com

ISBN: 978-1-958384-56-5

Chapter One

THE WHITE CANDLE'S FLAME FLICKERED and local attorney Marc Williams held my hand. We'd found a quiet corner table at Tuscan Tomato, Heyward Beach's new hot spot for romantic dinners. Instead of sitting opposite of me, Marc sat to my right. On our left, couples occupied most of the tables. A few people might have been here on business, but there wasn't a child in sight. Soft jazz music played in the background. The aroma of garlic, tomatoes, and fresh-baked bread stirred my appetite.

"Andi Grace, how do you feel about setting a wedding date?" Marc had proposed to me weeks earlier, but we'd never found time to pick a date for us to get married.

"I've enjoyed being engaged to you, but I'm ready to set a date." My heart pitter-pattered. My life as dog walker Andi Grace Scott would change in amazing ways once we tied the knot. "I bought a wedding magazine, and it suggests we start planning twelve to eighteen months ahead of time."

"Whoa." Marc shook his head.

"You know I'm pretty easygoing, and Heyward Beach is a small town. If you're okay with an intimate wedding, I think we could get married this fall."

The smile that always turned my knees to mush appeared. "Now we're talking. I'd be okay if it was just the two of us."

I laughed. "Nate and Lacey Jane would never forgive us if they weren't included, but we can keep it simple." My siblings and I were tight. We'd survived our parents' deaths, and I'd skipped college to raise them. It'd be unforgivable to exclude them from such an important event.

"Su-weet. How much help do you want from me?" His eyes sparkled in the candlelight.

"Plenty if we're going to get married in five or six months."

A tall woman entered our area of the restaurant. She wound her way around the tables looking at the people dining as if searching for somebody. After surveying each person, she left our section for the bigger dining area.

Curious, I leaned forward to see if she found her possible date. "Do you know who that is?"

"No, I'd remember if I'd met her."

Our waiter appeared and obstructed my view of whatever was about to happen. He left a fresh basket of bread and two salads.

Marc passed the bread basket to me. "One day your inquisitiveness is

1

going to get you in hot water. And I mean hotter than ever before. When we get married, do you plan to quit investigating murders?"

"Smooth. I appreciate you aren't telling me not to investigate any more suspicious deaths." I took a roll and dabbed Parmesan butter on it before taking a bite.

"I know better. You look out for people in need, and I imagine you always will. Add to that your deep sense of justice, and you'll most likely help others if the occasion arises."

A commotion from the other room interrupted our conversation.

"Where's my dog?" a feminine voice shrilled.

All conversations around us ceased.

"Copper's at the house. Safe and sound." The masculine voice sounded amused.

Two waiters ran past us toward the uproar.

I glanced around the tables near us. Most all of the patrons were focused on the action. Soon the blonde zipped past us, red-faced and wearing a frown.

"Whatcha gonna do?" a man's voice boomed, and people laughed.

A pale-faced Regina Houp entered our room and paused when her gaze met mine. Her eyes narrowed, and she disappeared the same way the blonde had gone.

Marc said, "It appears Regina might be connected to the scene we overheard."

I swallowed hard. "You may be right."

A balding, round-faced, husky man sauntered past our table.

Marc nodded at him, and when the coast was clear, he leaned close to me. "That's Dirk Cutter, the radio personality and podcaster."

"Did you notice his shirt is wet?"

"Sure did. Almost like one of the women threw a drink on him."

"Yeah. It's too much of a coincidence the three of them just happened to leave right after the altercation if they weren't involved."

Our waiter appeared. "The owner apologizes for the scene. Dessert will be on us tonight, and your main course will be ready soon."

"Thanks," Marc said, and the young man left us.

"Let's get back to planning our wedding." I stabbed a bite of salad and lifted it to my lips.

"I'm proud of you, for not going outside to see if there's a fight in the parking lot."

"Hey, I'm not a complete busybody. I only snoop if there's a dead body."

"Good to know." He chuckled. "So a fall wedding?"

"Yes. I know enough people who will be happy to pitch in. If we keep the guest list to under fifty people, it's definitely doable."

We ate our lovely romantic dinner and only discussed wedding plans, but once I was home alone my thoughts returned to Regina Houp, Dirk Cutter, and the tall blonde.

How did Regina know Dirk? Were they dating? I yawned and headed upstairs to my bedroom where Sunny, my German shepherd, had already conked out. Who was the other woman, and why had she come to the restaurant believing Dirk knew where her dog was?

Chapter Two

FRIDAY MORNING, my best friend, Juliet Reed, and I stood near the Heyward Beach Pier. The May sun warmed us like a cozy hug. Eighty degrees and only a touch of humidity. I studied the crinkled list of clues in my hands. "We're almost done. Only two items left. Take a picture of a pelican and take another photo of a swimming pool." When my comment was met with silence, I looked at Juliet. She'd been distracted all morning. Happy, but unfocused. More than once I'd caught her reading text messages or looking off and humming country love songs. "Um, Juliet? Did you hear me?"

"Yeah. Take two pictures, then we go to the pier and turn in our clues and findings." She flashed me a radiant smile.

"Right." Something was different about Juliet, and I'd discover the answer. Later. At the moment, we had more pressing matters to focus on. Heyward Beach's first ever Beach Scavenger Hunt to promote tourism had brought a lot of people to the island. The grand prize was a week's stay in one of the beachfront homes. Local business owners had pitched in to help defray the cost to the owner. The more people who chose to vacation here, the better it'd be for all of us.

Juliet and I had spent the morning going from one place to the next, gathering items on the list and solving clues. Some of the challenges were to take pictures of specific things, like a street sign, boat, or a bike. Other tasks required us visiting various businesses, like Daily Java, where our challenge was to get a receipt for a purchase. The coffee shop owner had cut all her prices in half for the contestants. In addition to the local merchants participating in the scavenger hunt, the church had a team providing free hot dogs and soft drinks to anybody who stopped by.

Excitement filled the air. People laughed and waved to each other. The event appeared to be a success.

My German shepherd stood at attention between Juliet and me, as I looked up and down the street. "I know lots of homes have swimming pools, but which one has easy enough access to take a picture?"

"Should we go back to the mainland to the community pool?" Juliet's blonde ponytail bounced as she moved.

"No, the point is to promote tourism. Houses with swimming pools appeal to some vacationers, and the photos will go on social media promoting our beach."

"Then it'll probably be easier to take a picture of a second-row home with a pool." She pointed behind us, then quickly dropped her hand, but not before the sun sparkled on the familiar ring on her finger. The sight of my mother's ring on a different hand surprised me.

"Juliet!" I squealed and snatched her hand. "Are you and Nate engaged?"

Her face bloomed bright red, and she nodded. "We wanted to tell you together, but there was no way I'd take the ring off once Nate put it on my finger."

Juliet had been the poster child for patience, waiting on my brother to propose. I hugged her, and Sunny barked. "I'm so happy for y'all! Can you believe we're both engaged at the same time?"

She stepped back. "It's a dream come true." Her smile wavered.

"Is something wrong? Do you want to have your wedding first?" It'd be understandable. I hadn't waited years for Marc to pop the question. Still, after our discussion last night, my heart was set on a fall wedding.

Juliet placed both hands on her face and wiped away a few tears. "Is it okay that Nate gave me your mother's ring?"

There were very few earthly items left from my parents, and as a little girl I'd imagined wearing the vintage ring with an oval-cut ruby nestled between two diamonds. I was an adult now and had come to understand I wouldn't wear my mother's ring. Marc had given me his deceased mother's diamond ring, and Juliet deserved the one Nate had given her. "I'm happy you want to wear it."

"What about Lacey Jane? Will your sister mind?"

"Don't worry about her. Years ago, the three of us kids discussed that Nate should have Mom's ring in hopes his future wife would wear it every day. I plan to wear Marc's ring forever, and one day my sister will be the same way with her own husband." If my parents hadn't died so young, it wouldn't be an issue. Mom would still be wearing her ring. "Mom and Dad would've loved having you for a daughter, and now we will be family."

Juliet beamed. "Life is good."

"Yes, it is." There were so many times I'd worried Nate was going to ruin things with Juliet. Only a woman deeply in love would've waited over ten years from the beginning of her crush on my brother.

Sunny barked again, and I laughed. "I guess we need to get back to the scavenger hunt, but it's going to be so fun planning our weddings."

"I know! But you're right. We need to focus on solving the current clue.

Let's head that way." She pointed to Crab Street. It ran perpendicular to Ocean Drive and intersected with Sand Piper Way. "There are plenty of homes to the south with pools."

"Lead the way." We turned, and I followed Juliet while stuffing the list into the pocket of my khaki shorts.

Tires squealed and a car horn honked. I turned toward Ocean Drive, where the sound had come from.

A scraggly shih tzu shivered in the middle of the street.

My heart raced. Leaving Juliet and Sunny on the sidewalk, I ran to the frightened creature. "Hey there. Whatcha doing in the middle of the street?" I scooped the dog into my arms, waved at the driver, and rejoined Juliet and Sunny.

Juliet's eyebrows lifted. "Whose dog is that?"

"I don't know, but he needs a bath." I checked the tag. Sandy paws and matted hair screamed of neglect. Unless he'd been playing in the ocean. Either way, the poor thing was in desperate need of grooming. "The fancy dog tag says his name is Copper. He belongs to Olivia Caswell, and the address is here on the island."

Juliet looked at the tag, then gazed toward Ocean Drive. She pointed. "It's the house right over there."

"How convenient. Let's find the owner. Ms. Caswell better have a good reason for letting Copper run wild." I headed toward the raised periwinkle beach house. Allowing a dog to roam unattended was dangerous. Irresponsible pet owners grated on my nerves.

Sunny matched my pace. She was accustomed to me caring for other pets and never showed a bit of jealousy when I paid attention to another dog.

Juliet said, "Andi Grace, you need to calm down. What if the owner had a stroke or something bad? Give the woman a chance to explain."

"You're right." I counted to ten in French and crossed the street. Giving myself time to calm down and thinking of something more pleasant like Paris was a strategy I often used to control anger.

The driveway of crushed clamshells led to a concrete pad that extended under the house. The open carport contained two vehicles, storage areas, an enclosed shower, and two sets of outdoor stairs. "Let's try the front door."

"Look at the Porsche. It's a Macan. Probably 2018." For some reason Juliet was passionate about vehicles.

"Nice." Even I knew a Porsche was a fabulous car and expensive.

Sunny scooted past me, and I trailed her up the pricey composite stairs.

Juliet followed on my heels. "This place is nicer up close than you imagine from a distance."

"You're right." The home was probably worth over a million dollars. Beachfront property near the pier added to its appeal. We reached the front porch with white furniture to match the white railing and trim on the house. "Juliet, the door. Look. It's open."

"That explains how Copper got loose, but why is he such a mess?"

I paused at the entry. "Ms. Caswell. We've got your dog." My belly churned. Something felt wrong. Could the woman be sick?

Groups of people walked up and down the street, working on the scavenger hunt. Laughter and happy voices filled the air.

The little dog wiggled in my arms.

I reached in and knocked on the door. "Ms. Caswell? I've got Copper. Are you okay?"

My German shepherd entered the house, looked in both directions, then trotted up the carpeted stairs.

"Sunny, wait." I hurried after her. "Ms. Caswell, if you're home, I'm here with your dog, Copper."

No reply.

From the top of the stairwell, I looked down at my friend. "Juliet, maybe you should call the sheriff."

She'd remained standing in the doorway, but we could see each other. "On it. And I'm keeping watch in case the owner returns. No need to get shot while doing a good deed."

Sunny turned from the upstairs family room to a bedroom, and I followed her.

The sight of a heavyset woman with long bleach-blonde hair sprawled across a king-size bed stopped me in my tracks.

"Woof." Copper leapt from my arms and landed on the firm mattress. He licked the woman's face.

It was the same lady who'd caused a scene at Tuscan Tomato the night before. No, if the dog collar was correct, this woman was Olivia Caswell. Not Olivia Cutter. Yet, it was the same woman. What was going on?

She lifted her head. "There's my sweet baby. Where have you been?" Her groggy voice made me wonder how long she'd slept there.

"Ms. Caswell?"

"Ack!" She grabbed her dog and leapt from the bed. "Who are you? What are you doing in my house?"

"I found your dog in the middle of the street and wanted to return him."

"Why didn't you ring the bell like a civilized person?" Up close, I calculated the woman was over six feet tall. She was definitely the person who'd accused Dirk Cutter of having her dog.

"I called out to you more than once. You didn't answer." I clenched my hands. "Your front door was wide open, and Copper almost got run over. I rescued your dog and brought him here. You should be more careful."

"He's been missing." Her eyes narrowed. "Why is he such a mess?"

"I wondered the very same thing." The woman hadn't even thanked me.

A dog frantically yapped nearby. Despite the muted sound, I could tell the animal was agitated.

"Do you have two dogs?"

She shook her head. "No. Copper is mine, and Peanut belongs to my husband."

"Where is Peanut? He sounds desperate." Chills swept up my back.

"I put him in Dirk's office." She breezed past Sunny and me.

"Are you Dirk Cutter's wife?" I raised my voice, not wanting to be ignored.

"Yes." The word came out like a snake's hiss.

I followed, but at the top of the stairs waved to get Juliet's attention. "She's alive. No need to call Wade."

Juliet jogged up the stairs. "Good, because I had to leave a message on his voicemail. What's going on?"

"May I present Mrs. Olivia Caswell." I pointed toward the blonde, who banged on a closed door.

"Peanut, be quiet. When you quit barking, I'll let you out."

To my shock, her threat worked. How often had she threatened the dog on the other side of the door?

Olivia pushed the door open with her empty hand and snuggled Copper to her ample bosom.

A brown, black, and white beagle appeared with his nose to the ground.

Sunny barked at the other dog, who didn't give my German shepherd the time of day.

Interesting. A couple who each had their own dog, and they'd fought the previous night about one of the pets. Now Olivia had her dog, and Dirk's pet seemed to be tracking something. His owner? "Olivia, where's your husband?"

She shrugged. "How should I know?"

"But you're his wife, staying at his beach house. Er, your beach house?" The woman had lost track of her beloved shih tzu and her husband. Based on the scene at Tuscan Tomato, I didn't believe she was still in love with the man. How could she be with that much anger? If that was the case, it wasn't surprising she didn't know where Dirk was.

Olivia sighed. "We're separated. This is Dirk's place, and I live up the coast."

The beagle brushed past me at rocket speed, as if on the scent of something important.

My stomach somersaulted. There was definitely something weird happening, but what? I met Juliet's gaze. "Let's follow the dog."

Olivia didn't try to stop us. In fact, she was so enamored with her beloved pet, she didn't question our intentions.

Peanut raced down the stairs with Sunny on his heels. Juliet and I followed the dogs to the glass door at the back of the house.

An outstanding view of the wide beach and the Atlantic Ocean greeted us. A pod of pelicans flew by, skimming the waves with their wings and conserving their energy. The sight always gave me a sense of peace, and it did again today. At least until the beagle barked, and I glanced down at him.

Peanut nudged his nose against the door, so I opened it. He headed down the stairs and paused at the square landing. He looked toward the fenced-in grassy area at the bottom steps before turning his attention to the enclosed swimming pool area.

Sunny wagged her tail, then hurried to the gate leading to the pool.

I'd wrongly predicted Peanut needed to relieve himself. He joined Sunny, and I looked at the pool. From my vantage point, it was easy to see a man floating in the water. I gasped and ran to see if I could help.

Juliet had remained in the house but stepped outside when I entered the pool area. "What are you doing?"

I glanced back at her. "Call Wade, again, and an ambulance. There could be a drowning victim."

My friend gasped but swiped at her phone.

My body buzzed, in a bad way. This was Dirk Cutter's home, and the beagle barking at the pool gate was Dirk's dog, so it made sense the man lying facedown in the water was the famous podcaster.

Chapter Three

TWO KIDS APPEARED FROM THE CARPORT right as I opened the gate leading to Dirk's swimming pool. The boys looked like middle-schoolers. One was skinny with a pale complexion, freckles, and red hair. The other kid was taller with cornrows.

My breathing hitched, and my fingers gripped the top of the four-foot-high gate as it swung a few inches open. The kids were too young to witness whatever was about to unfold between the victim and me. "Guys, what are you doing?"

The kid with cornrows frowned. "Lady, we got here first."

"Please go somewhere else. You don't want to see this." My heart raced.

The boys whispered to each other.

The dogs pushed past me and ran to the deep end of the pool. Peanut stopped at the edge and howled. Seeing a dead stranger would be traumatic, but if the boys knew the victim, it'd be worse. "Do y'all know Dirk Cutter?"

"Who? We're here for the contest. You know. Picture of a swimming pool." The redhead shook his head like I was nuts.

Juliet joined us. "The emergency dispatcher is sending an ambulance, and I left another message with Wade."

"Handle these kids." I left her with the boys before heading to the body. Kicking off my shoes, I dropped my phone onto the nearest chair and dove into the deep water. Chilliness froze my limbs momentarily. Brr. Sunny barked from the edge of the water, no doubt telling me to move. I kicked and pulled the man to the shallow end using maneuvers I'd learned years ago during lifeguard lessons. His unbuttoned Hawaiian shirt floated on each side of his body, almost like angel wings. As soon as my feet touched the bottom, I flipped him over, hoping he might take a breath of air.

No such luck.

Peanut sat near the pool stairs and howled.

Screaming from the back porch drew my attention for a moment. Olivia. Then the kids hollered.

Juliet corralled the three hysterical people, and soon all was quiet except for Peanut.

I felt for a pulse. Nothing. His chest didn't move, but I listened near his mouth and nose for breathing sounds. Zilch. Neither did I feel his breath against my cheek.

Juliet reappeared. "Olivia is with the kids and watching for the ambulance or fire truck, whichever arrives first. Is he alive?" Her voice trembled.

"He's not breathing. We need to start CPR. Help me get him onto the pool deck." I anchored my arms under the man's shoulders. Juliet entered via the swimming pool steps. She secured Dirk's legs, and we lugged his big-framed body out of the water and managed not to drop him as we laid him on the deck. "Do you want to do the chest compressions, and I'll perform mouth-to-mouth?"

"Yeah." She placed her hands on his chest and started compressions.

For drowning victims, rescue breaths were mandatory. I lost myself in trying to save the older man. He was tan and in the bright sunshine it was easy to see his scalp through thinning hair. His body was cool to the touch, but the water had been cold. I wasn't ready to give up.

Two EMTs appeared and took over.

Juliet and I left them to the rescue attempt. We huddled together on an adjustable chaise lounge at the far end of the pool. Sunny lay at our feet panting, and Peanut watched the medics perform CPR.

Juliet folded her hands together. "Dirk Cutter, right?"

"Afraid so." Goose bumps covered my arms. The sun beat down on us, but I still shivered.

Juliet wrapped her arm around my shoulders. "We need to find a towel or something for you."

"The cops won't be happy if we leave." My teeth chattered.

Sunny paced from me to Peanut, as if unsure who needed comforting more.

"It's okay, girl. Take care of your new friend." I reached for my phone on the other chair. "You're right. I need dry clothes or something."

"Let's see what we can find."

"Maybe you should stay with the body. I'll hurry inside and look for beach towels."

"No, thanks. I'll look in the area under the house. That way I can check on Olivia and search for a towel." Juliet moved away faster than I did, but her clothes were dry and she wasn't too cold to move.

"Sounds good." I walked toward the back door.

"Just where do you think you're going?" a familiar deep voice questioned, and the angry tone stopped me mid-stride.

My next shiver had nothing to do with my cold wet clothes and everything to do with our local sheriff. He was *not* going to be thrilled to find me with another dead body. I turned and braced myself for the lecture that was bound to follow. "Hi, Wade."

His frown confirmed my suspicion. Sheriff Wade Stone's anger blazed from his eyes, but I wouldn't slink away. If Peanut hadn't needed rescuing, I wouldn't be here, nor would I have found another body.

Sunny must've sensed I was in trouble because she trotted to my side, leaving the grieving Peanut with the emergency personnel. Sunny whined like she did when she was in trouble. I patted her back then met Wade's gaze.

Deputy David Wayne appeared and stood beside the sheriff. They presented a united front. Two men against a woman and her dog. The odds weren't good. Not good at all.

Wade frowned. "Andi Grace, I seriously can't believe you. What are you doing here?"

The two law enforcement officers stepped over to where I stood on the platform outside the pool area and looked at me.

I was friends with both men, and David was my sister's boyfriend. Both David and Wade had earned my respect as officers of the law, but times like this pitted us against each other. I shrugged. "Would you believe it's the dog's fault?"

Wade shook his head. "I should've known you'd blame it on a poor dog. First, what's going on here? Do you know the man they're trying to revive?"

"I haven't officially met him, but it's Dirk Cutter. The radio man and podcaster." My teeth chattered, and I crossed my arms. Hard to believe I could be so cold on such a warm day. "Juliet and I were doing the scavenger hunt to promote tourism, and we heard a car honk. That's when we found Copper, one of Dirk's dogs, in the middle of the street. Er, Copper is officially Olivia's dog. Peanut belongs to Dirk."

David patted my shoulder. "Olivia?"

"Yeah, Olivia Caswell. She's Dirk's wife. Evidently each one of them claims to have their own dog. She doesn't think much of Peanut, the beagle over there." I pointed with a shaky finger toward the pool.

The look on David's face confused me. Compassion, maybe? Had dating my sister led him to feel like he needed to watch out for me?

Wade took notes on a small pad. "I guess the woman in the carport with the tiny dog is the widow. Are those their kids?"

"N-n-no." I couldn't quit shivering. "The boys showed up to take a picture of the pool for the scavenger hunt."

Juliet bounded up the steps from the carport and joined us. "An EMT is with Olivia, and I walked the boys to the pier. They're staying with Leroy Peck and Chip Johnson. Andi Grace, I didn't find any towels."

"Don't go anywhere." Wade left us and strode with determined steps to the people kneeling over Dirk.

David said, "Andi Grace, when did the kids arrive? Before or after you found the body?"

"After, I think." I turned to Juliet. "What'd they tell you?"

"They were here to take a picture of the pool." She shrugged. "They're old enough to participate without parents, but too young to see a dead man."

David's eyebrows rose. "Care to elaborate?"

Juliet shifted from one bare foot to the other. She'd only gotten her feet wet, and her red Chucks lay on the pool deck. "I didn't see them until after we'd spotted the body."

I filled David in on the events leading up to his arrival.

When I finished recounting the details, David spoke to somebody through his mic then met my gaze. "I'm glad you sent them to Leroy, but if Dirk Cutter was attacked, his assailant could be lurking in the shadows. The kids need protection in case they saw something. It could be a detail they didn't even realize they observed. Leroy may not be able to protect both boys if danger follows them."

"Chip Johnson's with Leroy. He seems like a nice guy." I shivered again. "You don't think this was an accident?"

David said, "If you're involved, chances are it's intentional."

"Hey, that's not nice."

"Sorry. But just in case there's more trouble, I sent another deputy to keep an eye on the kids until their parents arrive." He adjusted his sunglasses. "Are you okay?"

"I think so." From the corner of my eye, I saw a different kind of movement from the EMTs. David, Juliet, and I all grew still.

The female medic marched over and talked to Wade in a tone too soft to hear from where we stood.

Juliet scooted closer to me and clenched my arm. "It doesn't look good."

"No." A lump formed in my throat. How could this be happening again? If David's theory was correct, Heyward Beach had another murder.

Chapter Four

I STOOD AND STARED AT THE POOL AREA. Supported by my best friend and my loyal German shepherd, I braced to hear the worst. My heart thundered against my ribs. What was the medic telling the sheriff?

At last, the conversation ended. A tight-lipped Wade headed to us. David angled his body until the four of us formed a circle. Wade cleared his throat. "Dirk Cutter is dead. We're going to treat this as an official crime scene."

"Not an accident?" Why was I questioning Wade? I'd known all along someone had intentionally killed Dirk.

Wade shook his head. "The paramedic believes there's more to this than an accidental drowning. Andi Grace, I refuse to go into details with you and Juliet at this point. Consider it a crime scene, but don't tell the whole town. There's a possibility Dirk's death was an accident, but there's no need to contaminate possible evidence only to learn later the victim was murdered."

David patted my shoulder in a brotherly manner. "I'll be right back."

I met his gaze and nodded. Had my sister put her boyfriend up to being protective of me? How embarrassing. My thoughts returned to Dirk Cutter.

The fact a man died was bad enough, but another murder? Today was supposed to be a day of community fun. Our town had come together to build up tourism.

It'd been a great week up to this point. Nate had proposed to Juliet. Marc and I were beginning to plan our nuptials. Happiness all around, except for Dirk and his poor dog. Peanut sat beside his master and threw back his head, emitting the most pitiful howl. "Wade, what about Dirk's dog? Can you bring him to me? I'll take care of the poor little thing until you find this man's kinfolk."

"You don't think the wife wants the beagle?"

"No. Once you talk to her, you'll see what I mean." I tried to rub away the goose bumps on my bare arms. My damp T-shirt and shorts clung to my body.

Wade narrowed his eyes then sighed. "I need to verify your assumption with the wife. If she agrees, I'll let you take the lead with Peanut."

"Me? I'd rather you bring him to me." I didn't want to drag the pitiful beagle away from his human.

Wade shot me a glance. "You're the one who has a way with dogs.

Once we have the widow's permission, we'll get his leash in case we have to physically move him away from the deceased."

Juliet said, "Sunny and I'll wait here for you."

David reappeared and handed me a dry towel and a faded orange hoodie. "They're clean, and you need to warm up."

"Thanks." I blotted my hair then my clothes with the rough white towel before slipping the sweatshirt over my head. "I'm ready, Wade."

David said, "Juliet, let's sit on the front porch. You can give me your version of what happened."

My friend's shoulders drooped. If she was stuck answering questions, she wouldn't be able to call our loved ones.

"What about Mrs. Caswell? Shouldn't you question her? After all, she was asleep while her husband drowned." I wanted to buy Juliet time to contact Nate, Lacey Jane, and Marc.

"She's with another deputy." Wade motioned for me to move, and I followed, burrowing my hands into the front pocket of David's soft hoodie. The combination of warm and soft took the edge off my anxiety.

Deputy Levi Sawyer met us inside the great room. I studied the scene with fresh eyes. Both a chair and the glass-topped wicker coffee table had been flipped over. A lamp lay broken on the floor, and a pillow had been tossed to the side. How had I missed the mess earlier? How had Olivia not heard the struggle? Although, she hadn't heard my arrival and calling out her name.

The deputy was a few years older than me and a shade taller than Wade. More muscular than the sheriff too. He nodded at me before focusing on the sheriff. "The place is clear, sir. Looks like the victim didn't make it." He pointed toward the swimming pool.

Wade ran a hand over his face. "Yeah. Besides this chaos, did you find anything suspicious?"

The deputy crossed his arms. "Sure did. He's the podcaster, Dirk Cutter. His program, *Where Are They Now?*, is one of the fastest-growing podcasts in the nation. He also has a local radio program focused on unsolved mysteries in the Low Country."

I said, "*Cut to the Truth*. It's usually interesting. This week Dirk mentioned on his radio show that he had some big news. Today he planned to reveal the surprise on his podcast. Do you think it's related to his death?" I'd never heard a complete episode of his radio program, but I'd caught bits and pieces going to dog appointments.

Neither man answered my question.

Deputy Sawyer wrote notes on a little pad of paper. "You and Mr. Cutter both have an interest in solving crimes. The only difference is he did it for profit and fame."

"And me?" I held my breath, waiting to hear what the men would say.

"Not sure, ma'am."

"Please, call me Andi Grace."

Wade frowned. "Andi Grace, as far as I can tell, you really don't get anything out of it. Justice for all seems to be your thing. No doubt, if this is officially ruled a murder, you'll look into it too. No matter how much I try to object, you insert yourself into my cases."

My heart skipped a beat. The man understood my intentions. "Thanks for not calling me a busybody."

Wade harrumphed then looked at his deputy. "Without seeing the body, how did you determine the man is Dirk Cutter?"

Deputy Sawyer lifted his chin. "First thing I noticed was the wallet." He pointed to the kitchen counter, where sunglasses, a late-model cell phone, keys, and a black leather wallet lay. "Follow me." He motioned for us to trail behind him.

I looked from the wrecked living area to the kitchen counter. How could I have missed so many clues? It was a miracle I'd ever solved a mystery.

The three of us headed upstairs. With the sheriff and deputy, I wasn't apprehensive like the first time.

"As I was saying, if you go into the office right here, it's obvious the place belongs to Dirk Cutter." Deputy Sawyer left us standing in the recreation room, or whatever the open space was called.

I met Wade's gaze, and we proceeded to the office. Every area of Dirk's beach house had a casual beach vibe, but this space was modern and sleek. A shiny blue desk sat in the middle of the room. There was a lamp that looked like a rock with a lampshade on the corner of the desk. Clear acrylic shelves full of books lined one wall. A credenza painted light blue matched the stripes in the window treatments. There was a power cord but no computer. "I wonder where the laptop is."

"Don't even start." Wade scowled. "Why'd I let you come up here?"

"Um, maybe because deep down you know I have a knack for finding clues?"

Wade huffed then pointed to the door. "You're here to get the dog's belongings then take him with you. Let's go back downstairs and review your statement about what happened this morning."

I studied the office one more time, wishing I could snap pictures with my phone without making Wade mad. Instead, I retold my story to the sheriff while we walked down the stairs. Together we hunted for the dog's leash and food. When taking care of a new dog, it helped to stay consistent with food and treats. Peanut had suffered a trauma, making it essential not to change more than necessary. The last thing we needed was for Peanut to have an upset tummy. "We could just ask Olivia where the dog supplies are."

"Not going to interrupt her conversation with Deputy Harris."

"Oh, I'm glad you have a female officer with Olivia." Denise Harris was older and one of the first Black deputies in our area. She could be tough, but she had a tender heart. If Olivia was upset, Denise would be the perfect match.

"So glad you approve of my decision. Why don't you look under the sink for dog supplies?" He opened various cabinets.

I followed his suggestion and only saw a lined trash can and cleaning supplies. "No luck."

"Here you go." Wade interrupted my swirling thoughts and placed a basket on the kitchen counter. "One skinny blue leash that should work for one very sad dog."

"Great. Now to see if we can get him away from the body without provoking him to attack us." With the leash in my hand, I snatched some dog treats out of the brown wicker basket and hurried to the pool area. No telling how Dirk's death was traumatizing the dog.

I paused before entering the pool area and surveyed my surroundings. Sun high in the sky, water pounding the shore, body covered with a sheet, and medics sitting in white lounge chairs. I stepped forward.

The bald man said, "We didn't want to upset the dog more than necessary, so we're just sitting here."

"Thanks for giving me time to work with him." I moved beside the beagle lying down with his paws covering his head. I sat on the warm deck and patted the dog's side. The sunny day didn't match the somberness of the moment. "Hey, boy. I know you're sad."

Peanut didn't flinch.

"It's going to be okay. I'll take care of you and find you a good home." I hoped Olivia wasn't interested in caring for Dirk's dog. Not likely, gauging from her earlier behavior.

For the next few minutes, I spoke to Peanut in soothing tones. Finally, his body didn't look quite so tense. "Let's go for a walk."

He turned his head and gazed at me.

I attached his leash, stood, and held out a treat. "Come on, Peanut."

The beagle stuck his rump in the air and ever so slowly raised himself to a standing position. His legs wobbled. I gave him the treat, and we walked away from Dirk's body. We puttered past Wade and down to the grassy area. The dog sniffed around and gazed through the slotted fence toward the Atlantic Ocean.

"Hey, boy, are we kindred spirits? I always feel better at the beach."

Wade appeared and leaned against the brown composite fence. "You got anything else to share with me?"

I inhaled the briny air and rewound the last hour in my mind. David's hoodie kept me from shivering in the breeze. "The missing laptop and the widow concern me. Be sure to question Olivia about the commotion last night at Tuscan Tomato. How did she wake up here after the altercation with her husband? I can't think of anything else."

"Okay. Great. Do I need to remind you that we're handling the investigation into Mr. Cutter's death? If anything else occurs to you, run it by me. Please don't go around questioning suspects." He lowered his aviator sunglasses and made eye contact.

I didn't blink. "No need to worry about me. I've got a wedding to plan and a potential dog groomer to interview."

"I'm glad to hear it."

"My shoes are by the pool, and so are Juliet's. If you don't mind grabbing them, I'll get out of your way."

It didn't take him long to collect the shoes. "I'll drop the dog's food off at your house when we finish up here."

"Thanks, Wade. Tell David I'll return his hoodie after I wash it. See ya later." I pulled on my shoes and led Peanut to the driveway.

"I see you convinced the dog to leave the man's body." Juliet and Sunny appeared from the shade of a palm tree, startling me. "Thanks for retrieving my shoes."

"You can thank Wade later." I passed the red Chucks to her. "Where's David?"

"Inside with Deputy Harris and Olivia Caswell. I think she's going to be a suspect."

Sunny stood on alert beside Juliet.

"I'm not surprised. Why don't we go check on Leroy and the kids?"

Juliet crossed her arms. "I don't know what Wade said to you, but David told me not to mess with their investigation."

"Yeah, I got the same lecture. I only want to say hi."

"Andi Grace, you look a fright. Your hair and clothes are damp, the sweatshirt is old and faded, and your mascara is smeared."

"David loaned it to me." A middle-age couple walked by and stared at us. I smiled and waited until they couldn't hear us. "It may be old, but it's warm."

Juliet stepped closer to me. "Let's go back to your house before people start talking."

My friend made a good point. "You're right. It won't take long to run home and change. Come on." It'd also give me time to collect my thoughts on the death of Dirk Cutter. What was the motive if he'd truly been murdered? Even if I didn't help Wade catch a killer, it couldn't hurt to take notes and gather my own evidence. Nothing official and nothing to take away from planning my wedding.

Chapter Five

IT TOOK LONGER AT THE HOUSE THAN I'D PLANNED. Juliet played with Sunny and Copper outside while I ran upstairs to change.

Many days I had to pinch myself to believe my luck at living in such a nice house. If possible, I would've been content still living in my former little home. The previous owner of this house had been murdered on the beach, and her daughter had made me a deal too good to ignore, especially since I'd just become homeless. My new place didn't lack for modern conveniences, but it wasn't exactly my style. One of the first projects I'd tackled was to paint the master bedroom walls a soft turquoise blue. A lattice-patterned throw carpet added warmth to the floors. In time I'd have my personality stamped in every room.

A speedy hot shower and slipping on dry clothes invigorated me. I was prepared to tackle the rest of the day. "Juliet, are you ready?" I ran down the stairs.

When there was no reply, I looked out back. "Ready?"

Juliet sat in a wicker chair on the covered patio and held Peanut in her lap. Sunny looked at me with her ears pointing straight up. "Do you think he's house trained? Is it safe to leave him home alone?"

"Peanut's had enough excitement for one day. Let's get him settled in one of my spare crates." I'd converted the back study into a casual office for myself. There were a couple of extra crates in there, and I readied one for the beagle. "Here you go, Peanut. Sunny will stand guard and make sure you're safe."

Juliet placed the smaller dog in the crate, and I shut the door. "Sunny, you're in charge. We'll be back in a while."

Peanut whined.

"Andi Grace, he's so pitiful. Are we doing the right thing?"

I looked at the beagle. "Uh, you're right. He's been through so much today."

Juliet let the dog out, and he tilted his head.

Sunny lay on the rug beside the now empty kennel. "Peanut, lay here. You'll be okay."

Peanut curled up next to my German shepherd, and we slipped out of the room, closing the door behind us.

Juliet's fingers flutter-patted her chest. "I feel so much better now. He about broke my heart."

"I know what you mean." We walked down my front stairs, and I paused in the driveway. "Between the scavenger hunt crowd and law enforcement around Dirk's beach house, I think it'll be quicker to walk to the pier than try to find a parking place."

"Yep, I agree." Juliet stayed at my side, and we strode toward the beach. "Did you learn anything when we weren't together?"

"Wade told me not to blab about it, but there was a struggle in the family room."

"How'd we miss that?"

"We were focused on Peanut, then the body." I described the disarray. "I also got to see inside his office. It's in good shape, but I didn't see his laptop or any kind of computer."

"Do you think the murder was the result of a robbery gone horribly wrong?"

A large SUV stopped in the middle of the road, allowing us to cross the street. A group of giggling teenage girls hopped out of the vehicle and reached the sidewalk before us. I slowed my pace, and didn't speak again until we were alone. "Dirk's watch, wallet, and phone were sitting on the kitchen counter in plain sight. If it was a regular robbery, why not take those things?"

"I see your point. We'll rule out burglary and robbery. Did Wade agree?"

I kept my voice low. "He wants to treat it as a crime scene just in case."

"Andi Grace, I'm sure your wheels are turning. What do you think about the death?"

"Once you rule out accident and robbery, I have questions. Why murder Dirk Cutter? And why here?"

"Where do you think he should've been killed?"

I pulled her into a band of shade in a pebbled driveway. "Did Dirk live here, or was this just a vacation spot? I saw him around town, but not often. At least not often enough to consider him a local."

"Some guests at the B and B mentioned meeting him on the beach a few weeks ago. Do you think he was renting the beach house?"

I shook my head. "No. Did you notice the name of it?" Many people on the beach gave their places charming names, like Beach Blessing, Island Time, Shore Thing and other cutesy titles.

Juliet's eyes widened. "Yes. The sign on the front of his place is a sailboat, and it says Cutter's Landing. Dirk Cutter. Wow, I completely missed the connection."

"We both did. So, I believe he owned the house." I flashed back to my conversation with Olivia. "His wife also mentioned it's Dirk's place. We have officially answered one question in my investigation."

Juliet nodded. "While you showered, I texted Nate, Marc, and of course Lacey Jane. We don't need another lecture from your sister for leaving her out of the loop."

"That's for sure." It'd happened more than once. "What did they say?"

She waved for me to follow her to the sidewalk, and we returned to walking. "Nate's in Georgetown landscaping a museum. Lacey Jane didn't reply, but Marc's going to meet us at the pier."

My heart swelled with love for Marc. When he proposed, I already knew he was the man I wanted to spend the rest of my life with. For better and for worse, and dealing with suspicious deaths fit the *worse* category. "I think Lacey Jane has a final today."

We crossed the street near the pier.

"Andi Grace!" Marc's deep baritone brought tears to my eyes.

Hold it together, girl. I waved to my fiancé. Six-foot-three-inches with dark blonde hair, the man was the picture of calm in a crisis. His gray eyes met mine from a distance. I opened my mouth, but words failed me.

Marc jogged my way wearing a black suit and a crisp white shirt. No tie.

Juliet said, "Don't you start crying, or I'll be blubbering too. I'm heading over to Leroy." She dodged people in the crowd.

"Be careful, Juliet." I watched Marc, and the tingly sensation in my belly appeared. After all the months we'd dated, he still had a powerful effect on me.

"Are you okay? What happened?" Marc placed his hands on my shoulders, and he looked me up and down.

"Juliet and I were doing the scavenger hunt. What could be more innocent?" My voice cracked.

Marc pulled me into his arms. "I'm so sorry, Andi Grace. I called Wade on the way over. He said you found a man floating in his pool. How?"

I absorbed his strength. He smelled of coffee mixed with something spicy. "Juliet and I were returning a lost dog to his owner. The man we found is Dirk Cutter."

"The *Cut to the Truth* guy on the radio? We just saw him at the restaurant last night."

"Yeah." I shared everything I knew about the man's death. "Two boys showed up and saw the body also. Juliet and I are here to check on them. Do you mind if we look for the kids?"

"Sure." He kept his arm around me while we walked to the table, where Leroy and Chip Johnson stood collecting lists from the participants of the scavenger hunt.

During a lull in the action, I waved to Leroy. "Hey, do you know what happened to the boys?"

The older man removed his fishing hat and ran a hand over his freckled head. "Juliet took them into the pier diner to get hot dogs and Cokes because they claimed to be starving. Their parents are on the way from Charleston. It's a long story, but they're fine."

Tension eased from my shoulders. "I knew they'd be safe with you."

"Andi Grace, have you met Chip Johnson? He's my landlord."

The tall, thin man with a long nose patted Leroy's back. "Hey, now. We're friends who just happen to share a duplex."

"We've met before, but it's good to see you, Chip. I heard you're going to let Leroy have a dog in his place."

"Yes, ma'am." Chip acted like I was older than him, but if I had to guess, he was at least forty.

I gritted my teeth and forced a smile. Maybe I needed a facial or better sunscreen. If many more people called me ma'am today, I was going to get a real complex. Although, I lived in South Carolina, so it was probably best to shake it off.

Leroy said, "It's time for us to find me a dog. Whatcha think, Andi Grace? Can you set me up?"

"You bet I can. In fact, I may have the perfect solution." Would Leroy be a good fit for Peanut? I leaned into Marc. As much as I wanted to ponder matching Leroy and Peanut, a man had died earlier. My rescue attempt had failed.

Two ladies approached the table, and Leroy excused himself and went to help them.

Marc said, "Chip, how do you like Heyward Beach?"

"The people are nice, and you can't beat the climate." He looked right and left then lowered his voice. "So, the boys were pretty upset. What'd they tell you?"

I shrugged. "Not a whole lot. They showed up to take a picture of the swimming pool and spotted the body before I could waylay them. What'd they say to you and Leroy?"

"Hardly anything. I couldn't help but see the cops and an ambulance over there. Did the dude die?" Chip's raised eyebrows and wide eyes led me to believe he cared. I was glad Leroy had a new friend.

"Yeah. Juliet and I tried to perform CPR, but we couldn't save him." The words hadn't come easy, but I'd managed to state the facts without crying.

He crossed his arms with thumbs up near his armpits. "Well, that's just too bad."

Juliet stepped out of the pier diner with the boys. Each kid carried a half-eaten hot dog and a red paper cup. Deputy Sawyer shadowed them.

"We should probably change the subject." I waved to Juliet. "I don't want to upset the kids."

Leroy finished helping the women and rejoined us. "I see the boys."

"If you gentlemen will excuse us a moment, I need to talk to Andi Grace." Marc led me to the nearest empty bench. "I know we'd planned to have engagement photos taken after work, but should we reschedule?"

We'd hired Zarina Mills, a newcomer to Heyward Beach, to be our photographer. "No, Zarina's a single mother and might need our money to buy groceries or pay bills. This place should be cleared out by the time we meet her, and my nerves should have calmed down by then. It'll be fine."

"Your heart for others is one of the reasons I fell in love with you, Andi Grace." He gave me a slow kiss. "I'll pick you up a little before five."

"Bring Chubb." Having the dogs would help me stay relaxed.

"Of course." He stood and reached for my hand. "How are you getting home?"

"Juliet and I walked over here together."

"Good. I've got to meet a man who's recovering from a car accident. The insurance company doesn't want to pay his medical bills. I'll feel better knowing you're not alone." He hugged me. "Please stick with Juliet and be careful."

"Don't worry about me. I'll see you later." I kissed his cheek, then strolled to Juliet. She and the boys were chatting with Leroy and Chip. The sunshine beat down on my head. People milled around the parking lot in small groups, probably waiting to hear who won the contest. If the old saying about safety in numbers was correct, I had nothing to fear hanging out with my friends.

Juliet passed me a Coke. "Thought you could use this."

"Thanks. Have they announced the winners?" I sipped the icy Coke, and my nose tingled.

Leroy said, "The judges are going over the results now."

The redheaded boy's face held more color than earlier. He bounced on the balls of his feet. "A week at a beach house would be cool. It's too bad our parents will make us include them."

I laughed. "There are some other great prizes. What about dinner at Tony's? Maybe you'll win it."

The other boy said, "It's the best pizza anywhere. That's what I'm hoping we win."

"Naw, a kayak rental will be more fun. We can go down the marsh without any of our family."

I laughed again. "I'm sensing a theme here. You guys think you're too old to hang out with your siblings."

The kid with cornrows flashed a smile. "We *are* too old."

Chip said, "Don't go wishing your life away, kid. Tonight, you may start remembering something from finding the dead man earlier. You two are going to need your families supporting you. Have you thought of anything else you might have seen?"

The child's smile faded. "No. We were only there to take pictures with our phones for the contest. That's all."

"Good. The less you saw, the easier it'll be to recover."

I stared at Chip. Was he trying to scare or comfort the guys? Either way, they were bound to have nightmares.

"Attention, ladies and gentlemen." Frank Hoffman stood on a platform with a squeaky microphone.

I waved to the retired military widower. He'd taken huge strides from his days of staying home alone and working in his yard. Even though he didn't own a local business, he'd volunteered to help the town with the scavenger hunt.

Frank winked at me. "If I can have your attention, we have winners to announce."

The crowd grew quiet, and I watched the hopeful faces in the crowd.

My friend Hannah Cummins had donated to the effort and used this opportunity to campaign. She'd decided to run for state representative and was working hard to win the election. While most eyes were on Frank, Hannah wandered to the nearest bench and sat. Her shoulders drooped, and her smile disappeared.

I didn't interrupt her moment in case she needed to rejuvenate before talking to more voters.

The other person not focused on Frank, besides myself, was Chip. He stared at the kids and frowned. What was that all about?

Chip's head jerked, and he met my gaze. In a quick heartbeat, a smile appeared and he nodded. "The moment of truth. It'll be good if the boys win a prize."

I returned his smile and turned my focus to Frank, hoping the boys would win a prize. Chip was right. The boys needed something good after having just seen a dead body.

Chapter Six

HOURS LATER, Marc and I walked onto the pier to meet Zarina Mills. No crowds in the parking lot and no emergency vehicles surrounded Cutter's Landing. What had happened to Olivia and Copper?

I shook my head. No. This wasn't the time to think about Dirk Cutter's death.

Instead of allowing a local murder to distract me, I turned my attention to Zarina. She was a young Black woman beginning her own photography business. Her four-year-old daughter lived in Charleston with Zarina's mother. I'd met Zarina at Daily Java one day, and she'd shared her dream of starting her business and being successful enough for her daughter, Shalita, to come live with her. Zarina longed to raise her daughter in a small town, and she'd set her heart on Heyward Beach.

Nobody understood the challenges Zarina faced like I did. The financial burden alone had intimidated me when I chose to raise my siblings after my parents died in a car wreck. I admired the young woman and had booked her on the spot for our engagement photos.

Zarina waved from the end of the wood pier.

I squeezed Marc's hand. "Here we go. I hope you like her."

"I'm not worried a bit." We stopped in front of the photographer. "Hi, Zarina. This is my fiancé, Marc Williams."

"Nice to meet'cha." Marc extended his hand and shook Zarina's.

"You too. Andi Grace, you look beautiful. Y'all, thanks for meeting me up here. First, we'll get some amazing pictures with the sun setting in the background. Then we'll head down to the beach, because I know you love it so much."

"I agree. Andi Grace does look beautiful." He kissed my temple.

"Thanks." I ran my hands down the blue sundress with a full skirt. I'd chosen chunky-heel sandals for the pier shots, but I'd go barefoot in the sand.

"Let's get going while the sun is good." Zarina gave us directions for where to stand and how to position ourselves.

The photo shoot was romantic and fun. Marc held me in his arms. We gazed into each other's eyes. We kissed. To spend so much time focused on Marc did my heart good. We moved from the pier to the sand, and the romantic feeling continued. Thoughts of death disappeared until near the end, when I caught sight of Dirk's beach home. Had he and Olivia been madly in love at one time? Had she orchestrated her husband's slaying?

Zarina pulled her camera back. "Andi Grace, what's wrong?"

I shook my head. "What do you mean?"

"You quit smiling, and there's a shadow in your eyes not due to the setting sun."

Marc met my gaze. "Are you thinking about Dirk Cutter?"

I nodded. "Yeah, I'm so sorry."

He hugged me. "It's natural you'd be upset."

Zarina stepped closer to us. "Are y'all talking about the man who died?"

I gulped in the beach air. "Yes."

Her eyes rounded. "I knew him. The other day I took pictures for his podcast and radio show. He was so excited about his announcement today. I can't believe he drowned."

Marc reached for my hand. "I hate to tell you this, but the coroner ruled it a homicide."

I gasped. "That was quick. How do you know?"

"The coroner was caught up and went to work as soon as he got the body. I ran into Wade earlier, and he said Dirk was strangled, then put into the pool. They think the killer wanted it to look like an accidental drowning."

"I've never known a murder victim before." Zarina crossed her arms and shook her head. "Poor man. I bet it's his wife."

My palms grew damp. "Have you met his wife?"

"Kinda."

Marc said, "What do you mean?"

"I didn't actually see her, but I overheard a phone conversation between Dirk and Olivia. It wasn't like I was eavesdropping though. Dirk had the phone on speaker, and he knew I was in the house." Zarina was turning into a real chatterbox. "They're separated. She has a fancy clothing boutique in Wilmington. North Carolina, not Delaware." Zarina lowered her voice. "She's one of the meanest people I ever met. If you count me listening to them a meeting."

I snatched a strand of hair blowing in my face. "He had you take pictures inside Cutter's Landing? Why?"

"He ran his podcast episodes from the office in the house. The man has a beautiful office, and I took many pictures in there."

"He lived here? Like full-time?"

"Oh, yeah. One thing we had in common was wanting to make this place our permanent home."

Marc said, "It sounds like you two were close."

"If you consider he was almost old enough to be my grandpa, then yeah. I guess so. I appreciated him giving me the opportunity to be his photographer. The pictures were for social media to promote his business. The man had huge dreams of being a top podcaster. He thought exposing this specific cold case would land him in the big time. The goal was to create a big stir and hopefully get more sponsors for his podcast."

Shadows stretched across the sand, and the sea oats danced in the breeze. An Atlantic ghost crab scooted sideways across the sand and disappeared into a hole.

"Ladies, how about we continue the conversation somewhere else?" Marc's gaze met mine.

Zarina placed the lens cap on her camera before putting it in her bag. "I'm heading to Charleston to see my baby girl."

Marc smiled. "Sounds like you could use a cup of coffee for the road. My treat."

Marc almost always considered others and their needs. It was one more thing I loved about the man. "We can swing by Daily Java."

"I rarely turn down a good cup of coffee, but I want to see my daughter."

"Let me at least get you a cup from the pier diner. I'll meet you two in the parking lot."

"Two creams and lots of sugar, please." Zarina patted her narrow hips. "I don't hafta watch my figure yet, so I enjoy doctoring up a cup of joe."

I laughed and followed Zarina to her vehicle. "I bet the drive gets tiring."

Zarina placed her camera bag in the car and slammed the door. "At first it seemed to take forever, but I'm used to it now. Still, it'll be wonderful when I get my own place here."

Marc appeared carrying three lidded cups in his large hands. "I was impressed with their selection. Zarina, here's your coffee and a pack of peanut butter crackers in case you need something to tide you over. Andi Grace, a coffee for you."

I waited until Zarina took the cup with her name on it, then I took mine. "Thanks."

"Anytime. So, what'd I miss?"

"Not much." I grinned at him before turning to Zarina. "I'm amazed how much you learned about Dirk in one session."

"What can I say? We're both big talkers. Only difference is that he gets—got—paid for it. What else would you like to know?"

"Did you notice if Dirk had a laptop?" Now that I knew he'd definitely been murdered, I believed his computer contained a clue.

Zarina stared at the pier. "You know, he did have a laptop. He patted it and joked about not letting it out of his sight."

My pulse leapt. "Do you think he had secret information about the cold case?"

"Either the case for his podcast, or it contained files on his wife, soon-to-be ex-wife."

"Interesting that you suspect it could be Olivia."

"Yeah. Those two for sure didn't get along, but the divorce was her idea. He made some comment about two playing the game."

I turned the cup in my hands. "What'd he mean?"

"You know, the cheating and getting back at each other game." She raised the cup to her mouth but paused. "I may be young, but I ain't naïve."

"It sounds like he believed Olivia cheated on him." I tried not to judge even though I believed in taking marriage vows seriously.

"That was my assumption. He kidded me that if I was older, he'd ask me out himself." Zarina wrapped both hands around the paper cup. "Yuck. I mean, the man must have been over sixty. It's a good thing he knew better than to ask me on a date. He paid me on time and even gave me a tip with a promise of hiring me again in the near future. It would be bad to lose his business, but I wouldn't have dated him just for a photography job." She glanced at her watch. "I better get going. I'll get the pictures to you by Monday."

"Thanks, Zarina. Be careful driving tonight."

"I'm used to it. See you Monday." She hopped into her car.

Marc and I walked to his truck. He took my hand in his and ran his thumb over my knuckles. "You look stunning."

My face grew warm. "Thanks. I know we'd planned to go out to dinner tonight. What do you think? Do you want to go to Tony's?"

He chuckled. "I know you well enough to realize your brain is racing with theories on what happened to Dirk. Why don't we go to your house so you can start taking notes while Zarina's words are fresh on your mind?"

"I love how you get me." It astonished me how well Marc understood my desire for justice. "The wife will be the first person I investigate."

He opened the passenger door for me and paused. "What will you do when Wade discovers you're interested in catching the killer?"

His question took the wind right out of my sails. "Oh, man. I told Wade this morning I wouldn't look into Dirk's death."

Marc's deep laugh held a note of surprise. "You what?"

"It's not fair to you. I told Wade not to worry about me interfering because I have a wedding to plan."

"Hmm, while that's true, it'll amaze me if you stay out of the murder investigation." He threw his hands up. "If you do start looking into it, let me know. I'll have your back, because the most important thing is keeping you safe."

"Aw, my hero." I lifted my lips to his and kissed him.

My little girl dream to be a newspaper reporter combined with my desire for justice had spurred me to investigate past mysteries. This time would be different. I had no reason to look into Dirk's murder. Nope, there wasn't a single reason to investigate. Hard as I tried to think of an excuse, nothing came to mind. Dilemma solved.

Chapter Seven

SATURDAY, I ENTERED WADE'S OFFICE midmorning with a fresh cup of coffee from Daily Java. "Hi, Wade. Thanks for seeing me."

"Andi Grace, I thought we were clear. No interference from you." He drummed two fingers on his desk.

I placed the paper cup in the center of his desk. "Patriotic blend. Erin assured me you'd like it. Now, get ready to take notes because I've got some information for you."

He reached for the cup first and took a sip. "Erin's right. I like it." He leaned back in his chair and pinched the bridge of his nose.

"Wade, I'm not trying to make life harder for you." I lifted my hands. "You told me not to keep secrets, which is the reason I dropped by."

He took another drink of the coffee before reaching for his laptop and opening it. "Shoot."

I leaned toward the desk. "Dirk Cutter was separated from his wife."

"We learned that from Olivia Caswell yesterday."

"Did she ever take his last name?"

Wade tilted his head. "Cutter is Dirk's stage name."

It made sense. "*Cut to the Truth.* Cutter. It's catchier than Caswell for Dirk's business."

"Um, Andi Grace?"

I met his blue-eyed gaze. His lips were pressed together. "I bet you imagine I've been investigating, but it's not what you think. I came into this information quite innocently." I explained about Zarina and the things she'd told us.

Wade managed to type while his gaze remained on me. "Okay. It never ceases to amaze me how people spill their guts to you."

"It's a gift." I gave him a saucy smile and walked to his door. "I hope you're giving me points for focusing on the wedding like I told you. Engagement pictures. Check. Staying out of your investigation. Check. See ya later, Wade."

He chuckled. "Bye."

I took two steps down the hall then returned. "Oh, yeah, I still have the dog, Peanut. I'd like to find him a home." Leroy came to mind. "Or at least a foster home until Olivia decides what to do with the beagle."

"I'll be in touch." Wade reached for his coffee cup.

"You know where to find me." On my way out of the building, a flash of red hair caught my attention. I did a double take. What in the world was Regina Houp doing here? She owned a fancy antique shop in town. We weren't enemies, but she barely tolerated me due to some imagined jealousy issues from our past. No makeup and messy hair spoke volumes. She hadn't come here to volunteer information like I had. There was something wrong.

If I had to guess, going by Regina's appearance, she'd been hauled in for questioning in Dirk's death. They'd been together Thursday night, and she'd been involved in the nasty scene at Tuscan Tomato. As much as I longed to hang around and find out what was going on, I left. It wasn't any of my business, and I planned to keep my word to Wade.

I hopped into my SUV and headed to a dog-walking appointment for Phyllis Mays. Whenever I walked Pumpkin and Captain, I tried to squeeze in a little obedience training. Poor woman thought she had it handled, but she was mistaken. The Australian–German shepherd mix was only a tad better behaved than Pumpkin, the full German shepherd. They were good dogs. Both were smart and loving, but they needed to learn how to behave.

Once I was inside the house, the dogs barked. I followed the cacophony to the laundry room. The animals clawed against the door, then there was a boom followed by a howl. I paused at the door, knowing they'd likely knock me on my backside if I didn't allow them time to settle down. "Quiet."

One dog continued to yap.

"Pumpkin. Captain. No barking." I'd learned years ago how to be firm without being mean.

When the commotion ceased, and there was only whining, I turned the knob. "Look how good you two can be. Let's go outside."

With one dog on either side of me, I led them out the back door. White clouds floated on a breeze in the azure blue sky. The dogs raced around the yard and did their business. I gave them plenty of time to burn off energy.

"Come." I pulled two treats from my bag and waited for the shepherds to join me. They ran, then skidded to a stop in front of my feet and panted. "Good job. Now sit." We'd worked on this for weeks but not consistently. Phyllis only scheduled me when she was busy with church functions or hosting a meeting at her house.

Both dogs sat. "Good job." I tried to use the same words over and over. After giving Captain and Pumpkin a treat, I threw balls with them to help them burn off more energy. Even though Olivia had told me she and Dirk laid claim to different dogs, I felt Dirk would've been inclined to play with Copper. Olivia playing with Peanut didn't compute. I definitely needed to find a good home for Peanut because Olivia wasn't a good option.

My thirty-minute stop had turned into an hour, so I took the dogs inside and settled each into their own kennel. "Why doesn't Phyllis put you in your crates instead of locking you in the laundry room? Don't give her a hard time. All three of you will be happier if you behave."

Had Peanut tried to attack Dirk's killer? It would explain why he was locked in the upstairs office. Had there been a confrontation upstairs at the beach house, even though there'd been no signs of an altercation? The killer might have grabbed the beagle and tossed him into the office before, or even after, attacking Dirk. If the murder was tied to the laptop, it made sense something bad had happened in the office. Although, the family room on the main floor had been in shambles.

It'd be helpful to know the time of death. Where was Olivia at the time of death, and when had she returned to the beach house? Could she and Dirk have fought in the main room and continued in his office? Maybe she threatened to delete the alleged divorce files off his laptop.

I shook off murder thoughts and headed home to check on Sunny and Peanut. Ahead of me, hobbling down the street was Regina Houp. I stopped beside her and lowered the passenger window. "Need a ride?"

Regina's head whipped up, and she straightened her shoulders. "No, I'm fine." Her limp red hair needed a good brushing. There was nothing fine about Regina this morning.

"Even a stranger could tell you're not okay. Come on." I patted the seat.

She looked both ways.

"Hoping for a better offer?" I bit back a smile, knowing it'd only irk her.

With a sigh, Regina walked over and slunk into the passenger seat of my Highlander. "Thanks."

"What's going on? I noticed you were at the sheriff's department." I started driving once she fastened her seat belt.

Her knuckles whitened on her purse strap. "They took me in for questioning in Dirk Cutter's murder. Can you believe it?"

My foot jerked off the gas pedal. "Why? Because you were dating him?" I returned my foot and tried to act natural driving down the street.

"We were not in a relationship, regardless of what you heard at the restaurant the other night. We were on a date, and it may have been the biggest mistake of my life." She threw back her head. "Scratch that. Going to dinner with Dirk was most definitely the dumbest thing I've ever done."

"Thursday was your first date?"

"Yes."

An image of the dead man floated through my mind, and I shivered. "You must've liked him, right? Why'd you agree to dinner?"

She fidgeted with the cuticle on her thumb. "Dirk was fun to be around, and when he invited me to dinner I agreed. He had his big announcement planned for Friday, and he wanted to celebrate. We had a good time speculating on the different ways his career would change. The evening started out pleasant."

"Do you know what he planned to say on the podcast?"

Regina stared straight ahead. "No. Dirk didn't share details about the show, but he believed it would change lives and close an unsolved homicide. He called the cold case in California his Triple C threat."

California? The murder couldn't have been much farther away from South Carolina. But if Dirk was going to reveal information that would solve an old cold case, maybe the killer had found out and done away with Dirk first. I returned my attention to Regina. "It sounds like you were having a fun evening."

"Sure, it was a delightful date until Olivia Caswell showed up claiming to be his wife. I was mortified." Her tone was laced with pain.

"I'm sorry, Regina."

"I thought he was divorced, but in reality, they were only separated. The whole thing is humiliating. I'd never break up a marriage. You may not like me, but I do have scruples."

"I believe you, and I like you." I turned into Regina's little neighborhood. "It must have been awful to discover the truth in a public place." So many questions ping-ponged in my brain. How did Olivia know where to find them? Did Olivia know about their date? What about the cold case? Had Dirk confided in his wife about the show before their marriage became turbulent? How long had Regina and Dirk known each other?

Regina sighed and leaned back into the bucket seat. "I don't know how much you and Marc heard, but Olivia caused quite a scene."

She wasn't exaggerating, but I didn't want to make her feel worse. "It sounds like Olivia was upset before she laid eyes on you. I wonder why she was so mad, and how did she know where to find you and Dirk?"

"She tracked us by his cell phone. Evidently, she'd received a notice from the divorce attorney. Dirk wasn't giving in to all of Olivia's demands, which infuriated her. When Olivia got to our table, she reached for his whiskey and drained the glass. Then she threw my drink in his face, dumped the lasagna in his lap, and stormed off. Everybody around us watched the scene. Some even stood to get a better view." She clicked her thumbnails against each other. "There was also an issue about her dog. I know people were taking pictures with their phones, and I was beyond humiliated at that point. I kept my focus on Olivia and Dirk."

I pulled into Regina's driveway and parked. "What did Dirk do?"

"He laughed, threw a wad of cash on the table and said, 'Whatcha going to do?'" Regina sighed.

Her words confirmed what I'd heard. "Anything else?"

"He waved and told everybody not to miss the next episode of *Where Are They Now?* One of the qualities that attracted me to Dirk was his ability to laugh off things that would drive me nuts." Regina grabbed my arm. "Andi Grace, you've got to help me. The sheriff thinks I killed Dirk."

"Why? What would be your motive? You were on a date with Dirk." Wade must have some reason to question Regina.

"The entire scene upset me. While I thought it was great that Dirk could shrug off such a stressful situation, I'm not the same way. We got into a big argument in the restaurant's parking lot, and somebody overheard us." Her fingernails dug into my skin. "That's probably what got me on the sheriff's radar.

"What did you say that was so terrible somebody reported it to the sheriff's department?" I unclenched my hands from the steering wheel and dropped them in my lap in hopes I didn't look judgmental.

"It might not be the words exactly, but more like my tone. I was embarrassed and angry. Life should be nice and tidy, at least in public. If you're going to have a fight, it should be in private. Not in front of a respectable restaurant full of people. Olivia dropped a real stink bomb, and I overreacted."

I patted her hand, hoping she'd quit squeezing the life out of my arm. "What exactly did you say, Regina?"

"I'm so mad I could kill you, Dirk. Take me home." She released my arm. "It's bad, isn't it?"

"The situation could be worse." Like somebody could've seen Regina drag Dirk's body out of the house and dump it in the swimming pool.

Chapter Eight

I TOOK A DEEP BREATH AND COUNTED TO TEN IN FRENCH. Regina's words could easily have been seen as a threat, especially when you considered the man had died the next day. No wonder she'd been reported to the sheriff. "I see how that looks bad. You threatened to kill Dirk for embarrassing you. Or was it because he dated you while still married? Either or both reasons could be a motive." Regina was a prideful woman.

"I'd never kill Dirk." She wrung her hands and looked down. "But you're right. I was humiliated. And a little hurt. At this stage of my life, I had dreamed of being married and having children. I'm forty. Forty!" Her voice grew louder with each word.

"Hey, that's not too old to have a baby."

"But I'm not in a relationship." Her voice took on a whiney quality. "Peter broke my heart, and then he died. It took me a while to recover. Then I met Dirk, who was entertaining and exciting. He knew so many people and had great stories."

Fascinating. Two men Regina had cared about had been murdered. If she wasn't careful, she'd get accused of being a black widow. "Calm down, Regina. Tell me, who do you think killed Dirk?"

"Olivia Caswell. She's a freak. Anybody at Tuscan Tomato would agree with me." Regina met my gaze. "I'm telling you, she was furious Dirk rejected her demands in the divorce settlement. Plus, she couldn't find her dog."

"Okay. Her motive would be anger regarding the divorce." Good to know a motive existed.

"Don't forget scorned in love." Regina gripped my arm again. "Andi Grace, you've got to help me."

"How?" I dreaded hearing her request. Not that I didn't want to assist Regina, but I dreaded breaking the news to Marc. It'd be worse when I told Wade.

"Catch the real killer and prove I'm innocent." Her brown-eyed gaze implored me.

I shook my head. "You don't need me. Sheriff Stone is good at his job."

"He has to be politically correct and follow the rules. You don't. Besides, you have a knack for solving murders."

My hands grew damp. "I'll help you, but don't tell the authorities what we're doing. I'm not asking you to lie, but don't advertise the fact."

She leaned close, giving me the impression that she might hug me. In the blink of an eye, she backed toward the passenger door. "Great. Where do we start?"

"I need a notebook, and you're going to tell me all you know about Dirk Cutter from the first time you met him."

"Come inside. I've got plenty of journals you can choose from."

I followed Regina up the sidewalk to the front door. The portion that wasn't glass panels had been painted bright red, making it the perfect color choice on the gray house. To say the door popped would be an understatement.

We crossed the threshold and entered the great room, consisting of an open living area, dining area, and kitchen. The interior was immaculate. No shoes, magazines or unfolded afghans littered the area.

Regina said, "I'll be right back."

I wandered around her living space filled with priceless antiques. It wasn't fun vintage items like I preferred. Regina had a taste for costly European items. Her place was beautiful and would be perfect for a home tour.

"Here we go. Choose your favorite." Not only had she gathered supplies, she'd brushed her hair and applied lipstick.

I picked a blue journal with angels, swirls, and a dark binding. "How about sitting at your table?"

"That'll be fine." She handed me a stainless-steel pen then walked to the end of the square glass table for eight.

I sat next to her in a white upholstered dining chair and was glad we weren't eating spaghetti. "Where did you meet Dirk?"

"At a bar up in Murrells Inlet in April." She folded her hands together. "It's not the best place to meet a man. Maybe I'll resort to online dating if I don't go to prison for Dirk's demise."

Regina had gone to a bar to meet men? What was the world coming to? I steeled my expression to remain neutral instead of revealing my surprise. If she'd said an art gallery or estate sale, it would've been easier to believe. "Stay calm, we'll figure it out. You suggested Olivia Caswell as a suspect. Anybody else?"

Regina shrugged. "Maybe the focus of Dirk's *Where Are They Now?* podcast for Friday's episode. Instead of a prerecorded show, Dirk had planned a live event. According to Dirk, the announcement, er episode, was going to be a major boost to his number of listeners."

"Why would a live show make it better?"

She pushed back a cuticle. "Dirk could be paranoid at times. He didn't want to risk the show leaking. Keeping the topic a secret was important. He also thought it'd be more exciting."

I added those tidbits to my notes. "Was Dirk the only person aware of the big reveal topic?"

"As far as I know."

"There's no producer for his show?"

"That was the next step he wanted to take. He believed yesterday's show would put him on the map. He hoped to get sponsors and a producer and maybe even a book contract."

"Duly noted." I continued adding to my notes. "We didn't find a computer in his office. No laptop either, but we did see cords."

"I bet Olivia stole it." Regina slapped the table so hard, the pop made me jump.

"If you believe she's the killer, why steal the laptop?" I worked to keep my voice steady.

"There could be divorce documents in it, or some other incriminating evidence to make her look bad to a judge. Dirk had a knack of uncovering secrets. If he had some dirt on Olivia, it'd give her extra incentive to kill her husband."

"I'm not sure about your theory. If she was going to steal the computer, why kill him?" I met her gaze. "Do you have any other thoughts on where it might be?"

"Dirk was paranoid. He had a storage unit somewhere and hidden safes in his beach house. The cops should look behind all of the pictures."

"You need to call the sheriff, Regina. Tell him about the safes."

"The less I'm involved with Sheriff Stone, the better. What else?"

I closed the blue journal and stood. "Let me see what I can find out. If you think of anything else, let me know. Remember, it'll be safer for both of us if we keep our investigation private. The killer won't want us to prove you're innocent."

"I understand. If I'm innocent, then the cops will continue looking for the real murderer." Regina walked me to the door and gave me a hug. Desperation must have led to the move because she liked to have squeezed the breath out of my lungs. "Thank you so much, Andi Grace."

I patted her back until she released me. "We'll get through this. Have a little faith." I left her, and the dead bolt clicked behind me.

I texted Marc. *We need to talk.*

His reply was immediate. *Let me guess. You're looking into Dirk Cutter's homicide.*

I laughed. *Yes. Do you want to meet at my house?*

A smiley face and thumbs-up emoji appeared.

I drove to the island and fixed a fresh pitcher of tea while waiting to discuss the case with Marc. If I was going to help Regina, I needed to rule her out as the guilty party. Although, it'd be a pretty sneaky maneuver for her to pull if she was behind Dirk's murder.

At this point my money was on the wife. Olivia had been in the house when his body was found. How had she not known he was dead? She'd also been angry with him on Thursday evening. Motive could be anger, or embarrassment. With Dirk dead, would Olivia inherit the house? What about a will? Who was the beneficiary? So many questions needed answers, and I was ready to tackle the task.

Chapter Nine

WHILE WAITING FOR MARC, I DIALED OLIVIA'S NUMBER.

"Who is this and how'd you get my number?" Her haughty voice almost made me want to disconnect.

My pulse throbbed in my neck. "Olivia, this is Andi Grace Scott. The dog walker." After a few seconds of uncomfortable silence, I plunged on. "We met yesterday at Cutter's Landing."

"I remember now. Do you have Peanut?" Her words were slurred.

"Yes." Was she drunk? Stoned? "Do you remember agreeing to let me take care of Dirk's dog?"

No reply.

"Hey, are you okay?"

Olivia cleared her throat. "This situation with Dirk has thrown me for a loop. Why are you calling?"

"Mostly to check on you and verify you're giving me custody of Peanut."

"I'm fine and you're welcome to keep the dog." She sniffed, then coughed. "Is there anything else?"

"Do you know if he has any favorite toys?"

"He was Dirk's dog, and Copper is mine. I really don't know much about what the beagle prefers. If that's all—"

"While we're on the phone, I was wondering how you knew where to find Dirk on Thursday night."

She launched into her explanation about the phone's tracking device. Same story Regina had told me earlier. "If you're married, I highly recommend doing the same thing."

"Oh, well, I'm engaged." If Marc and I track each other it will be for security reasons. Not because we're fighting.

"In that case, get a good prenup. Don't make the same mistakes I did." She sighed. "I tracked my husband to the Italian restaurant. He'd been dodging my calls about the divorce, but I never expected to find him on a date with that little tart."

I opened the blue journal and began taking notes. "Oh, I thought maybe you were trying to catch him with another woman."

The slight pause gave me a feeling I was on the right track. "No, no, no. I only wanted to talk to Dirk."

"Okay. Where'd you go after the scene at the restaurant?"

"I drove to Charleston to spend a few nights at my favorite spa."

My doorbell rang, and I hurried to let Marc inside. He kissed my cheek then whispered, "Who're you talking to?"

I led him to the kitchen table and pointed to the spot where I'd written down Olivia's name.

He nodded and moved into the kitchen area.

Meanwhile the woman hemmed and hawed about all sorts of places, including the gas station. One word caught my attention.

"Wait a minute. Did you say you went to a spa?"

"Yes. My nerves were shot after the confrontation, so I decided to treat myself to a few spa days. No phones. No distractions. You know the kind of place I'm talking about."

Yeah, I'd heard of those kinds of places, but who had the time or money for such an extravagance? Wait, her answer didn't make sense. "We found you at Dirk's beach house Friday morning. I can't think of any spas that are open in the middle of the night."

"Not that it's any of your business, but it's a spa and resort combined." Her voice dripped with derision. "They were booked, so I came back to Cutter's Landing."

"Why? If you were so mad at Dirk, why go to his place?" I pushed the speaker button so Marc could hear both sides of the conversation.

"I tried to pull a switcheroo on Dirk. I should've known, it's impossible to get ahead of the man." A dog barked, and Olivia murmured to him.

"I'm still here. You were saying—"

"Yes, I came here, to the beach house, after the restaurant. Peanut was in the yard, and Copper was inside. I couldn't get into the place, so I took Peanut with me. I texted Dirk that I had his dog and was willing to trade if he'd agree to my divorce demands."

"I don't understand how you could get one dog but not the other. Is there a doggy door?"

She laughed. "Peanut doesn't mind being outside. He was in the fenced-in backyard, and I snuck off with him Thursday night. Remember, I said it's impossible to get into his house? I stole Peanut to exchange for Copper."

"Did you take him to the spa with you?" What a twisted woman, and the poor dogs.

"As a matter of fact, I did. They have a special area for pets, and my plan was to indulge myself and let them handle Dirk's mongrel."

Marc rolled his eyes.

"Olivia, with Dirk's passing, is Peanut legally yours? If so, I'd like you to sign a release making me responsible for the beagle." I drew circles around her name until I wore a hole in the page.

"Fine." She ended the call without so much as a goodbye.

I met Marc's gaze. "The widow. She's one cunning woman."

Frown lines spread across his forehead. "She doesn't sound like a grieving widow."

"You can say that again. I kept trying to verify she'd given up her rights to Peanut." I closed the journal. "Let's go for a walk, and I'll update you."

"Great. Chubb's in the backyard with Sunny and Peanut." He walked behind me and massaged my shoulders. "How's that?"

"If I was a cat, I'd purr." The tension eased from my tight muscles at his touch. "You could put Olivia's favorite spa out of business."

He chuckled. "Not likely."

"Wait until you hear who begged me to find the killer." I stood and faced him.

"Who?"

"Regina. As in Regina Houp."

Marc's eyes widened, then he threw back his head and laughed. The deep rumble in his chest never failed to assure me everything would be okay.

All of a sudden, the day brightened. "I know you came over to help me brainstorm the latest Heyward Beach homicide, but we're not going to spend all day discussing Dirk's murder. We've got a wedding date to pick."

"Su-weet! I like the sound of that."

I secured Peanut in the comfy crate and gave him a little treat, then we harnessed and leashed our dogs. "Let's head to the pier."

"You don't want to include him?" Marc pointed at the beagle.

"No, I feel like he may need some quiet time. He's been through a lot since Thursday night." I ran my hands over my face.

"What's wrong?"

"I never got an answer from Olivia about how she could be napping at the house while Dirk was dead in the pool." I opened the front door, then locked and bolted it when we were all on the porch. "She drove from Dirk's place to Charleston and back. How did she get inside the second time if she couldn't enter on her first stop?"

Marc said, "From what I heard of the conversation, she's either ditzy or very clever."

"I agree, which makes her hard to figure out."

"Do you want to go past Cutter's Landing on our way to the pier?" He paused for Sunny and me to catch up with him and Chubb.

"Of course. We might find a clue." I strolled beside him on the sandy street, giving the dogs freedom to have more space to roam and sniff. Heyward Beach wasn't the biggest tourist destination, and my little street has very little traffic, making it safe.

"First I want to know why Regina asked you to find the killer. What's the deal?"

"My guess is getting hauled to the sheriff's department for questioning made her desperate, and my services are free."

"Ouch. No, I bet it's because you do a terrific job solving murders." Marc wore athletic shorts, a T-shirt, and a ball cap. I caught my reflection in his aviator sunglasses and adjusted my ponytail. *Life is better with a boat* was emblazoned across the back of his light blue T-shirt.

"Do you miss working with boats?"

"Some days I do, but it got lonely. I'd see very few people on a daily basis, which tended to make me like a hermit. Starting my own law practice allows me to help lots of people. I'll never be rich, but I tried the big-money road. It wasn't a good fit."

"I'm glad you're happy." My fiancé had a huge heart, and being in his life was an enormous blessing. "This morning I stopped by the sheriff's department to see Wade. That's when I spotted Regina. You know how prissy she is? Always dressed perfectly and all that? Her hair hadn't been brushed, and she wore no makeup." I continued the story of my day.

"Olivia sounds like a piece of work. I can't believe she stole Dirk's dog."

"Poor Peanut. Dirk and Olivia didn't have children, and I think it's probably a good thing. I may try to match Peanut up with Leroy." We paused while Chubb sniffed around a fence at the corner of the street.

Marc laughed. "You never quit trying to rescue people and dogs. I was a goner the day you asked me to take care of Chubb."

I smiled. "Best day of your life, right?"

"No, meeting you was the best day of my life despite the fact it was over a dead body."

"I love you." Marc pulled me into his arms, and we kissed until the dogs barked.

Chapter Ten

I WOKE UP SUNDAY MORNING with the realization I needed to question Olivia. Peanut was probably the best way to get to the woman.

I slipped on shorts and a T-shirt before taking the dogs to the backyard. The beagle still showed signs of nervousness. He yelped and darted away from a moving shadow.

Sunny went to his side and nosed him affectionately. The two stuck together until Peanut had enough time to do his business. Pride filled me at how sensitive and caring my German shepherd was toward the other dog.

My dog-walking schedule was clear for the day, so I went for a run then got ready for church. These days we usually occupied the back corner of the little community church. It used to be Nate, Lacey Jane and myself. In the past year, we'd grown to include Marc, Juliet, David, and Ike Gage. David had started dating my sister a few months earlier, and Ike was Lacey Jane's biological father. Some weeks we all ate lunch together after church, but today there was too much happening to meet. After Pastor Mays's sermon on loving our neighbor, we took off in different directions.

Marc followed me home, and we ate on the back porch while the dogs amused themselves. Chubb played with Peanut, and Sunny sat at my feet while watching the others. Marc's golden retriever was fun and full of life. With support from our dogs, Peanut would hopefully begin the healing process. Plus, I planned to lavish the beagle with love.

Marc and I ate grilled cheese sandwiches, apple slices, and baked potato chips. "I've got a surprise for you."

"Really?" He'd been quiet all through lunch, like when we'd first met.

"Yeah, I made chocolate bars for dessert."

His eyebrows popped up. "Su-weet."

I reached for his hand. "Is something wrong?"

"Yeah, I wasn't sure whether to bring it up or not."

I met his gaze. "We should be able to discuss anything. Tell me what's on your mind."

A few seconds passed before he answered. "You know my friend Lincoln Zane?"

The popular country singer and Marc's friend. "Sure. He recorded one of your songs."

"He's in town, running from the tabloids. His oldest son, Thomas, got in trouble for smoking marijuana at a high school party. The kid's only fifteen. The cops showed up and read all the kids the riot act, but nobody was arrested. Even though Lincoln's a celebrity, he lives in a small town. The police chief decided to give the partygoers a good scare. He treated each youth the same. Case closed." He pushed his empty plate away and leaned back in the all-weather wicker chair. "Problem is, the tabloids caught wind of the story."

"Oh, no. There goes his shot at grace the police chief tried to give him."

"Exactly." Marc crossed his arms. "Lincoln actually came to Heyward Beach and rented a place. He'd scheduled a meeting to discuss the situation with Dirk Cutter. Lincoln will do just about anything it takes to protect his wife and kids."

My heart leapt. "A meeting with Dirk? Does that mean he's running from all the tabloids or just Dirk?"

"Not exactly sure. We do know there was going to be a podcast episode about celebrities and athletes. It was going to focus on how fame affects family life." Marc wadded up his paper napkin. "Lincoln came here to find out if Dirk was the only person who caught wind of the party. With a little luck, he'd hoped to persuade Dirk to drop the story."

"When did your friend get to town?"

"Wednesday. Dirk was murdered either Thursday night or Friday morning. It could look bad for Lincoln." Marc frowned.

"Where is Lincoln's family?"

"Lincoln's wife took the kids to visit her parents in northeast Georgia, near Helen."

"It sounds like we've got more than one reason to help catch the real killer." I swallowed hard. "Let's go back to the area around Cutter's Landing. Maybe one of Dirk's neighbors heard or saw something. We need to gather clues if we're going to catch this killer."

"Sounds like as good a place to start as any." He stood and rubbed his hands together. "How about we eat your chocolate bars later? I have to admit that I'm anxious to get started proving Lincoln is innocent."

"Give me five minutes." I hurried to change into shorts and a blue T-shirt, slipped on my beach tennis shoes, and grabbed my phone from the charging station.

Downstairs I found Marc sitting on the couch petting the dogs. He'd changed into khaki shorts but still wore the same green polo from earlier.

"We should leave the dogs here in case we run into Olivia Caswell. I want to try to get inside the beach house, and she claims the place is half hers. Maybe I'll spot some kind of evidence." I got the dogs settled, and we headed outside.

Marc was quiet on the walk, and I didn't interrupt his thoughts.

Regina and Lincoln both felt like they were suspects. Regina had been questioned, and she thought Olivia was the most likely culprit. Zarina also believed Olivia might have killed Dirk. I now had three official suspects, but I doubted Regina or Lincoln was guilty. Rudeness didn't mean Olivia was the killer, but there was more to the wife than being ill-mannered. Dirk's mysterious announcement could also be a factor in his murder. Who was the subject of Friday's podcast? Could it possibly be Lincoln?

We turned the corner from Charleston Street to Ocean Drive and would approach Cutter's Landing from the south.

A lady walked her tall, thin yellow-haired Afghan hound, and I crossed the street. "Hi, your dog is beautiful. May I pet her?"

Marc didn't join me. In fact, he was looking at his phone.

My gaze returned to the woman, who was tall and thin like her dog. She flipped her long blonde hair over her shoulder. "Gypsy doesn't always take to strangers."

"I'm a dog walker and animals usually like me. Can I try?"

Her face didn't change expression. "Knock yourself out."

I held the back of my hand toward the Afghan hound. "It's too bad about Dirk Cutter's dog getting loose during the scavenger hunt."

"Is that the man who died?" The woman's skin was flawless.

"Yes, ma'am." I rubbed on the hound. "Dirk had two dogs, but his wife claims the shih tzu is hers. Peanut, the beagle, was Dirk's dog. Did you notice anything weird this past week?"

She pushed up her puffy three-quarter sleeves and held a portable fan with a bracelet attached to her wrist in front of her face. "One of the dogs was yapping late Thursday night. Very late. I almost called the sheriff. There was more barking Friday morning, but I chalked it up to the commotion of the scavenger hunt. You know what I mean?"

"There was a lot of activity." I straightened and smiled. "Did you know Dirk well?"

"We saw each other on the beach and spoke of the weather, but not much more. He often walked both dogs. The shih tzu and beagle. I don't remember seeing a woman ever spend time with either pet. Anyhoo, watching Dirk with the beagle reminded me of the cartoon. You know. *Snoopy.*"

"I love that comic strip." Maybe that's where the beagle got his name. "Did you ever listen to Dirk's radio show or podcast?"

She lifted her chin and waved the fan around her neck. "No, I don't like to dwell on negativity. I listen to the oldies radio station. Rock and roll is my thing."

"I understand." No other questions came to mind. It appeared our conversation had come to an end.

The woman surprised me though when she opened her mouth again. "There was yelling Thursday night. Like an argument, you know what I mean?"

"Yes. Could you hear any words?"

"No, but the voices were angry." She turned off the fan and met my gaze. "Dirk's wife blew her stack more than once. She's not very nice, but Dirk was always polite. If somebody was going to get killed at that house, it seems like it would've been her. It's not hard to imagine she goes around making enemies with that hot temper."

"Did you hear about the scene at the restaurant Thursday night?" I caught sight of Marc talking on his phone across the street.

She nodded. "Tuscan Tomato. Yeah, it's all over town. I think her name starts with an *A* or an *O*."

"Olivia."

The dog tugged on the leash, and the woman followed Gypsy's lead. "She was here Thursday night, but it was earlier than the argument. Olivia banged on the front door and screamed like a banshee. Even though it was earlier than the argument, it doesn't mean she didn't return. I gotta go."

"If you ever need help with your dog, I'm Andi Grace Scott. I'm a dog walker, dog trainer, and we also board animals at my place, Stay and Play. Soon we'll do grooming."

"I'll keep you in mind." She waved and left me standing in her wake.

I recrossed the street and waited for Marc to end the call. When he finished, he smiled. "Who was that?"

"I'm losing my grip because I didn't get her name. She seemed a bit skittish, so I allowed her to lead the conversation with only a few questions from me."

"Did you learn much?"

"The neighbor confirmed Olivia was at the house Thursday evening, pounding on the door. She also heard an argument later that night, and it could've been at Dirk's house."

"You said Olivia went to a spa."

"Yes. I see where you're headed. Olivia claims she went to Charleston to check into a spa after she stopped by the beach house to get her dog. The house was locked, so she dognapped Peanut. The spa was full, but maybe we can find out what spa she tried to check into and verify her claim."

"I doubt the staff will share with you."

"Then I'll just have to ask Olivia to convince them to tell me."

"How do you plan to persuade her to share?"

"It'll be a step in proving her innocence. I can tell her once she's cleared from my list of suspects, I can focus on proving Regina is guilty."

"But Regina asked you to prove she's innocent."

"I know, but Olivia doesn't know that."

Marc laughed. "Sounds like a tangled web."

"When a wife and potential mistress point the finger at each other, it's definitely a tangled web." Images of the women flitted through my mind. "With some luck, I won't get eaten by either one." I didn't voice my ridiculous thoughts about Regina being a black widow, but the men in her life had a habit of dying under mysterious circumstances.

Chapter Eleven

I REACHED FOR MARC'S HAND and put aside thoughts of murder, motives, and suspects. "Who were you talking to?"

He cocked his head to the right. "Lincoln. Do you mind if we meet him in a while?"

"Fine by me." As long as Marc looked at me with those amazing gray eyes, I'd agree to just about anything. "Do you still want to go to the pier? Do we have time?"

"Yes, and yes. We might see somebody we know." He squeezed my hand in his while we strolled the short distance.

Leroy and Chip walked across the parking lot. Leroy carried a cooler and his fishing gear. He spotted us and changed directions. Chip followed.

I smiled at the men. "Hi, guys. Leroy, I've got a potential dog for you. I'd like to spend a little more time with him, then I'll bring him over for you to meet."

The older man's face lit up. "That will be real good, Andi Grace. A big reason for me moving was to have a dog. It didn't hurt the rent is better too." He clapped Chip on the back.

Chip glanced up from the latest-model cell phone. "It'd be a shame not to let a buddy have a pet. In fact, I'm a dog person myself."

"Oh, do you own one?" I'd never seen him with a pet, but I barely knew the man.

"Not right now. It broke my heart when my Doberman died last year, but one day I'll get another one." He dropped his hand holding the phone and focused on us.

"I understand. It's hard to say goodbye to a pet." I couldn't stand to think about the day Sunny passed on.

Marc said, "Andi Grace plans to start a shelter. When you're ready, maybe she can help you find the right canine companion."

Chills popped up. Canine companion. Maybe that's what I'd name my shelter.

"That'd be right nice." Chip wore faded denim shorts, a Heyward Beach T-shirt, and a high-tech watch. He appeared to be a down-to-earth sort of guy, but also a man who enjoyed nice electronics.

I nodded. "Just let me know when you're ready. Leroy, I'll see you later."

"Sounds good." The two men walked to a black sedan, and Chip got behind the wheel.

"I wonder why they didn't bring Leroy's truck. Who wants that smelly stuff in their car, especially if you have the option of a truck bed?"

Marc shrugged. "Maybe Chip just likes to drive."

"Could be. He's been a good friend to Leroy."

"Or the other way around. Chip came to town to run the low-income apartment complex, but Leroy has introduced him to many of the locals." He pointed toward the pier, and we walked to the building that not only held the diner but allowed access to the pier.

I pulled my hair back into a ponytail to keep it from slapping my face in the Atlantic breeze. "Where are we meeting Lincoln?"

"He'll call when he arrives. It might be better to talk on the beach where we'll have some privacy."

Lots of people fished on both sides of the pier. Sun worshipers filled the beach, and families played in the sand and waves. "It's going to get more crowded every week until after Labor Day. I hope the scavenger hunt helps promote the small businesses in the area."

"The tourists who come here are looking for a different experience than vacationers who flock to Myrtle Beach. This is a place where you're content to entertain yourself and enjoy nature. Myrtle has everything imaginable to keep a person entertained."

"And Charleston is full of history and culture. We're lucky to have so many options nearby."

"Don't forget the golf courses, plantations, museums, and state parks."

"You could do a tourism commercial, but if I never visited those places it'd be okay. I'm a beach purist." For as long as I could remember, the beach had been my happy place. It'd never been hard to entertain myself in the sand or water.

Marc's phone dinged, and he looked at the screen. "Lincoln's here."

A bad case of the nerves hit me like a semitruck. "Wait, why don't you spend time with your friend? You don't need me."

"Of course I need you. We're a team." He tilted his head. "Is there a problem?"

"You mean besides the fact that Lincoln Zane is a big country superstar? I don't want to embarrass you."

"Hey, you'd never embarrass me. Lincoln's my friend, and I plan on inviting him to the wedding. Come on. It's time for you to meet my friend."

I did my best to ignore the butterflies in my belly as we returned to the parking lot.

Lincoln stood near a big blue pickup truck. He wore athletic shorts, a T-shirt, and a Yankees ball cap pulled low, shadowing his face. "Hey, man." He threw his arms around Marc like good buddies do. They slapped each other on the back, then Lincoln said, "Thanks for meeting me."

"Always." They pulled apart, and Marc signaled for me to join them. "Linc, this is my fiancée, Andi Grace Scott."

Lincoln looked at me over the rim of his sunglasses. "It's good to meet you. I was glad to hear Marc found a woman who could convince him to settle down."

Marc laughed. "There's no settling down with this one. Andi Grace has kept me on my toes from the moment we met." He reached for my hand.

"We literally met with a dead body in the room between us." I intertwined my fingers with Marc's. "It seems like that's why we're meeting you today."

The country singer shook his head. "I hope we don't stumble over any dead bodies today."

My face grew hot. "I didn't exactly mean that. I just meant, you came here to talk to Dirk about you know who, and now he's dead."

A group of women walked near us, giggling and pointing. They wore bikinis and carried towels and water bottles.

"If you don't mind, why don't we go for a walk?" Lincoln pushed up his dark sunglasses, concealing his amazing brown eyes.

"Would you rather go to my house, where we won't have any distractions? It's a couple of blocks from here." I thought about my old house then shifted into picturing my new house as home. One day I'd get used to it.

Lincoln studied the parking lot full of people. "Might be a good idea. Hop in."

I got in the backseat of the truck while Marc rode shotgun.

Music blared as soon as Lincoln started the Silverado. "Sorry about that. I was listening to some demos. Marc, when are you gonna write me a new song?" He turned off the music.

"There are only so many hours in the day." He pointed. "Turn left here."

I watched the interaction between the two friends. Maybe if I didn't drag Marc into all my crazy adventures, he'd have more time to write music. One of the things I loved about Marc was how talented he was in so many areas.

"Nice way to avoid my question." Lincoln's melodious voice filled the cab of the truck.

Marc pointed to my house. "Pull into the driveway right there."

He whistled. "Very nice. Is this where you two plan to live after you get hitched?" We idled in the street.

"Yeah. I'm going to list my place with an agent and move to the island with Andi Grace. Wait until you see the inside. It's plenty big for us now and even after we start a family," Marc replied before I could answer, and his words touched me. He hadn't hesitated. In fact, he sounded happy to live on the island instead of his place on the Waccamaw River.

I removed the seat belt and leaned forward. "I'm a beach girl at heart, but I would've agreed to move out to the country with Marc if he'd asked."

My fiancé tweaked my nose. "As long as we're together, I'm happy."

"Aw, that'll be the title of the song I sing at your reception. Now you've really got to help me write it." Lincoln's throaty laugh filled the truck.

Marc's face grew red. "We'll see."

My heart swelled with love for my boatbuilding, lawyer, music-writing future husband.

Lincoln cleared his throat. "Any chance you have a garage?"

It was possible to park under my raised house, but it was full. "I'm sorry, but it's too full to get your truck in there." My face grew warm. It was past time to organize the space. "Why don't we move our vehicles? You can back into the driveway so nobody sees your Georgia tag."

"That'll work."

Marc and I hopped out and in less than five minutes, my Highlander blocked Lincoln's truck in the driveway, and Marc parallel parked on the street. The garage would've been better for privacy, but it couldn't be helped. The three of us walked inside, past the stairs leading up to the master bedroom, past the front room and the narrow hall under the stairs leading to the guest rooms. The main hall opened into a large room where I spent most of my time. "I think the appropriate name for this is an open floor plan, but I call it the family room slash dining room slash kitchen. Why don't you two have a seat? I'll get us something to drink."

Lincoln whistled. "This is right nice."

"Thanks, but you didn't come for a house tour. Marc, would you grab my journal? Let's get started before Lincoln's fan club tracks him down." I opened the back door for the dogs to go outside, but Sunny stayed with us while Chubb and Peanut ran around.

After arranging the chocolate bars on a pretty antique lace dinner plate, I prepared glasses of unsweet tea because I was learning to watch my sugar intake. I joined the men and sat close to Marc on the couch. Sunny lay at Lincoln's feet.

Lincoln eyed the sweets. "Those smell great."

"Thanks." I loved Marc with all my heart, but it was hard to ignore the fact Lincoln Zane was sitting in my house. Focusing on the murder would help ground me. "Why are you concerned about Dirk's demise?"

"I know he planned to do an episode on my family. My oldest son, Thomas, went to a party and smoked pot. He assures me it was the first time, and he did it to impress a girl. Still, he did it. Neighbors reported a loud party, and the cops showed up. The parents hosting the party called the chief of police, who arrived before any arrests were made. He talked to the group of kids and scared them to death. Then he called every single parent with kids at the party and had another little chat. Then he individually lectured each kid and parent in an interrogation room. As you might suspect, this took all night long. But there were no arrests, and we all appreciated how the situation was handled. Kids will be kids and all that. Why ruin their future for a stupid mistake? Somehow Dirk Cutter learned about the incident. He had the decency to contact me first, and I asked if we could discuss it man to man. It's too bad the guy never had kids, or else he'd understand better."

Marc twirled the pen in his fingers. "We've all made dumb decisions in our lives."

Lincoln took a deep drink of his tea. "Yep, but life with a celebrity father makes it harder. We're under a microscope and judged harsher than normal people."

I reached for my journal to jot down Lincoln's story. "Did you meet with Dirk?"

"Yeah. We got together Wednesday after I settled into the beach house I'm renting."

"Where'd you meet?"

He ran a hand over his face. "His place, so my fingerprints could be there."

"How'd the conversation go?"

"He listened to my side of the story, but he didn't agree to forget about it." Lincoln finished his drink. "Dirk mentioned the big story about a man who murdered a woman years ago on the West Coast and had never been caught. He was proud of himself for solving it."

My pulse accelerated. "I heard California, so that matches. Did he mention the people involved?"

"No, he was drinking, and I don't think he meant to let that much slip out. He asked me to keep it to myself, and I didn't play the blackmail card."

"Blackmail? Did you know the guy from out west?"

"No. What I meant is not blackmailing Dirk. Like I'll keep your secret if you don't tell the story about Thomas."

"Oh, that was nice of you." I sighed.

Lincoln turned his hands palms up. "Hey, I'm a nice guy trying to make a living and protecting my family at the same time."

I jotted down what he'd said while Marc took Lincoln's glass and refilled it.

Lincoln munched on a chocolate bar. "This is so moist, and the frosting is like candy. Not as thick as fudge, but you could eat it by itself."

"Thanks." His compliment pleased me. I wasn't the best cook and usually baked treats from a box. This was a rare made-from-scratch dessert. "What else did you learn from Dirk?"

"My focus was on convincing him to drop the story on Thomas. Protecting my family is my top priority, and I know Dirk's death makes me look bad."

Marc returned and set the glass beside Lincoln. "We're trying to find other suspects."

Lincoln said, "Dirk was a womanizer. In fact, he was waiting for a woman from his past to stop by."

I stopped writing. "His wife?"

"Nope, but I believe she was an old flame. By the overwhelming amount of cologne Dirk wore, I suspect he was happy to reconnect."

"Interesting. He was still married to Olivia, dating Regina, and meeting an old flame. How'd he find any time to work while juggling three women? Maybe we can look at old yearbooks or something to figure out the mystery woman from his past." Would she turn out to be a suspect? I made a note about her with a fat question mark.

Marc said, "It might be a good idea for us to meet with the sheriff and get on top of this. It'll be worse if word gets out you were at Dirk's place the week he was killed."

"Sheriff?" Lincoln tilted his head. "Doesn't Heyward Beach have a police department?"

"Yeah, but they're going through a reorganization process. Sheriff Stone will oversee the murder at this time." Marc leaned against the couch cushions and folded his hands together on his flat belly. "He's a good guy."

"I don't guess it's possible he'd come here." Lincoln's mouth turned down. "Walking into the sheriff's office is bound to hit the news."

I laughed. "Wade's been here plenty of times. Let me text him."

Lincoln stood and paced with Sunny at his side, matching his steps. "I'm glad you two are on my side."

"Team Linc, all the way." Marc stood and pointed to the back of the house. "Let's go outside and get some fresh air."

My phone showed three missed calls from Olivia. I texted Wade first, and he replied right away.

Hannah and I are at Daily Java. We'll head your way.

Hannah Cummins had adopted one of my rescue dogs. She and Wade had been dating for a couple of months and seemed to enjoy each other.

I called Olivia.

"I expected you to answer when I called the first time." Her disdain dripped through the line.

"I'm sorry, but I have company." Why was I apologizing? "What do you need?"

"Copper seems out of sorts. Can Peanut come over for a playdate?" She sniffed. "I'm at Cutter's Landing."

"I can meet you in a couple of hours. Will that work?"

"Now would be better."

I clenched my fists. "Like I said earlier, I have company. You can always come here."

A long pause followed.

"Mrs. Caswell, are you still there?"

"Let me know when you're on the way over." The call ended. Like before, she'd gotten the last word.

Chapter Twelve

NOT LONG AFTER MY CONVERSATION WITH OLIVIA, the doorbell rang. I walked to open the door for Wade and Hannah. "Thanks for coming over."

Each wore casual clothes, confirming I'd probably interrupted a fun date. Wade frowned. "Did you call us over here to discuss Dirk Cutter's murder?"

I raised my hands and backed away. "Kinda, but I didn't go looking for this. In fact, it's going to be a nice surprise."

Wade shook his head. "Somehow I doubt it."

Hannah elbowed Wade. "Give Andi Grace a chance."

He pasted a fake smile on his face. "Hi, Andi Grace. Thanks for inviting us over. What's the surprise?"

I bounced on my toes. "Lincoln Zane, the country singer, is in my backyard."

"Get out of town." Hannah squealed. "How did that happen? I love his music, and Wade does too."

"Can't deny it, but what's he got to do with Dirk's murder?"

"Come on back." I led them to the family room. "Make yourself comfortable while I get him."

I hurried outside. "Wade and Hannah are here."

Lincoln removed his ball cap and ran a hand through his dark hair with strands of gray. "May as well face the music and get it over with."

When we entered the family room, Hannah and Wade sat on the couch whispering.

I cleared my throat. "Lincoln, this is Sheriff Wade Stone and Hannah Cummins."

"Nice to meet you." Wade stood, and the two shook hands.

One side of Lincoln's mouth quirked up. "I hope you feel the same way after we talk."

Marc stepped closer to them. "Wade, we need to make an official statement, but it'd be better if we don't go to your office because of Lincoln's fame. The main thing to keep in mind is we're coming to you."

"Sure. I understand. We don't want his fans to riot our office."

Lincoln chuckled. "I doubt there'd be a riot, but I'd appreciate discretion."

"Not to worry."

Hannah's gaze darted from Lincoln to Wade and back like a spectator watching a tennis match. When all three men agreed to have their conversation at my house, Hannah said, "I'll step out of the room and give you privacy."

"Me, too. Hannah, let's go to my office. We can catch up while they have their conversation."

The men remained quiet until Hannah and I entered the office at the back of the house, and I shut the door. I even turned some music on so Wade couldn't accuse me of eavesdropping. "I haven't seen you in a while. Is the election going okay?"

"Much better now that Danny's out of the picture. Forget politics. I'm dying to know how you met Lincoln Zane."

"A while back, Marc worked on a boat for Lincoln. When Lincoln went to pick up the boat, he heard Marc singing an unfamiliar song. Marc sings to himself often, and I think he's amazing. Anyhow, they got to talking, and Lincoln recorded it. They've been friends ever since."

Hannah's eyes sparkled. "Is that why he's in town?"

My face grew warm. "I'm sorry, Hannah. I shouldn't say too much about the situation."

Her mouth dropped open. "Oh, honey, I wasn't thinking straight. Of course, you can't tell me. If I had to guess, I'd say it's related to Dirk Caswell's murder."

"He goes by Dirk Cutter." She had my full attention, and my pulse beat in my ears as I strained to hear her answer to my next question. "How'd you know his name is really Caswell?"

Hannah hopped up and walked around the room, pausing near the rolltop desk with glass windows in the hutch doors. She moved on to the window looking over the backyard. "You've got a great view, and I'm glad we're neighbors."

"Hannah, what aren't you telling me?" The swirling in my belly warned something was wrong.

She kept her back to me. "Dirk Cutter. Don Caswell. What's the difference? It's the same man."

"Don Caswell? Hannah, you're scaring me. Tell me what you know, or at least tell Wade."

Her hunched shoulders shook.

I hurried to my crying friend and touched her back. "What's wrong? Did you know him?"

She nodded and swiped at falling tears. "We met at a fundraiser."

"And what? You meet lots of people at political functions. Right?" A cloud of confusion swirled around me. Hannah was strong and confident. She'd faced political foes during her campaign. Why was she upset about Dirk?

"This was different. He wanted me to promote his business." She snatched a tissue from the desk and blotted the tears running down her face.

"Was he pressuring you somehow? Blackmail?" I handed her another tissue.

"I haven't done anything to be blackmailed for."

"I'm sorry. What about your dad?" It'd be hard to imagine Asher Cummins doing something worthy of extortion.

"No. Listen, I need to go. Tell Wade bye for me." Instead of exiting through the front door, Hannah rushed out the back.

I turned off the music and wrote in my journal. Hannah feared something. The question was what? Dirk had tried to push her for support. Had he threatened Hannah to the point she'd resorted to murder?

Lincoln's voice carried more than the other two men's. I heard mention of a white Volvo and the word *mystery*.

Sitting alone in my office was driving me crazy.

I called Olivia. "I can come over now, if that's okay."

"I'll be here." Again, she hung up. The word *bye* must not be in her vocabulary.

I counted to ten in French then texted Marc. *I'm taking Peanut to see Olivia. Be back soon.*

The beagle sat on the back patio beside Chubb.

"Did you guys have fun?" I attached the leash to Peanut's harness, then opened the back door. "Chubb, go inside. Find Marc."

The golden retriever barked once before following my command. I led Peanut to my SUV and settled him in the back. We took off for Cutter's Landing. On the short drive, I practiced different speeches for greeting Olivia. I didn't know if she'd murdered her husband, and I didn't want to tip her off that she was at the top of my suspect list.

Chapter Thirteen

OLIVIA OPENED THE FRONT DOOR. Once more, I was struck by her size. She was a big woman. Not fat, exactly. Tall, big-boned, and curvaceous. Long bleached hair flowed out of a floppy beige straw hat.

"I'm glad you're here. Copper's not his normal self. He seems depressed, and I thought playing with Peanut might improve his mood." Olivia waved me in.

Her words were like a sledgehammer to my gut. "Do you want to keep Peanut?"

"No. I just need him to perk Copper up."

My dogs always raced me to the door when the bell rang, but there was no sign of the shih tzu. "Where is your dog?"

Olivia pointed to the kitchen floor where the little pooch lay.

"What's wrong with him?" I released Peanut from the leash and knelt beside Copper, placing my hand on his side. Peanut trotted to the other side of the unmoving dog.

"I gave him part of my diazepam."

I gasped. "You shouldn't have done that. His breathing is slow."

"He was so despondent, I had to do something." Her whining didn't soften my stance.

"Olivia, you need to take him to a veterinarian."

She sashayed past the back door, where a white bag of garbage sat, and moved to the long table. Olivia waved her hand over a box. "Is there something here you can use to make Copper better?"

"I doubt it. What do you have?"

"Food, treats, a leash, special doggy shampoo, pee pads, and toys. His bed is upstairs, but we'll probably sleep together."

"Um, pee pads?" How would they help revive her dog? "Give me a treat."

She batted thick false eyelashes at me then handed over a small twisted bone.

I waved it under his nose. "Wake up, Copper. I've got a treat for you."

No movement.

"Olivia, I'm serious. He needs more help than I can provide. Take him to the vet."

"Would you be a dear and handle it for me?" She tapped a manicured finger on her cheek. "I'll be in town a few days. Would you want to train him when he feels better? I'll pay you well."

I would've done it for free if it meant more access to one of the suspects on my list. I'd also be able to keep an eye on Copper to make sure he was well. That is, if he survived Olivia's anxiety medication. "Sure. Do mornings work for you?"

"Afternoons are better. At my age, it's more important than ever to get my beauty sleep."

How could any one person be so self-absorbed? I counted to ten in French before I uttered regrettable words.

I retrieved a business card from my brown leather cross-body purse and handed it to Olivia, even though she knew my cell number. It was best to stick to business if I was going to train Copper. Scratch that. The dog was trained. Momma was the one who needed to learn how to take care of her shih tzu. "Call me later, and we'll work out a time."

"Fine." She left me in the kitchen with both dogs. "Be sure to lock the door when you leave."

Peanut growled at Olivia, and I couldn't blame him for being upset.

"Would you like me to take out your garbage?"

"That'd be great."

Yes. Her trash might be my treasure, if I found anything useful. I rubbed the sleeping dog's side. "Hey, Copper, can you wake up?"

He twitched but didn't rouse.

I got comfortable on the floor and continued to speak to him until he shook his body and stood. He blinked at me, and I ran a hand over his head. "We're going to see Doc Hewitt. He'll know what to do."

He cocked his head but appeared too tired to react.

"Poor boy. Let's get out of here." I harnessed Peanut and carried Copper. On the way out, I studied a wall of awards Dirk had won over the years. No family pictures on the walls or coffee tables, but there were plenty of pictures of Dirk with celebrities and politicians.

I pulled out my phone and snapped pictures of the awards and anything I thought useful to my research before we walked out the door. I made sure to grab the garbage bag with the hand holding the leash. Unable to lock the door with both dogs and the bag, I left it for Olivia. The woman wasn't helpless.

I settled Copper into a kennel in the back of my Highlander, and Peanut joined him. I kept the travel crate for emergencies, and this seemed to fit. In Copper's drugged state, if I hit the brakes too hard, he might slide out of the passenger seat and onto the floor. I didn't dare risk hurting him.

Despite my anger with Olivia, I jogged back to the front door and locked it. If she wasn't the killer, she might need the protection. In no time, I backed out of the driveway and paused to study Cutter's Landing. One of the blinds flickered from upstairs, as if Olivia watched my departure.

Was Dirk's wife aware she was a suspect? Would she stick around Heyward Beach or return to Wilmington?

Doc Hewitt took Copper with a promise to contact me when he knew more. I made the short drive to my house. Lincoln's truck, Marc's truck, and Wade's official SUV were still there. Great. I'd be able to tell Wade about Olivia before he left. The beagle and I entered the house and joined the men in the living room.

"Sorry to interrupt. Wade, Olivia Caswell is still at Dirk's beach house if you have any questions for her. She drugged her shih tzu with diazepam. So, I took her dog to the vet. If she'd drug her beloved pet, imagine what she'd do to an angry spouse. Or a spouse she was angry with."

Wade stood so fast he bumped his shin on the coffee table. "What else can you tell me?"

"She went by the house Thursday evening to get her dog, but Copper was locked in the house. Peanut was in the small yard, so she stole Dirk's dog." With as few words as possible, I revealed what the neighbor had told me earlier.

"I still don't understand why people spill their guts to you. I'm outta here." Wade stomped away.

Marc and Lincoln followed me to the back patio, where we could enjoy a view of the yard from our raised position. We stood, feeling the sea breeze, and listening to the waves pound the shore.

Chubb and Peanut ran down the steps, and Sunny followed at a more sedate pace. After a few minutes of sniffing around, Peanut settled in a shady spot. Sunny and Chubb lay on each side of the beagle.

"Poor little thing lost his master, and the dog he usually plays with was drugged by Olivia. He's got to be torn up."

Marc gave me a quick hug. "He'll be okay, because he's got you on his side."

Lincoln sat in one of the chairs. "Marc, I'm glad you encouraged me to talk to Wade. It doesn't sound like he suspects me."

Marc left me and sat beside Lincoln. Marc propped his right ankle on his left knee. "I think you're in the clear. Do you plan to stick around town?"

"It beats staying with my in-laws." He grinned. "I'll work on writing some new songs. Who knows? Maybe I'll get lucky and create a hit tune."

I kept an eye on the dogs while listening to the men chat.

"We should get together while you're here. We could go fishing, kayaking, or surfing."

"Sounds good." Lincoln made no move to leave. "Andi Grace, you've got a special place here. You also are marrying one of the good guys. I predict you two will be happy."

"Thanks." I met his gaze. "I feel blessed."

Marc laughed. "You two are going to make me feel like I'm dying. Knock it off."

Lincoln placed his hand over his heart. "Don't take each other for granted. The wife and I are struggling, and Dirk's stunt didn't help our situation. Yes, she took the kids to her family with the story of escaping the media sharks. In truth, it's a trial separation." Grief etched lines on his tanned face.

"I'm so sorry, Lincoln." I was always in favor of happily ever after.

"Aw, man. I hate to hear it." Marc's jaw twitched, but he leaned forward and slapped his friend on the knee.

Lincoln stood and avoided eye contact with either of us. "Don't know why I dumped all that on you two. I best get going."

"I'll walk you out." Marc held the door open for his friend.

"Hey, Marc. Would you bring back the bag of garbage with you from my SUV? It's unlocked."

"Evidence?"

"Possibly. Olivia said I could take it out for her." I held my hands up in an innocent gesture. "We might find something incriminating."

"Linc, Andi Grace is the only woman I know who enjoys going through other people's garbage."

The country music star laughed. "Nice."

Their voices faded away, and I sat on the steps watching the dogs. Chubb had begun nosing around an azalea bush. Peanut watched with his head propped on his paws, and Sunny kept her eyes on Peanut.

Had Olivia and the beagle been home when Dirk was killed? Or were they still on their supposed trip to Charleston?

If Peanut had been home at the time of the attack, what would the killer have done? Bad guys feared my German shepherd, for good reason. She'd attack anybody who came after me. Would Peanut have gone after

Dirk's killer?

What time had Dirk died? When had Olivia and Peanut returned? Why had she been able to get inside the second time and not earlier when she dognapped Peanut? There were so many unanswered questions. I needed to get busy if I was going to help catch the killer.

Marc appeared with the white garbage bag and the worst frown I'd ever seen on him. He dropped the bag at my feet and looked toward the yard. "I can't believe Savannah isn't being more supportive. Linc's got a lot to juggle, and he needs her to stand strong by his side."

My heart raced. My big strong fiancée had grown up in foster care with few people supporting and loving him. He needed to believe in the sanctity of marriage. I moved to where he stood and wrapped my arms around him. "Marc, you know I'll always stand by you. Right?"

He held me tight and nodded.

"I love you. There's nothing you could do that would make me walk away." I knew Marc wasn't perfect, but he loved the Lord, and he loved me. I trusted him. "I won't leave you alone to deal with life's trials like Savannah has done to Lincoln. We'll never be like Olivia and Dirk. We may face problems, but we'll deal with them together."

"I love you." Marc stepped back, cradled my face in his hands, and kissed me.

I got lost in the kiss. Marc would always come first. Solving Dirk's murder could wait.

Chapter Fourteen

MONDAY MORNING WAS BUSIER THAN USUAL for no reason I could figure out. I walked dogs and checked on pets for families who were out of town. Vi Thompson had scheduled me to walk her bichon frise three times a day while she recuperated from knee replacement surgery. She lived at the Waccamaw Retirement Community and had plenty of friends, but she wanted to make sure Fluffy got a good walk three times a day. My stop at her place had taken double the normal amount of time because the lady was a real chatterbox on a normal day, but today she'd been especially long-winded. In case she was lonely, I hadn't tried to rush her.

At noon I needed to be at Marc's office to meet him and Zarina to choose engagement photos. He'd looked so handsome when we'd posed, and I couldn't wait to go through the photographs.

I checked my watch. There was time to take Peanut by Leroy's duplex, and see how the two felt about each other. The low-income housing community Leroy lived in bordered the marsh and was a short drive to the island. As a child, our parents took us to the community on Thanksgiving and Christmas with food and gifts for the residents. When I pulled onto the property this morning, the conditions appalled me. Bushes needed to be trimmed, buildings needed a fresh coat of paint, and window screens needed replacing. If this was evidence of Chip fixing up the place, I was glad I hadn't seen it before he took over management.

I waved to Jeremiah Prichard, a veteran who rode his bike all around Heyward Beach. Jeremiah was good with his hands and did odd jobs for locals. Sometimes he got paid and other times he didn't. Many years earlier, his wife had left him when he returned home from Desert Storm with severe PTSD. Our community looked out for the veteran without hurting his pride.

Leroy's truck sat in a sandy parking space in front of a duplex. "This must be the place." I glanced at the beagle.

Peanut barked from the passenger seat while I parked. After attaching the leash to the beagle's harness, we got out of the SUV.

Leroy appeared. "Hi there. You should've called, and I'd have fixed a pot of coffee."

"I did call but you never answered." I winked.

His eyebrows rose, and he pulled out his phone. "Dead. Well, I'm glad to see you. Who's this little fellow?"

"Leroy, I'd like you to meet Peanut. He's full of life and energy this morning."

"Is this the dog you want me to keep?"

"Maybe. At times he's rambunctious, but other times he's docile. His owner was Dirk Cutter, and I think he's a little depressed."

Leroy nodded. "Heyward Beach's latest murder victim."

"Yeah. That's why he's so sad. His basic instinct is to be playful, and I think he'll recover. Would you like to foster him for a bit? If it doesn't work out, I'll keep looking for a better match."

The older man held out his freckled hand, and I passed the leash to him. "Let me take him for a walk. Get to know the little fellow."

"Alone?" Most people wanted me involved in the getting-to-know-you process.

"Yes, ma'am. Consider it a little man-to-man time." He chuckled. "We won't be long."

I debated if the older man could keep up with Peanut, but they both seemed eager to try. "Sure. Take your time."

I sat in a shellacked wooden rocker on Leroy's front porch and got lost in checking the email on my phone.

"Woof. Woof. Woof."

Peanut's fierce barking brought me to my feet, and I ran toward the sound. Around the corner of the duplex and down the sand-covered blacktop lane, I stopped at the sight of Leroy, Peanut, and Chip a short distance away.

Peanut lunged toward Chip. Leroy tightened his grip on the leash. Chip laughed but backed away at the same time, holding out his hands in a protective gesture.

With bated breath, I watched. Would Leroy be able to handle the situation?

He spoke in a stern tone to the dog. Peanut growled then sat, but he didn't take his gaze off of Chip.

With the situation under semi-control, I walked over to them. "How's it going?"

Leroy adjusted his ball cap with his free hand. "Something spooked the little guy. Possibly an owl, or a squirrel, or a feral cat. Yeah, most likely a cat."

"It's probably me. Most dogs don't like me for some reason." Chip laughed again. "I'll skedaddle. See you later."

Weird. Dogs often were a good judge of character. What did that say about Chip Johnson? To be fair, Peanut was still traumatized from Dirk's death. Maybe the way the light and shadows played across Chip's body had spooked the beagle.

"Andi Grace, I won't be able to adopt a dog if he don't like Chip." The older man looked like a little boy who'd just lost out on a special prize.

"Do you want to watch him this afternoon and see how it goes?" I wasn't feeling confident about the choice either, but I rarely failed matching dogs and people. Then again, Leroy wasn't the problem.

He shrugged. "It's not me I'm worried about. I don't want the little guy to be frightened."

I rubbed the man's arm. He had such a big heart, and I wanted him to have a good pet. "I've got a better idea. What if you meet me at Stay and Play around one thirty? I'm going to interview a dog groomer then, and you can play with Peanut."

Leroy leaned close. "I like your idea. He won't be distracted by Chip. Maybe if he gets comfortable with me, there won't be any more outbursts."

Leroy walked me to my Highlander and handed over the leash. "I appreciate your faith in me, Andi Grace. I know we didn't start off on the best of turns."

"Aw, water under the bridge. We're friends now, and that's all that counts. See you soon." I settled Peanut into the passenger seat and drove to Marc's office once the beagle was calm.

Marc stood in his law firm's small parking lot looking oh, so handsome.

I checked my hair and applied lipstick. Lacey Jane would be proud after all her lectures about working on my appearance.

Marc opened the passenger door. "Hey, Peanut. You've got my seat."

The dog gave a happy bark and hopped into the back.

Interesting. He didn't mind Marc. Yesterday with Lincoln had been fine, unless he'd felt more confident with the other dogs around. Still, he was okay with Marc today. "I thought we were meeting Zarina."

"She dropped off some photographs and this memory stick. Something about double booking and see what we liked. She even offered to post our favorite shots on social media and release one to the newspaper."

"Less for us to do. Yay. Have you got time to eat?"

"How about a quick sandwich at Daily Java?"

"Perfect. I can sit on the patio with Peanut, and you can order me something healthy." I drove out of the lot. "Do you have a favorite picture?"

"I've narrowed it down to a couple, but let's see what you think. Then we can negotiate."

"Oh, no." I pretended to pout. "That's your area of expertise. We may as well just publish the ones you prefer."

Marc shook his head. "Don't try to pull that on me. How many times have we worked to solve a murder against my better judgment? Most of the time I feel like I'm trying to catch up to you." His chuckle assured me he wasn't complaining.

I backed into an empty spot near Daily Java. "I'll eat anything you order, but please get me an iced coffee."

He handed me the packet of pictures. "Yes, ma'am."

I snagged my cross-body bag and the dog's leash and led Peanut to a shady table on the patio. Seagulls circled overhead, and the day was already warm.

Two men wearing slacks and dress shirts passed by us. They were deep in conversation, and Peanut didn't make a peep.

I turned my attention to the photos. Marc and me on the pier, on the beach, with the sun setting behind us, and some with waves crashing in the background. Without seeing what was on the jump drive, my favorite so far was the one with the waves crashing. In it I was looking at Marc with adoring eyes.

A young couple sat at a nearby table. The guy's voice was deep, and the girl had a squeaky sound. She was so short her feet didn't touch the ground. The guy sat on the edge of his seat and his feet did touch, but if he'd lined his spine against the back, his feet would dangle too. Once again, Peanut paid them no attention.

Dirk and Olivia had been a large couple. Individually each one was tall and dramatic. Put them together and they probably intimidated a few people.

What had Wade thought about Dirk's wife? I couldn't stop myself from smiling as I imagined his second conversation with Olivia.

"Whatcha thinking about?" Marc sat across from me with two sandwiches and two bowls of fruit. There were also two iced coffees and a cup of water.

"Wade interviewing Olivia. It would've been fun to watch him deal with Dirk's wife yesterday. On Friday, he treated her with respect as the grieving widow. I imagine his questions were different yesterday, especially after he knew she'd dognapped Peanut." We divvied up the food. "Is the water yours?"

"It's for Peanut." He removed the lid and held it out for the dog, who lapped it up.

"You're so nice." I checked my sandwich. "Turkey, avocado, tomato, lettuce and a vinaigrette. It looks amazing."

"The bread is some kind of sprouted wheat, and Erin assures me it's good for our health." His eyes cut to the food. "Did you have time to go through the pictures?"

"The three on top are my favorites." I plucked a grape out of my fruit cup. "Do you want to hear something interesting?"

"Everything you say is interesting." Marc winked.

"Ha, ha, very funny. It's obvious you've been hanging out with Lincoln." Despite trying to laugh off his compliment, I grew warm.

"What do you mean?"

"You wouldn't usually say something so mushy. Spending time with a country music star famous for his love songs is getting to you." I bit into my sandwich.

"Look who's funny now." He looked at the pictures. "Hey, this is one of my favorites too."

"Sounds like we've got a winner. I'll let Zarina know."

"You never told me the interesting thing."

I wiped my mouth. "Earlier, Peanut went ballistic when he saw Chip Johnson. What makes it more intriguing is that he hasn't gotten upset at a single other man in the last twenty-four hours."

Marc tilted his head. "Did Chip threaten him?"

"Not that I'm aware of." I shrugged. "Leroy took him for a short walk by himself, so I'm not positive what happened. Chip claims most dogs don't like him."

"Oh, boy. That puts him on your naughty list for sure." He met my gaze. "Give Chip a chance."

"Hey, dogs are a good judge of character." I took another bite of my sandwich, and we discussed the weather and the wedding until I dropped him back at his office. "I'll check on Chubb while I'm close to your place."

"Thanks, he'll enjoy seeing you." Marc gave me a quick kiss before heading into his office.

According to my dash clock, I had enough time to pick up Chubb and take him with me to Stay and Play. It'd be good to see how the applicant for my new dog groomer dealt with different dogs. I was also curious to see how Peanut acted with Leroy. If it turned out Peanut distrusted Chip, then I would take heed of his warning. I'd never encountered a dog I didn't trust. If Chip had never met a dog who liked him, alarms wailed in my head.

Hold on. Chip must think I'm plumb crazy. He'd already told me his old dog died. The man had lied to me at some point. At least one dog had liked Chip during his lifetime. The immediate question was why didn't Peanut like Chip?

Leroy and Chip got along fine. Peanut was the one who'd gone nuts around Chip. Whose judgment was more dependable? Man or dog? Peanut or Leroy?

Chapter Fifteen

DOG GROOMER MELANIE BRADSHAW was older than I'd expected, and she was short. Really short. I wouldn't judge a person on their size, but how would she manage working with big dogs? Who would handle who? We stood in my dog barn on Kennady Plantation, which I'd inherited not too long ago. "Your application shows you started working in your teens."

"Yes. We didn't have much money when I was growing up, and it eased the burden on my parents when I got a job." She pushed the glasses up her nose. "Do you have questions for me about this job specifically?"

I did my best to ignore the snippiness of her tone. "It looks like this is your first job as a dog groomer."

"Yes, but I've had my training. As you can see, I have lots of experience working retail, but it's more fun to work with animals. Either way, the customer always comes first."

First check for a good answer. "I get it. Why Heyward Beach?"

Her long blonde ponytail swayed. "I'd rather not say in case you don't hire me. It's personal."

"Oh, I'm sorry." My face warmed. "I didn't mean to pry. Your application says you're from Charleston. Do you plan to commute, or do you have a place here?"

"I need to find an apartment, but it can't be too expensive."

We'd just added an apartment to the stand-alone old kitchen. Juliet's brother had converted the place into rooms for guests staying at Kennady Plantation Bed and Breakfast. The back patio had been transformed into a small place to live. Before I offered the little apartment, I needed to witness Melanie at work first. "I'd like to see you interact with a couple of dogs."

"Sure." Her voice screeched and gave me pause. How would dogs respond to her high-pitched tone?

"Let's start with Chubb." The golden retriever lifted his head and trotted in our direction but remained in the play area.

A truck's rumble outside grew louder, and a quick glance showed it was Leroy. Right on time.

"Melanie, I'm going to let my friend know where to find us. Play with Chubb, and I'll be right back."

"Sure thing." She entered the play area and rubbed Chubb's head. "Hi, boy."

Standing in the barn's doorway, I waved to Leroy while keeping an eye on Melanie and the dogs. She was professional but not all lovey-dovey. Firm yet gentle. I saw her potential.

"Andi Grace, I apologize for upsetting Peanut earlier." Leroy limped my way with his arthritic gait.

"Hey, you've got no reason to apologize. It's possible no dog will like Chip, then you'd have to be a cat person." I elbowed him. A cat had caused him to fall off a roof years earlier, and he was not fond of any cats these days.

His head jerked back, and he narrowed his eyes. "Don't hold your breath, missy. I'll go without a pet before I resort to a cat."

I laughed. "Come on in. I'm interviewing a lady for the dog grooming position. Let me know what you think later."

We approached Melanie, who took turns throwing a dog toy to each of the animals. "I'd like you to meet my friend Leroy Peck. He may foster Peanut until we find him a forever home."

She reached over the fence and shook his hand. "Nice to meet you, sir. I believe Peanut will give you a nice workout. He's fun and high-spirited."

"We'll see how it goes. I may not be able to keep up with him." Leroy turned to me. "Andi Grace, do you know how old he is?"

"Good question. I need to ask Olivia more about him." It'd be a good reason to probe deeper. The bag of garbage she'd given me had literally been trash. Not a clue to be found. "Melanie, let me show you the grooming area."

Leroy puffed out his chest. "I was one of the first people to use it when I found a little dog. He was a pure mess, and Andi Grace was on crutches. I found him, so I cleaned him."

"And we've been friends ever since." I patted his arm then motioned for Melanie to follow me. "We've got a big tub for large dogs, and here's the ramp for them to walk up."

She pushed up her glasses. "I see. Very nice. The little dogs won't be a problem to lift into the smaller tub."

"The washer and dryer are over there." I pointed to them. "This cabinet holds towels—"

Melanie stood by the shelf of grooming supplies. "You've got a good selection, including hypoallergenic."

I counted to ten in French. Maybe she didn't mean to be rude, cutting me off. It was possible she was nervous. "Thanks."

"It all looks amazing. How do I get grooming appointments?"

"Interestingly enough, I have a waiting list. You can groom dogs, and we can offer specials where owners pay for grooming and stay all day to play."

"What about shut-ins? I might take a day or two a month and go to homes and groom dogs." She pushed up her glasses again.

I'd give her credit for wanting to be successful. "Let me look into liability issues. It might work better to pick the dogs up and bring them here. If you got hurt in somebody's home, it could be a nightmare."

"I get it." She walked around and inspected each section of the grooming area. "I have some discounts available on dog grooming products. Every graduate from our program got them."

"Nice. So what do you think? Are you interested in the job?" I didn't know if I wanted her to say yes or no.

"I like it here."

"Then I'm offering you a job on a probationary period. Two weeks?"

She gave me the first genuine smile I'd seen, and for a moment it felt like we'd met in the past. "You won't regret it."

"Melanie, have we met before today?"

Her eyes grew wide and she shook her head. "No, I would've remembered. Listen, thanks again. I best find a place to live if I'm going to work here."

"Hold up. I've got a little apartment at the old kitchen area. This place is a bed-and-breakfast, but we created a couple of apartments for my employees. If you'd like to stay there for a bit, it'll lessen the pressure of finding an apartment so fast." Dylan was another of my employees, and he lived in a nice apartment in the dog barn. His place was a legit studio apartment, and he enjoyed living there.

"Andi Grace, I promise not to disappoint you. In fact, why don't I groom Chubb to show you my appreciation?"

"Chubb belongs to my fiancé, and Marc will love it. I'll check on Leroy, but let me know if you have questions. You've got my number." I wandered outside and found Leroy and Peanut walking to the main house. He probably hoped to get a cookie from Juliet, but I needed to talk to him first. "Hey, hold up."

He spoke to Peanut, and they both stopped and waited.

"Thanks. I was wondering if you knew Dirk Cutter when he was alive?"

"I met him one day at the pier. He was drinking coffee and leaning against the rail watching the surf. Nice fellow, but he wasn't into fishing."

"Taking in the ambience? I prefer that to fishing myself." I smiled at him. "How'd you meet Chip?"

"Also at the pier, except he was trying to fish. Didn't know much, and I took him under my wing." He cut his eyes to me. "What are you up to, Andi Grace?"

I didn't back down from Leroy's scrutiny. "You know me. If a dog doesn't like you, I have to ask myself why."

"Right. Don't forget it wasn't too long ago you considered me a suspect in Tabby Malkin's murder."

"I know, but don't you think it's weird that the dog belonging to Heyward Beach's latest murder victim reacted strongly to Chip?"

Leroy sighed. "I'm chalking it up to coincidence. Nothing more." He returned to walking, and I fell into step beside him.

"Okay, Leroy. Convince me that Chip's an upstanding citizen."

"He runs a housing development for people who don't have a lot of money. Chip treats each person living there the same as he'd treat the mayor or governor. He doesn't judge people based on how they dress or where they live." Peanut moved to a tree and hiked up a leg.

"You got me there." I needed to keep my mind open. Accusing somebody of murder just because a sad dog reacted to them wasn't nice.

"Besides, what would Chip's motive be? He ain't no fancy movie star for Dirk to feature on his podcast. He hasn't lived in South Carolina long enough to make Dirk's radio program of unsolved crimes in these parts." Leroy grimaced. "I just don't see how it's possible. You need to look for another suspect."

"I'm sorry, Leroy, but Chip's basically a stranger to me. I know very little about him, and it's illogical to think he could commit a murder." I crossed my arms. "If Peanut hadn't reacted so strongly to the man, Chip wouldn't even be on my radar."

"I hear ya. Trusting dogs is what you do." Leroy adjusted his cap. "Somebody killed Dirk Cutter, and you want to look into it. I don't believe it's Chip though. Keep your eyes open to other possibilities."

"As long as you stay alert for danger, I'll look for more suspects."

"I don't believe Chip killed Dirk or anyone else, but for your sake, I'll keep my eyes open."

I couldn't ask more from my friend. "Thanks."

"You're welcome."

"Take your time with Peanut. I'll be in the barn." I started to move away then met Leroy's gaze. "It's just that I'd hate for anything to happen to you. I couldn't live with myself if you got hurt and I could've prevented it. Please watch your back."

He gave me a little salute then continued walking with Peanut.

I stared at them, hoping my warning would help Leroy be aware and not put him in danger.

Chapter Sixteen

My PHONE VIBRATED as I walked back to the barn, and Zarina's name popped up. I swiped it. "Hi, Zarina. The pictures were fabulous." I changed direction and settled into an Adirondack chair under an old oak tree.

"Oh, good. That's why I'm calling. Do you have a favorite?" Her voice sounded tired.

"Yes. Should I bring the photographs by later?"

"Don't bother. You can take a picture of it with your phone. I still have a copy and can touch up the ones you like best. I'll submit them to the paper once they're ready."

One less thing for me to handle was amazing. "Great. I also need to finish paying you."

"Your future hubby settled the balance, so we're good."

"Isn't he wonderful?" I relaxed in my chair.

"Yeah, he is." Her voice lacked sparkle.

"Zarina, is everything okay?"

"As my momma would say, I'm juggling too many batons on fire." She sighed. "Nothing for you to worry about."

"Have you found a place to live yet?"

"Nothing I can afford, or at least nothing affordable where I feel safe with my baby."

Piney Woods Apartment Complex came to mind as being affordable, but safety issues might be a problem.

Peanut barked, and he and Leroy hurried past me. A squirrel scurried up a tree. Peanut lunged toward it. Leroy spoke firmly, then led him in the opposite direction.

Zarina said, "That dog sounds familiar. Where have I heard it before?"

"Maybe when you were with Dirk Cutter?" I waved to Leroy.

"Yes. It's the beagle, isn't it?"

"I'm impressed. If you ever decide to give up photography, you might have a career working with animals."

She laughed. "Definitely something to consider. I discovered that Peanut's a good watchdog. Whenever the doorbell rang, he barked his head off."

I leapt out of the Adirondack chair and paced in the shade. "Exactly how much time did you spend with Dirk?"

"A normal amount, I guess. We first focused on pictures for publicity, then he had another shoot with a darker theme because of his big reveal on the podcast. I was there two days."

"Okay. Did anything weird happen? Dangerous even?"

She paused. "I'm not sure if this fits your definition of weird."

"Try me."

"One day when I was over there, Dirk had to take a call. He told me to make myself at home. His old college yearbooks were on a shelf, so I looked through them. I don't know if he had girlfriends back then, but a strip of pictures slipped out. You know, like you get in a photo booth?"

"Yeah." My heart beat harder. I knew Zarina was about to tell me something good. "And?"

"The girl he was with looked familiar, but I couldn't quite figure her out."

"Did you ask Dirk about her?"

"Yes. He said the lady was married to a local bigwig, and her daughter wouldn't be thrilled to learn they used to date."

My mouth grew dry. Bigwig. Daughter. "Uh, did he give you a name?"

"Nope. He only said the woman he'd known was a real peach, but their relationship didn't last. Andi Grace, I gotta run. Trust me to take care of the pictures though."

"Thanks." I ended the call and leaned against the oak tree while typing notes in my phone.

From what I knew about Dirk, there was possibly an underlying meaning behind his words. If I could decide what he meant, maybe I could prove Regina was innocent.

The cops thought Regina was a suspect. There was also Olivia. Hannah had acted weird on Sunday, and she knew Dirk's real name. Peanut alerted me that Chip might not be the good old boy he pretended to be.

One problem I'd face solving Dirk's murder was the number of people who knew him. It wasn't just locals. Because of the radio show, he was known throughout the region and possibly the entire state of South Carolina. The podcast made him possibly known around the world. Lincoln had been concerned Dirk would leak the news that his son Thomas had smoked pot. Not just smoked it at a party, but hadn't been punished when the law got involved. I didn't believe Lincoln was the killer, and it appeared as if the police ruled him out. The guilty person could be a complete stranger to me.

Love and money were two common motives when it came to murder. Old secrets or cold cases could play into the reason behind Dirk's murder.

Bigwig. Zarina had used that specific word. The peachy girl from college had married a bigwig and had a daughter.

I didn't know where to look next, so I joined Melanie at the grooming station. "How's it going?"

She held a fluffy towel in her hands and dried Chubb. "Good. He wasn't happy about the hair dryer, so I'm towel-drying him."

Her sensitivity to Chubb's fear touched me. "Nice. Why don't we let him into the play area, and I'll show you the apartment at the old kitchen?"

"Sure." She gave the golden retriever a treat and led him away from her grooming station and to the play area. "Good boy, Chubb."

After she secured the gate, we walked to the back of the old kitchen. The original patio had been converted into an efficiency apartment. It was smaller than Dylan's place in the dog barn. "It's tight, but you've got a kitchenette, bathroom, and a daybed. If it was New York City, they'd call it a studio apartment." I studied her. She was calmer than when I interviewed her earlier. The way she'd handled Chubb had been kind. Maybe she'd been nervous before, and now that she'd been given the opportunity to work for me, she'd settled down.

Melanie walked into the space and studied the kitchen, then sat on the daybed. "Nice and firm. I like it."

"I won't charge you anything for the next two weeks. We can reevaluate your job performance then. And of course, you may decide you don't like it here."

"Andi Grace, you won't be sorry for giving me this chance. I just know I'll like this job."

"I believe you." I handed her the key. "Juliet runs the B and B. Dylan works with the animals, and he's my general maintenance man. He helped build this place. I'm not out here every day, and if you can't reach me, Dylan is the person for you to contact. People come and go daily, and they don't always schedule ahead of time. Some of Juliet's guests think just because they made a reservation for themselves the pets are included."

"Oh, that's probably a challenge. What do you want me to do when I don't have grooming appointments?"

Good question. She didn't appear to be lazy. "I'll pay you for a full-time job. Let me make some calls and set your schedule. When there's not an animal needing to be groomed, you can always play with the animals we're watching. Socialization skills are important. I need to introduce you to the others, and you can take off the rest of the day. Get settled into your apartment."

"Is there a Target nearby? I need towels and sheets."

"No. Paula's Pickings has interesting things. The owner, Regina Houp, may have towels there. If you drop by, tell her I sent you. There's also a dollar store, if you're in a pinch and don't want to drive far."

"Where is Paula's Pickings?"

I gave her directions to the shop on the island, then we found Juliet in the little herb garden near the main house, and I introduced them.

Leroy waved to me from the barn, and I left Melanie and Juliet talking. "How'd you do?"

The big grin on his face was all the answer I needed. "We got along just fine. I'll take him home with me for a trial run."

I patted Peanut. "Let me get you some supplies and enough dog food for a couple of days. If you have any trouble, call me. Day or night. It doesn't matter."

"If it wasn't for Chip, I wouldn't be concerned. Maybe they'll get used to each other. What do you think?" Leroy's eyebrows lifted, and I could imagine him as a little boy asking for a special treat.

"It's possible. Chip needs to let Peanut approach him. We don't know how Dirk and Olivia treated the dog, and maybe it was the way your friend moved or the sound of his voice. If it doesn't work with Peanut, we'll find you another dog and keep looking for a good home for this little one."

We settled the beagle and dog supplies into Leroy's truck, and the man gave me a gentle hug. "I appreciate this."

"You're my friend, and Peanut's lucky to be going home with you. Have fun."

After waving him off, I looked around Kennady Plantation. In the past it'd been a rice plantation. After the Civil War, the owners had sold off parcels. Marc owned a section along the river. He had a modest home, a good shed to work on boats, and easy access to the river. It'd been perfect for a boat builder, but he'd returned to practicing the law. On his terms. Marc took a stand for the underdog, and I couldn't be prouder of the man he was.

My favorite part of the property was the dog barn. Inheriting this place had allowed me to pursue my dreams of expanding my dog-walking business. Not only was I walking dogs and giving obedience lessons, but with Melanie on staff dog grooming was about to begin. Of course, that meant I needed to start making calls to people who'd requested this service in the past.

I walked to the barn and got Chubb. "Let's go to my place. You can hang out with Sunny while I call Doc Hewitt to check on Copper." We listened to an episode of Dirk's podcast on the way home. Dirk had a smooth voice and a nice sense of humor without being crude.

What had the man said or done so awful that a person would want to murder him?

My phone vibrated, and Olivia's name appeared with a text message. *I need to see you ASAP.*

Chapter Seventeen

IN LESS THAN AN HOUR, I rang the doorbell at Cutter's Landing.

Some dogs enjoyed a nap after being groomed, and others were ready to burn off energy after being good for so long. Chubb fell into the napping category, and he was snoozing at my house with Sunny.

I pushed Olivia's doorbell again and studied the front of the periwinkle blue beach house. Dirk had been clever in building his career right down to giving his beach house a name to draw attention to his business. He'd probably found a way to take it off his taxes. The horizontal oval sign for Cutter's Landing with the sailing vessel was attractive and stood out nicely at the front of his white stairwell.

Olivia swooshed open the door wearing a lacy black cover-up over a black one-piece bathing suit. Under her right arm she held Copper. "Andi Grace, I'm glad you're here. My baby's not eating like he used to."

"He's been through a trauma from Dirk's death, and the overdose of your diazepam didn't help. What did Doc Hewitt say when you picked up Copper?"

"He told me to never give any dog my medications again. Ever. I don't know how he has any clients. He was very rude." She sniffed and lifted her nose in the air.

"People recognize how much he cares about the animals he treats." It didn't surprise me a bit that Doc had gotten mad at her. "Olivia, is it possible Copper witnessed Dirk's murder? Could it be the reason he ran away from home Friday morning?"

"I honestly couldn't tell you for sure. Peanut and I got here long after midnight. It may have been closer to two, and I don't know what Copper did before we arrived."

"How'd you get inside?" Boom. I'd finally gotten to ask one of my burning questions.

"The front door was locked, but I came around to the back and found the door ajar. I secured it behind us and took Peanut to Dirk's office."

"Where was your husband when you arrived?"

Olivia shrugged. "When I didn't see him, I assumed he was sleeping in the master bedroom. I did call out and announce myself, but Dirk was a heavy sleeper. Copper found me, and we went to the guest room. I fell asleep, and the next thing I knew you were yelling at me about finding my dog in the street." She waved me into the house, so I entered, then shut the door and followed her to the kitchen area.

Olivia kissed the dog's head. "What should I do?"

"I'm not an animal psychologist, but I think you should keep showing him he's safe. You know, just in case he witnessed the murder while you slept. Make sure he eats and drinks plenty of water. When the weather turns warm, I make sure my dogs have plenty to drink." Yes, I was claiming Chubb as my dog because I'd known him most of his life, and once Marc and I married, the golden retriever would live with us.

She leaned a hip against the kitchen counter. "Should I give him more treats? Better food?"

"No, this is nothing you can fix with money or food. Copper needs your attention, and it will take time for him to heal. Even if he didn't witness the murder, he was wandering the streets alone, and we don't know what he experienced." I took a breath. "Time and attention will be the best way for him to recover."

"I have a business to run." She straightened her shoulders, making me feel smaller. Olivia was a big woman, but I was also tall. Not many women dwarfed me. "I guess he can stay in my office at the store."

I didn't agree with her plan, but she hadn't asked my opinion. "Do you want me to take him out to potty?"

"Sure." She handed the shih tzu to me.

"I need his leash."

"It must be here." She looked through the basket of dog supplies and came up empty. "Maybe Dirk left it in the pantry."

"Olivia, have you taken Copper out since he's been home?"

She batted her eyes at me. "No. We've been snuggling, and he used the pee-pee pads."

"Good grief. You need to be consistent. If you want Copper to go potty outside, he's got to have time out there."

"You're right." She opened the pantry door and disappeared into the little room. "I never understood Dirk's organization system."

Shame on me. Olivia was a grieving widow and I needed to cut her some slack. "I always keep an extra leash in my SUV. You don't need to search right now."

She appeared with a gray plastic container marked *Dog Supplies*. "Maybe we'll find one in here."

Copper got restless in my arms, and I set him down. He headed straight for a pad.

"No, Copper. Let's go outside." I snapped him up and headed out the back door. "Come on, Olivia, it's a small yard. The fence will prevent him from running away."

I jogged down the composite steps, paused at the landing to glance at the empty swimming pool, then hurried down the next section to the fenced-in yard. "Okay, Copper. Go potty." I set him in the grass.

Olivia clopped down the stairs with her sandals smacking each step loudly.

The wind blew my hair loose, and I adjusted my ponytail while watching Copper. Waves crashed on the beach hard, like when a storm brewed in the Atlantic.

"I'll have to give Dirk credit for picking the perfect spot for a beach house." Olivia stood next to me. "How long should it take him to do his business? Is there anything I should do?"

"Give him time to sniff around." Patience didn't appear to be Olivia's thing. "How'd you meet Dirk?"

"It was at a charity show in Wilmington. The community food bank was raising money to replenish their provisions. I provided clothes for the fashion show and helped volunteers get dressed. Dirk emceed. We met at the rehearsal, but it was the after-party where we got to know each other. I found him charming."

"How romantic. While doing good for others you found love. I guess you knew him as Don Caswell since your last name is Caswell." I kept an eye on the dog, who'd hiked his leg at two azaleas but continued to sniff the grass and other small bushes.

"No, he was Dirk Cutter when we met. His fame was growing, and we decided if I went by Caswell, it'd protect our privacy. I always called him Dirk, but once we started dating, he told me his given name. Don Caswell. He just never seemed like a Don." The dog positioned himself and did number two. "Do you expect me to use one of those plastic bags and pick up his dog droppings?"

"You have two options. Leave it and risk stepping in it later or picking it up. If you don't want to use a bag, there are scoopers you can use."

She shivered. "Ugh."

"It's part of being a dog owner. What'd you do with the pads after he used one?"

"I threw them away and lay out a fresh pad." Copper came to Olivia and whimpered. She picked him up. "Good boy."

"Olivia, what happened in your marriage? It sounds like you loved Dirk."

Her eyes narrowed. "Are you sure you're a dog walker and not a shrink? Or even worse, a reporter?"

I grinned. She hadn't asked if I was an amateur sleuth. "I promise."

She walked up the steps, and I followed. "I had trouble dealing with so many women throwing themselves at Dirk. He was handsome, but there are better-looking men. It was Dirk's charisma that drew people to him. Did you ever meet my husband?"

"No, I'm afraid not." I couldn't help looking at the pool again on our way past it.

"Trust me. Women wanted to be with him, and men wanted to be him. I can't remember where I heard that expression, but it fit Dirk." She opened the door and walked to the dog bed and placed Copper on it. "Would you like some water, Andi Grace?"

The day before she couldn't wait to get rid of me. Today Olivia offered me a drink. "Sure."

"Or something stronger? Dirk liked his liquor and there are plenty of options to choose from." She opened a liquor cabinet. "That man could drink almost anyone under the table." She paused, as if awaiting my response.

"I'm good with water. Thanks."

Olivia opened the refrigerator and removed two bottles of spring water and passed one to me before turning to the box on the table. "Let's see if there's a leash in here." She removed the lid of the gray box.

"Were you young when you met Dirk?"

"Close to forty, but don't try to do the math. I refuse to reveal my exact age." She shook her head. "Oh, dear. This is so typical of Dirk. He tended to be a tad paranoid about his research."

"What do you mean?"

She unscrewed the blue top of her bottle. "He feared somebody would scoop him on the good stories, so he liked to hide his notes. I don't know how he kept track of all his secret places."

"Can I look?"

"Are you sure you're not a reporter?"

I laughed. "I promise. I'm curious though."

She pushed the box my way. "Knock yourself out."

"Who do you think killed Dirk?" I gripped the sides of the box.

She tilted her head. "Did you send the sheriff over to question me?"

"Trust me, Sheriff Stone doesn't take orders from me." If I wanted Olivia to trust me, I needed to be entirely honest. "We're friends though, so I did tell him we'd been communicating about the dogs."

"I thought it was fishy when he arrived right after you left." She sat in a chair at the table. "Sheriff Stone treated me like I was a suspect, but I told him he was barking up the wrong tree. He needs to look into Dirk's love life, starting with that Reba woman."

"Do you mean Regina Houp?" I drank from my water bottle.

"That's the one. They were dating, but she claims she didn't know he was married. I saw them at Tuscan Tomato Thursday night, and she appeared startled to learn I was married to Dirk." She played with the blue lid. "You were there too. I remember now. Maybe Regina was innocent about my marriage, but I still think she's the killer."

"You probably look guilty because you tracked them down at the restaurant. Stopping by the house probably didn't help your claim of innocence." I kept my voice soft and sat across the table so it wouldn't seem like I wanted to intimidate her. Although it was doubtful many people frightened the woman.

"I believe we already had this conversation. I wanted Copper and settled for Peanut."

"Do you know Chip Johnson?"

"The name doesn't ring a bell. Who is he?"

"He runs an apartment complex on the other side of the marsh. A friend of mine took Peanut for a walk, and the dog went crazy when he saw Chip. I haven't known Peanut for long, but he doesn't seem to get upset around many people."

"It is odd for him. Dirk took him lots of places, so he's been around all kinds of people. Maybe he was just having a bad day."

"Could be. Chip said most dogs don't like him."

Olivia pointed at me with her French-tip fingernail. "And that disturbs you because you're a dog person."

I shrugged. "I can't deny it, but I'm also aware people rub us wrong for no apparent reason."

"So true." She finished her water.

"Do you know who Dirk dated in college?"

Olivia laughed long and hard. "He has dated so many people, you'd need a spreadsheet to keep up. His college yearbooks are around here somewhere. You're welcome to them if you can find any."

Zarina had already given me a clue. I moved into the family room and looked at the shelves full of books and games. "I love your beach house, and having a pool makes it more special."

"Once Dirk got sponsors for his podcast, he bought this place. He took risks looking for a good story, but he was careful with our money. He thought this was a good investment as well as a nice house."

"I guess he could even deduct part of it from his taxes since he named the house for his business. He also recorded the podcast from here, and I guess that works for tax purposes."

Olivia's eyes widened. "Aren't you clever? Not everybody understands that."

I turned my attention to a small bookshelf near the stairs. "I used to have an accountant friend." Peter had been the first murder victim I'd found. On the bottom shelf were four college yearbooks. I pulled them out and walked to the table, where Olivia stood going through the box from the pantry. "I wish I could find Dirk's will. No attorneys have reached out to me, but he was too smart not to have written one."

Drat. Our conversation had distracted me from going through the box. "You didn't have a joint will?"

Olivia flipped her long hair over a shoulder. "No. We never had kids, so we kinda had the mindset we'd each have separate wills."

Cold. Or maybe it was smart. "Is there anything I can do?"

"Look behind me in the pantry. Maybe there's another box with the real dog supplies."

I turned on the light. "Wow, he was organized."

"And a minimalist. That makes it easier to be neat."

"Good point." I moved cereal and cracker boxes but found nothing. The cookie shelf contained the best, most expensive cookies from a local bakery. I checked behind and under each item, until I touched one cardboard container that felt lighter than the rest. I peeked inside and found index cards. "No leash, but I found notes."

I showed the white lined cards to Olivia.

"Oh, yeah. He always carried a few blank cards with him for when inspiration struck. One night we were out eating in a romantic restaurant. A football player for the Carolina Panthers entered the place and was ushered to a booth in the back. I didn't recognize the man, but Dirk pulled out a card and started taking notes. Not only did he recognize the football player, but he knew the woman wasn't his wife. Dirk researched until he discovered the woman was the football player's sister, and he discarded the notes."

"It sounds like Dirk had scruples."

"Yeah, but if you were in the wrong, watch out. Kill your spouse, embezzle from your boss, have an affair or anything like that, and he didn't hesitate to go for the jugular."

It seemed odd he'd date Regina while still married to Olivia if he'd go after others having affairs. Maybe deep in his heart they were divorced. "If Dirk's death wasn't related to a woman, who had the most to gain?"

"It must be somebody he exposed on the podcast." She yawned. "I didn't sleep well last night." My cue to leave.

"Let me run down to my SUV and get the spare leash for you."

She waved her hands over the table. "You can have any of this stuff."

My heart leapt. "Even this container?"

"Yeah, I doubt any of those papers are important to me. The only document I'm interested in locating is Dirk's will."

"Okay. I'll be right back." The plastic bin was too full to add the annuals, so I ran to my SUV with the books and the index cards.

When I returned, Olivia stood at the large window looking at the rough Atlantic. "It's hard to believe he's gone. I know we were separated, but I did love Dirk in the beginning. Honestly, I didn't fall out of love, but we weren't good together."

Believing her declaration, I patted her shoulder. "Death is always painful."

"I don't usually spill my guts to strangers. Thanks for listening."

I handed the leash to Olivia. "Call me anytime."

"Do you know a good lawyer?"

"A divorce attorney?" Why would she need one now?

"No." She shook her head. "You know, in case they arrest me for Dirk's death."

Marc had agreed to help me prove Regina was innocent, so he wouldn't be able work for Olivia. "Um, you probably need a really good defense attorney. Somebody used to murder trials. I don't know if the person has to be licensed in South Carolina to handle your case, but I'd look for one in Charleston or Myrtle Beach because they aren't too far away. You won't want to waste money paying attorneys to travel to Heyward Beach and visit you in jail."

"You keep impressing me, Andi Grace. At hundreds of dollars an hour, I shouldn't pay for travel time." She yawned again and picked up Copper. "I may need to go back to the spa to combat all this stress. This time I'll be sure to schedule an appointment before showing up."

"If you go, I'd be happy to take care of Copper." I turned and picked up the gray tote. "Do you want me to leave the container and just take the papers?"

She waved me off. "Take it all, but if you run across the will, and I don't think it's in there, but if you do, please return it."

"Of course. Take care of yourself, Olivia." I left her standing at the back door, holding her little dog. The normal hoity-toity expression she wore had been replaced by a forlorn look. Droopy mouth and a frown.

Either she was a superb actress or she was innocent of Dirk's murder. If Olivia didn't commit the deed, I was back at square one. Who killed Dirk?

Chapter Eighteen

MARC KNOCKED ON THE FRONT DOOR, then entered my house. "Andi Grace, you home?"

"I'm in the office." I'd placed blank index cards in the first two annuals to mark places where I'd found pictures of Don Caswell, also known as Dirk Cutter. The items I'd collected from his beach house lay scattered on the glass-top coffee table.

"Are you working on the murder?" Marc sat beside me on the white couch and kissed my temple.

"Yes, but I made myself wait until I'd lined up grooming appointments for Melanie. She'll be my dog groomer for two weeks on a trial basis. If it works out, she's hired. Dylan took over today's dog-walking appointments, freeing me up to investigate." I shared my impressions of the potential new employee with Marc.

"Two weeks should be long enough to see if Melanie can handle bigger dogs. It'll also give you time to determine if your customers like her."

"Exactly. People don't usually hesitate to complain, and that's a good thing when it comes to their pets." I smiled. "She groomed Chubb today."

He slapped his hand against his chest. "Without asking my permission?" The teasing tone assured me I had nothing to worry about.

"Your fiancée thought it was a good idea."

"She is one smart cookie, and I trust her opinion." He pushed a loose strand of hair behind my ear.

"Aren't you curious about all this?" I pointed to the books, Dirk's index cards, and the gray box from Dirk's house.

The dogs barked, and Marc walked to the back door. "Tell me about it in a minute. Why is Chubb here?"

"After Melanie groomed him, I hated the thought of taking him back home and leaving him all alone."

"You're a softie, Andi Grace." Marc let the dogs inside and the sound of running water in the kitchen told me he was filling their water bowls. He returned and sat beside me while loosening his tie.

"How was your day?" I turned on the couch so I could face him.

"Busy but good." He laughed. "It appears your day was more exciting. Tell me about all this stuff. Why are you looking at college yearbooks?"

"These are Dirk's annuals. Zarina somehow got a look at them, and she believes one of Dirk's classmates is somebody she's met in Heyward Beach.

She couldn't be sure though, and I managed to get all this from Olivia." I circled my hands over the table of potential clues.

"Wade won't be thrilled." Marc drummed his fingers on the arm of the couch.

"Hey, they had the opportunity to search the house and question Olivia." I lifted my chin. "I practically handed them Olivia on a silver platter."

"I hear ya." He grinned. "What can I do to help?"

"This box is labeled *Dog Supplies*, but it's paperwork. I also found the index cards in the pantry, and Olivia claims Dirk always kept some around in case he got inspired." I told Marc the story about the football player in the restaurant.

"It's hard to get a handle on Dirk's character, but I'm here to assist. Let me start with the box."

I clapped my hands. "Great, you're much better at organizing than I am."

He rolled up his sleeves and pulled all the papers out.

With my phone app, I started my playlist of country music, and the songs drifted out of the surround sound in the office. I lost track of time until Sunny appeared and nudged my leg. "Goodness, it's getting late. I bet you're hungry."

Marc patted his flat stomach. "She's not the only one who's hungry."

"I didn't go to the grocery store today, but I can fix eggs, toast, and fruit." I headed to the kitchen.

"Do you want me to pitch in with fixing supper or keep going through this box? I'm almost done."

"Keep working, and we can compare notes while we eat." I fed the dogs and refilled the water bowl. "Sorry, y'all. I got lost in my research." I rubbed their heads then got out of their way.

After washing my hands, I cut up an apple, an orange and the few remaining red grapes in my refrigerator. I pulled sourdough bread from the freezer and eggs and shredded cheddar cheese from the fridge.

Marc appeared. "Dirk's handwriting was atrocious, but from what I can decipher, he was checking out a cold case in California. He wrote the word *killer* and underlined it four times."

"Regina mentioned California to me. Would you look in my journal? I'm sure I wrote it down."

"Are you talking about the one on the kitchen table?"

"Yes, Regina gave it to me. Isn't it pretty?"

He picked it up and leafed through the pages. "It's nice."

I drizzled extra virgin olive oil into the pan, added the eggs, and began to stir them over medium heat. "Any luck?"

"Yep. Right here you wrote down Triple C threat."

"Yes, that's how she referred to the California cold case."

"Three Cs. I get it now." He ran a hand over his face. "I guess this could be what his big podcast episode was going to cover."

"When you looked through Dirk's notes, did you find anything similar?"

"No." Marc washed his hands and fixed two glasses of water.

"Hey, why don't you find a list of all Dirk's podcast episodes? If one is about a cold case in California, we can eliminate it from real clues to his murder."

"What?" His forehead crinkled.

"If he already aired the case, he wouldn't be a threat to the alleged killer."

"Unless his death is about revenge for exposing a murderer." Marc swiped and studied his phone. "I had no idea there were so many seasons of *Where Are They Now?*"

"I feel like Dirk had multiple podcast seasons each year." I moved the pan off the burner and divided the eggs up on each of the white plates, then sprinkled the cheese on top. "When we get married, I'd like to register for colorful plates."

"Like what?"

"Maybe those Fiesta dishes." Oops, I'd forgotten the toast, so I stuck two pieces in the toaster and pushed them down on the frozen setting. "Any luck?"

I carried our plates to the table then got the bowl of fruit and silverware.

The toast popped up with a click, and Marc stuffed his phone into the pocket of his slacks. "I'll get it. From what I can see, there is no episode with the items we're looking for."

I let the dogs out back, and sat beside Marc at the table. "Then it's possible this was the mysterious episode he was promoting. Let's eat our eggs before they get cold."

Marc ate with gusto and fixed more toast for himself. "How about the yearbooks?"

"I agree with Zarina. There's one female classmate who stands out, but I can't decide who she is." I gathered the books from my office and lay them on the table between us. "She's tall and thin with long hair, maybe blonde. Some of the pictures are grainy, adding to the challenge of identifying the person." Because of the well-placed index cards, it was easy to show Marc the pictures I'd found of the same woman with Dirk.

Marc leaned close to the page. "Hmm, show me more."

"I didn't see her in the book covering his senior year." I flipped the page.

"It's possible she was older than Dirk, transferred colleges, or quit school altogether."

"Good points." We went through each annual in chronological order. I drummed my fingers on the table. "Maybe if we sleep on it, we can reach a logical conclusion tomorrow."

"I'll help you clean the dishes, then I need to head home."

We cleared the table, and I turned to my fiancé. "I've got this. If I know you, there's a brief, or contract, or something needing your lawyerly attention tonight."

One side of his mouth shot up. "I can't wait until we're married and I don't have to leave you here all alone." He called the dogs inside and locked the door.

I leaned against his chest. "It's been an adjustment living here by myself with only Sunny for company. I miss Lacey Jane, but it's nice to have the place to myself at times." It was the first time in my life I'd lived alone.

He rubbed my back. "I feel better knowing you have a security system."

"You need to get going so you're able to sleep tonight." I took his hand in mine and led him and Chubb to the front door.

"I love you, Andi Grace."

"I love you, too." We kissed until Chubb pushed against Marc's thigh. "Be careful going home."

"See you tomorrow, and please stay out of trouble."

"I'll do my best to behave." I never meant to push the boundaries too far, but when dealing with a killer, it was sometimes unavoidable.

The authorities were looking at Regina and Olivia as suspects. It seemed like Lincoln had been ruled out. Because of his friendship with Marc, I'd never believed he killed Dirk. I was also curious about the mysterious woman from Dirk's past. Something was odd about Chip, but I couldn't quite put a finger on what. If the murder was related to the radio show or podcast, the list of suspects could be endless.

I turned out all the downstairs lights, and Sunny followed me to my bedroom and lay on the floor next to my side of the bed.

"Girl, if Chubb is used to sleeping in the room with Marc, this place will get real small, real fast. At least you don't sleep in bed with me." When my parents died, there were many nights Lacey Jane climbed into bed with me and even a few when Nate joined us and lay at the foot of the bed. Sunny had always slept on the floor, as if she felt the need to protect us. From the moment she'd appeared, she'd been instrumental in our healing process. I'd named her Sunny because she'd brought sunshine into our lives, and I considered my German shepherd to be a gift from God.

I rubbed her back before turning off the light. "Let's get some rest. Tomorrow will be here soon enough to look for more clues."

The sound of Sunny's soft snores relaxed me, but thoughts of Dirk's demise kept me awake. One potential way to rule out Chip would be to see if other dogs reacted badly when he was around. He'd claimed no dogs liked him. If I found his claim to be true, I'd take him off my suspect list. Which dog would I take to visit Chip? Sunny or Chubb? Visiting Leroy could be my excuse. Whether Chip's statement was true or not, it didn't mean he had murdered Dirk. What would be his motive? Did it involve Piney Woods Apartment Complex? Drug smuggling? Human trafficking? Or could it involve bids on work projects? Was Chip monkeying around with the finances? It was possible, but he hadn't worked there very long.

I yawned. Tomorrow would be soon enough to dig deeper.

Chapter Nineteen

A CLAP OF THUNDER WOKE ME UP TUESDAY MORNING. I'd changed my ringtone to the song written by Marc and sung by Lincoln, "Love Ripples." The tune played, and I checked my phone. There were three requests from families to come walk their dogs. Two were elderly ladies who lived at Waccamaw Retirement Community, and one was Phyllis Mays, because she didn't want to ruin her new hairdo before a meeting with the church ladies.

You never knew what to expect with Phyllis, but I agreed to all three requests. "Sunny, you need to go out now, but I'll let you stay home and snooze. No need for you to spend more time in the rain than necessary." We ran down the stairs and to the back door. After deactivating the security alarm, I let Sunny out.

Before I even had time to fix a cup of coffee, Sunny whined at the door. I snagged a towel and dried her off on the porch before we reentered the house.

A flash of lightning was followed by a boom of thunder, and it shook the earth. Sunny barked, and my heart leapt. "Let's go, girl"

She zipped past me and clambered up the stairs.

When I reached my bedroom, her tail stuck out from under the bed. "Your favorite hiding spot. How about some music to soothe your nerves?"

I turned on the radio and got ready in record time. The radio personality said, "Expect flooding on the island streets this morning. We've got a king tide, high tide, and it's raining, folks. Batten down the hatches."

"Oh, I better hurry before the roads are impassable." Driving through floodwaters was the perfect way to rust out a car in no time. Salt water was not kind to any metals, and I owned a nice SUV. In my opinion, dealing with your belongings getting rusty was the only downside to living on the island.

I hurried to the Highlander and took off. Water had already accumulated along the edges of Sea Turtle Drive, forcing me to stay in the middle of the road.

My phone rang from the cupholder phone mount. Leroy's name popped up, and I touched the button to answer on speaker mode. "Good morning, Leroy. How are you?"

"Morning. Andi Grace, we did good last night, but when Peanut saw Chip this morning it was bad. Real bad." His voice shook.

"No problem. We knew it could be an issue. Why don't you and Peanut meet me at Stay and Play in an hour or so?" I explained my three stops, and I'd rushed right out of the house without my morning coffee. Daily Java would be the fourth stop on my list.

"I hate to let ya down." A dog whimpered in the background.

"No, it's not your fault. We'll find you another dog who's a better fit." There were many reasons for a dog and owner not to jibe, and I never minded taking back a dog. "With all this bad weather, let's make it two hours. If you beat me, make yourself at home in the barn with Peanut. I'll see you later."

I zipped into the parking lot of Daily Java. If I waited until after my appointments, the parking lot and street might be flooded. Five other vehicles were parked in front of the coffee shop. I wasn't the only one needing their morning fix.

Flipping up the hood of my rain jacket, I dashed into my favorite coffee shop. On the way, my right foot landed in a deep puddle, soaking my shoe and sock. I also twisted my ankle, sending a dull pain up my leg. I'd had worse accidents.

Erin Lane smiled at me when I stumbled through the door. "Good morning. I see you're trying to beat the king tide."

"Absolutely. What's your morning brew?" I stood on my good foot and turned my right one in a circular motion, hoping to work out the kink.

"Georgia pecan. It's especially good if I add my secret peach sauce." Her eyes sparkled.

"Sounds great, and I'll take whatever muffin you recommend to go with it."

"Cinnamon crunch. Definitely." She rang me up and took my money. "I'll hurry so you can get out of here before the streets get worse."

"Thanks. I've got dogs to walk on the mainland, so I definitely need to get out of here. But I won't watch over your shoulder." I wandered to the sitting area. No matter how long I'd been walking dogs, it still made me nervous when some clients watched me closely.

Regina and Chip were sitting together at a table for two.

I may have gasped because they both looked at me.

"Hi, Andi Grace." Regina waved.

"Hey there. I planned to come see you later today after the tide recedes. How do you two know each other?"

Chip leaned back in his chair and puffed out his chest. "This sweet lady took pity on me and joined me for coffee."

So many questions raced through my pre-caffeinated brain. "Where'd you meet?"

Regina giggled. "We recently met at an organizational meeting for the town scavenger hunt."

Dirk had been murdered the morning of the scavenger hunt, meaning she'd met Chip before then. Thursday night had been her last date with Dirk. Had she dated both men at the same time?

One side of Chip's mouth slid up. "Might say it was my lucky night."

I snapped my fingers and hoped I didn't appear flustered. "Oh, maybe it was the meeting I missed due to helping a client with a sick dog."

"Andi Grace, your order is ready," Erin's voice interrupted our conversation.

"It's good to see you both this morning. Stay safe." I needed to quit gawking at the two of them and get off the island.

"You, too." Chip's deep voice vibrated in an attractive way.

I hustled to get my coffee and muffin and hit the road before embarrassing myself more. It'd be hours before low tide, but once the streets became drivable, I'd track down Regina and look into her relationship with Chip. Here I'd been worried Regina was pining over Dirk. It'd never occurred to me she was interested in another man.

With my wipers struggling at full speed to clear my windshield, and wind blowing against my Highlander, I turned my focus to the treacherous driving conditions. Solving the murder could wait.

Chapter Twenty

THE DOWNPOUR TURNED INTO A DRIZZLE by the time I'd walked all three dogs and reached Stay and Play. I parked as close to the dog barn as possible and limped inside.

Dylan King, my first employee at the plantation, stood near the play area fence talking to Marc and Leroy.

"Gentlemen, what's going on?" My heart pitter-pattered at the sight of my fiancé.

Marc smiled. "The police closed the roads on the island, so I've got the morning off."

"Nice." Except for the fact I no doubt looked like a drowned rat. Maybe the shadowy barn would disguise the damage from the rain.

Melanie appeared from the grooming area holding a little dog wrapped in a towel. "Hi, Andi Grace. The apartment is perfect for me, and thanks for lining up appointments. I guess you know Gus."

"I sure do. He belongs to Hannah Cummins, who's running for state representative. Actually, Leroy rescued Gus, and Hannah adopted him."

Leroy stood taller. "He was a mess the day we met. It looks like Hannah's taking good care of him."

Melanie lifted one of the dog's little paws and waved to Leroy. "Time to trim his nails."

Dylan said, "I need to call a man about a dog pool. Talk to ya later." He headed in the direction of my office.

Leroy glanced both ways. "It kills me not to be able to keep the beagle, but I'm not up to another move this year. If only he didn't get upset around Chip, it'd be perfect."

"Hey, you can come play with him whenever you want. We'll take good care of Peanut until we find his forever home."

The man's eyebrows lifted. "We didn't get in a full walk with the rain earlier. Maybe I should take him for a good long stroll around here. It'll help him burn up some of his energy.'

"Perfect. Thanks." I reached for a leash hanging on one of the support beams. "Have fun."

I turned to Marc. "Will you get slammed this afternoon trying to make up your missed appointments?"

"More than likely, but if we get to spend time together this morning I can't complain. The streets should be passable in a few hours."

"Let's go to the main house and grab a cup of coffee." I squeezed his arm. "No, wait. You're not going to believe what I discovered this morning. Regina and Chip know each other. They were drinking coffee together at Daily Java."

"You don't say."

"Yeah. I do." When Marc talked like an old man, I always smiled. "They met a few weeks ago at a town meeting for the scavenger hunt. You know what that means, don't you? While Regina was dating Dirk, she knew Chip."

Marc's head shook slightly. "I don't see how it can be a motive for murder."

I sighed. "You're right, but there's still something about Chip that rubs me wrong."

"I know, honey, but right now we need to stick to facts. There's nothing to show a relationship between Dirk and Chip."

"True, but what do we really know about Chip?"

"Leroy hangs out with the man and thinks he's okay. Why don't you ask Regina what she knows about his background?"

I snapped my fingers. "Brilliant. I can update her on the investigation and sneak in questions about him."

Melanie appeared. "Are you talking about Regina Houp?"

"Yeah, did you go to her shop?"

"Yes, but boy, is it expensive in there. Way over my budget." She lifted her hands in a surrender gesture.

"I should've thought about that before sending you over there. We just don't have a lot of shopping options in Heyward Beach except for dollar stores and gift shops." The prices at Paula's Pickings had left me staggering before. "When her aunt owned the place, she sold vintage and decorative items. The prices were more reasonable then. Not that I'm being critical. Regina just has a taste for finer things, which translates into paying high prices."

"Oh, I wondered why it was called Paula's Pickings when it's more like Regina's Royal Relics."

I laughed. "Touché."

"To be fair, she had been to an estate sale where she'd bid on a box that had her fancy linens as well as a quilt and soft pillowcases. She gave those to me at a steep discount."

Marc leaned against the play area fence. "Good for her."

The sound of an approaching car ended our conversation.

Melanie headed to the door. "I bet it's Hannah Cummins."

I glanced at Marc. "I had a question for her but can't remember what. It's probably in my journal, but I was in such a hurry to leave home this morning I even forgot my coffee, which is why I stopped by Daily Java."

Marc laughed. "Just talk to her, and it may come back to you. Meanwhile, I'll got get us some coffee from Juliet."

"Tell her I said hi." I squeezed Marc's hand because he wasn't much for public displays of affection.

He winked and took off, only pausing a moment to greet Hannah.

When Hannah entered the barn, I walked over to her. "Hey, do you have a minute to talk?"

Her mouth flattened. "I'm kinda in a hurry."

"How about if we meet for dinner?"

Her gaze dropped to the ground. "Andi Grace, I'm running for public office and can't afford to get involved in another one of your murder investigations."

Ouch. "I'm concerned about you. Do you want to come to my house so nobody will see us together?"

Melanie backed away. "It seems like you two need to talk. Hannah, I'll meet you back in the grooming area when you're ready for Gus."

"Wait." Hannah opened her purse and fished out a credit card. "Go ahead and charge me and give yourself a twenty percent tip."

Melanie took the card and left us alone.

I kept my voice low. "Hannah, what's really wrong?"

"I already told you Dirk wanted me to support his podcast. I didn't want to, and it probably makes me a suspect. So I broke up with Wade. It'll make his job easier." She pressed her lips together.

If my friend had punched me in the stomach, I couldn't have been more surprised. "You broke up with Wade? You two are so perfect together."

"He's a wonderful man, but it didn't work. My fault." Her voice trembled.

I threw my arms around Hannah. It took a moment before the tenseness left her body.

Hannah broke into sobs. "I thought he was going to be the one. You know what I mean?"

"Yeah." I patted her back. "It can still work out. Once Wade finds the killer, you two can get back together."

"No, it's too much to ask him."

"Oh, Hannah, I'm so sorry."

Gus barked, and Hannah pulled away. "I thought he'd be used to my crying by now. Poor thing is probably exhausted from listening to me."

"You're a strong woman, and you'll get through this."

She pulled a tissue from her purse and dabbed at the tears. "I didn't imagine how much it'd hurt."

"Tell Wade you made a mistake. You want him back."

"It's better for his career not to be involved with me."

I leaned close and whispered, "You didn't kill Dirk, did you?"

"No!" Her voice echoed through the barn. "I was furious with the man, but I didn't murder him."

"Did you say he knew your mother?" Often, when a clue hit me it was like a kaleidoscope coming into focus. This time was no different. Yearbook images flashed through my mind. "Your mother was Dirk's college girlfriend."

Dylan walked by and glanced at us but kept moving.

"Leave us alone, Andi Grace. My mother's been through enough this year helping my aunt fight cancer." Hannah left me standing there. I went to my empty office and propped my foot on the desk.

I pulled a yellow notepad from a drawer and reached for a pen.

Georgia Cummins and Don Caswell. What had happened in college?

Chapter Twenty-one

AFTER THE FLOODWATERS RECEDED, I returned to the island. My first stop was Paula's Pickings. It'd be a lie to say Regina didn't intimidate me. I ran a brush through my frizzy hair and pulled it into a ponytail. Lipstick. Check. Battle armor on. Time to enter the store. The front door bell announced my entrance, and I glanced around the store.

Regina was helping a mother and daughter duo, and the words *wedding registry* kept recurring in the conversation. I'd never considered Regina's store as a place to register for wedding gifts, but it'd be good to support a local business. Fine bone china and pieces from Europe filled the store. All were beautiful and unique, but my taste leaned toward casual pieces.

If a dog or child bumped a table and broke a dish in my home, there'd be no need for a scene. Priceless heirlooms weren't my thing. Various pictures hung on the back wall, and one caught my attention: the sun setting on a river with a man kayaking under a Spanish moss–draped oak tree would make a perfect gift for Marc.

When he'd opened his law practice, I'd helped him decorate his office. The painting in front of me would add Marc's personality to his office. I checked the price. Whoo-wee.

Stepping back, I continued to study it. The soothing scene would be ideal for Marc to look at on a stressful day. He deserved it. Besides, Marc spoiled me all the time. Here was an opportunity for me to do something special for him. Gingerly, I lifted the picture off the hook and carried it to the counter.

The other customers walked out the door, chatting excitedly. They'd had fun picking items for the wedding registry.

"Andi Grace, I'm glad to see you found something." Regina took the picture from me. "That's right. Marc's a boat man."

"Yes, he is. We've discussed going to Maine for our honeymoon. It'll be fun to go hiking and kayaking and whatever else you do in Maine."

"Brr, it sounds cold to me. I'd rather go to a warm Caribbean island. But to each his own." She removed the price tag and wrapped the painting in brown paper.

Her words and tone came out insulting, but I refused to react. Besides, there was a murderer to catch. "Hey, you know, I'm curious about Chip. He's fairly new to the area. Right?"

Regina met my gaze and narrowed her eyes. "Yes, and he's a good guy."

"Leroy said the same thing. Do you know where Chip is from?"

"Atlanta. He was a contractor until the work got too physically demanding for his body. Before you ask, he's forty-eight. Chip tried selling real estate but decided it was boring." She finished wrapping and leaned the picture against the wall.

"I always thought it'd be fun to sell homes. You'd be a good real estate agent, Regina."

"Not really. Patience isn't my strong suit. If a customer asked me to take them to dozens of houses, I'd probably give up." Regina announced the total of my purchase, and I handed my credit card to her.

"Because you asked me to help find the real killer, I have a favor to ask."

Regina rolled her brown eyes. "You want a discount?"

"No, we're both businesswomen. If I couldn't afford the price you put on the picture, I wouldn't have taken it off the wall. Don't worry about me dickering with you."

She inserted the card into the reader. "What's your favor?"

"Don't tell others about what we're doing."

She tsked. "You don't want me to tell Chip, am I right?"

"Honestly, yes. We don't know him very well, and we also don't know who the killer is. If you confide our progress to the wrong person, we could be the next ones to appear facedown in a pool of water." I shivered.

She turned the screen for me to sign my name. "I see your point."

"Did you already tell Chip what we're doing?" I signed the screen and put the credit card in my purse.

"I'm afraid so. He's such a good listener." The dreamy look on Regina's face made me wonder if she was one of those women who always needed a man around.

"Do you trust me?" If she replied no, I'd walk away. We couldn't sabotage ourselves.

"Yes." She managed to sound contrite while holding her head high.

"Then we need to do it my way. Once the real culprit is caught, you can spill your guts to Chip." I sighed. "For now, don't give him any updates. Our goal is to prove you're innocent."

"I don't see how he could possibly be involved. He's a newcomer. I mean, what in the world would his motive be?"

She voiced the same question I'd been asking myself. "Regina, I don't know. You suspected Olivia the other day. Have you thought of anybody else with a motive to kill Dirk?"

She shook her head, but the red hair remained firm in the smooth bun. "If I was a gambler, I'd put my money on Olivia. Dirk was going to change his will, but the lawyer rescheduled their appointment to next month. If he left everything to his wife, she'll be even richer than if she'd received a divorce settlement."

Alrighty. A new clue. "Did Dirk tell you where he kept his will?"

"No. Is it missing?"

"Maybe. Wait a minute. I thought you didn't know Dirk was married."

Regina avoided eye contact. "I thought he was divorced or at least in the process of divorcing his wife. As far as I knew, Olivia was out of the picture."

I'd play along with her story. "Do you have any proof he wanted to change the will to prevent Olivia from inheriting his wealth?"

"No proof he planned to change it, but maybe I can go through my text messages and emails and find the name of his lawyer."

"That would be awesome." I leaned toward her and kept my voice low even though there were no other customers in the store. "I don't want to scare you, but if the killer realizes you were dating Dirk, you might be in danger."

"Oh, dear. I never thought of that. What should I do?" Her eyes grew wide.

"My suggestion is to stay with your aunt or a friend. You need to be around people and not alone."

"Aunt Paula's out of town on a cruise." She drummed her nails on the counter.

"Do you want me to see if there's a room available at Kennady Plantation? Juliet will feed you, and there are plenty of people around. It should be safe there as long as you don't blab."

"That's kinda rude, don't you think?"

The bell over the door tinkled, preventing me from replying.

Chip walked into the store. "Andi Grace, twice in one day. Good to see you again. Leroy said he returned Peanut."

I shrugged. "It happens often, which is one reason I assure people they can bring pets back anytime. I never want a dog to be mistreated or abandoned if the relationship isn't a good fit. I'll keep looking to find a good match for Leroy."

Regina came around the counter and placed her slender hand on Chip's arm. "What are you up to this afternoon?"

"I need a birthday gift for my mother."

"Sounds like my cue to leave. Have a nice afternoon, Chip. Regina, thanks for wrapping the picture." I took it from where it leaned against the counter and headed to Marc's office.

Regina was either doing a supreme job of acting like nothing was different with Chip, or my warning hadn't been effective.

My original reason to suspect Chip was because Peanut didn't like the man. Most people would consider me crazy. Regina and Leroy had both vouched for Chip. Maybe it was time to quit being stubborn and look for more suspects. Starting with who? Hannah? Hannah's mother, Georgia? Or a culprit Dirk had highlighted on his radio show or podcast? Or planned to expose of committing a crime? This case would be much easier to solve if I could determine the motive.

Chapter Twenty-two

RYLEE PROSSER, MARC'S OFFICE MANAGER, insisted on leading me to Marc's office when I arrived. As usual, she wore a green blouse, emphasizing her brilliant green eyes. The woman always deserved credit for knowing how to dress. Her overprotectiveness of Marc was duly noted. "Mr. Williams, Ms. Scott is here to see you."

I squeezed by her, gripping the large picture in my hands. "Thanks, Rylee."

"You're welcome." She left us alone.

Marc rounded the desk and gave me a kiss. "This must be my special day. Time with my best girl this morning and again now. How's your ankle?"

"Much better. I took some ibuprofen, and I'm wearing an ankle ice pack that Dylan loaned me." I pointed to the black and blue wrap on my foot and ankle.

"Good. Whatcha got there?"

I eased the picture to the floor. "Open it."

"It's not my birthday."

"I know. This is just because you're a wonderful man, and I love you like crazy."

His laugh was one of the first things I'd loved about Marc, and he laughed now. "Not sure about the wonderful part, but I'll never turn away from opening a present."

His comment made me want to surprise him more often with gifts. Had he received many gifts growing up in foster care? Probably not, but he didn't discuss his childhood often. I couldn't change his past, but I could give him little gifts often as an adult.

Marc used care removing the protective wrapping. When the kayak picture was revealed, he slapped his hand over his mouth.

"Do you like it? I thought you might hang it in your office."

He nodded. "It's amazing."

I screwed up my courage. "Also, I agree we should go to Maine on our honeymoon."

"Girl, it's no wonder I love you." He took me in his arms and lifted me off the ground in a bear hug.

I wrapped my arms around his neck and kissed him.

"Ahem." A knock on the door ended the kiss. "Your next appointment is here."

"Thanks, Rylee. Tell them it won't be much longer." He lowered me to the floor but didn't release me from his arms.

The door closed behind Marc's office manager with a thud.

I giggled. "She is one protective watchdog. Remind me to stay on her good side."

"Rylee is a great employee, but I'll be glad when your sister finishes final exams and comes back to work." He lowered his voice. "Having a third person here helps divert Rylee's devotion to me."

"I better go." I stepped away from my fiancé. "You're hanging out with Lincoln tonight, right?"

"Yeah, he's coming to the house. We plan to grill steaks and maybe work on a new song for his upcoming album." He carried the picture to the sitting area of his office and propped it against the wall.

I gathered up the wrapping paper and folded it into a square to be recycled. "Do you hear yourself? It sounds like writing a song for a country artist is no big deal."

He shrugged. "It won't affect my career, but if we write a hit, I'll have extra money to invest in your dog shelter."

"Aw, man. There's no outdoing you when it comes to being nice." I swallowed hard, delighted by how well Marc understood me. "Thanks."

"Hey, you're the one who gave me a fabulous painting and promised to go kayaking in Maine for our honeymoon." He kissed me, then walked me to the office door. "I'll miss you tonight."

"I'll miss you, too. Tell Lincoln hi for me."

"Will do."

I walked to my SUV on clouds. It was nice to see Marc with a friend from his past, and I was glad they were spending quality time together. At home, I added notes to my journal regarding all that had happened before I forgot important details. When I finished updating my progress in finding Dirk's killer, I took Sunny for a walk.

The gusty wind kept us on the streets instead of the beach. Sand in the eyes wouldn't be fun for either one of us. There were a few hours before the next high tide and more flooding, so we had time to walk to Daily Java. My light windbreaker wasn't keeping me warm, and I craved another cup of Erin's pecan coffee with the peach syrup. Sunny had been able to rest at the house most of the day, so I headed to the island's small business district.

It sprinkled on and off, confirming my good decision to get coffee. I opened Daily Java's door and stuck my head in. A table in the back corner held a group of ladies my age holding their book club meeting. Farther away their husbands or boyfriends sat at another table talking about sports. One of the men stood holding a baby in a contraption wrapped around his trunk and securing the baby in front. The man rested his hands on the child's back, and took part in the conversation.

Would Marc wear one of those things to hold our future babies? I turned my attention away from the sweet sight.

Erin looked up and smiled. "Hey, what are you doing?"

"I've got Sunny with me. Would you fix me another cup of coffee like this morning? We'll wait on the patio. And I've got a huge favor to ask."

Her face grew serious. "What?"

"Can I pay you tomorrow morning?"

She busted out laughing. "That is not a huge favor. Pay me whenever you like."

"Thanks." I moved to the patio with Sunny at my side.

The drizzle vanished. I considered sitting, but all of the seats were wet, so I walked around the patio area and looked toward Paula's Pickings. Would I catch Regina and Chip together again? Regina's Lexus was in the lot, but there was no sign of Chip's black sedan. It didn't mean they weren't together though.

In the shadows at the far end of the parking lot sat a red sedan. I couldn't make out the details. Too bad Juliet wasn't with me because she knew all about cars. I took a picture with my phone to show her later.

Erin stepped out with my drink. "Here you go."

"Thanks so much. Erin, you used to have employees. When Lacey Jane worked here, she always came home with fun stories about your staff. Are you running the place all by yourself now?"

Her smile faded. "It's going to take me a while to catch up from the money Corey embezzled from me. When the summer crowd hits, I'll hire a part-time employee, but I'm okay for now."

Her husband had been a scoundrel before his death. "The money's never been found?"

"No. My guess is it's in a foreign bank, and it'll stay hidden."

"Too bad Dirk Cutter's not still alive. He could probably help you find it."

"He was a good customer. I'm surprised you never bumped into him here." She smiled. "He was pleasant and a good tipper. I'm going to miss him."

"I regret not getting to know the man. Regina has insinuated that I'm a snob to people who haven't lived here for years."

"I think it's just that you're comfortable with the people you know. It's hard to walk up to a stranger and introduce yourself. When they come in here, I wait on them and get to know them. It's completely different. Regina has newcomers and visitors in her shop too."

"Maybe I should work for you for free and get to know the new residents."

Erin shook a finger at me. "Don't let her accusation bother you."

The truth often hurt, and maybe I did need to push myself out of my comfort zone. I sipped my coffee. "This is just as delicious as my cup this morning. Do you by any chance know who that red car belongs to?"

Erin looked in the direction I pointed. A vehicle pulled up to the coffee shop and the lights flashed across Erin's face. "Sorry, I don't see it."

"No worries. I'll let you get back to work. Thanks for the coffee, and I promise to pay you." Sunny and I skirted the car and then crossed the street. I held her leash and my coffee in one hand and took another picture of the red car.

The driver started the engine and drove off.

I forwarded the pictures to Juliet by text. *What kind of car is this?*

Had the driver seen me taking pictures? None of the shops were open, so why was a car sitting in the parking lot? I stared at the empty beauty shop. Juliet had owned it before taking charge of Kennady Bed and Breakfast. The salon had reopened, but I hadn't given the new owner a try. Maybe Regina's assessment of me was correct.

Was I a snob? I didn't believe so, but making an appointment with the new owner would be on my to-do list. Right after I solved Dirk's demise.

Chapter Twenty-three

EARLY WEDNESDAY MORNING, I went for a run on the beach. The sun rose slowly, spreading glorious red, orange, and yellow streaks across the sky. I usually called Marc to join me for morning runs, but he had a very early meeting. Sunny had only blinked at me when I got up, so I let her continue sleeping. Running solo gave me time to gather my thoughts on the murder.

I reached the north end of the island and circled around a sand castle that had been battered by the sea. You'd never know I had twisted my ankle the day before.

The ocean was flat and water gently lapped the shore this morning. The early brackish fragrance was one of my favorite smells.

I slowed to a fast walk and lifted my arms to stretch them over my head and to the sides. If I tried such a maneuver while running, it'd more than likely lead to a fall.

In the distance near the pier, a man swept a metal detector back and forth. Tourists rented metal detectors for fun, but a few people owned them, hoping to supplement their incomes with various treasures they could sell to pawn shops or auction off online.

Two women walked toward me, pumping their arms to match their long strides. I transitioned back to jogging until I drew close enough to recognize the women. "Hi, Hannah. Mrs. Cummins. I don't usually see you two this early." If not for Marc's influence, I wouldn't have begun early morning runs on the beach.

"Morning. We're trying something different. Mom, do you remember Andi Grace Scott?"

"Of course. You made your political announcement at her plantation, and she almost got killed." The older woman appeared to be in excellent shape.

"I wouldn't exactly say it was almost my last day on earth." I thought back to the day in question. "Actually, you're right. It was a close call."

Mrs. Cummins said, "I've been out of town helping my sister and her family while she battles cancer, but I kept up with Hannah's campaign." The older woman's hair wasn't quite shoulder-length, but the ends curled up. The wind blew her bangs back, making me glad my hair was long enough for a ponytail. Her eyes narrowed. "I fully support my daughter's effort to become our next state representative."

"Mrs. Cummins, Hannah has my full support." Did she imagine I didn't want Hannah to win? "I was honored to host her announcement at the bed-and-breakfast, and I'd never do anything to damage her campaign."

"Very well then." Her smile looked forced. "Please, call me Georgia."

"Yes, ma'am."

Hannah jogged in place. "We're not going to get our metabolism up high enough if we keep talking. Andi Grace, I'll see you later."

"Bye." I jogged in the direction of the pier. Had Mrs. Cummins been trying to give me a warning? What had Hannah told her about me? Could the strangeness of our encounter be related to Dirk's death?

Jeremiah Pritchard turned out to be the man with the metal detector. The neat gray ponytail, tucked-in shirt, and faded jeans were his trademark wardrobe. The older Black man nodded when we made eye contact.

I moved closer and started talking even though it was doubtful he heard me, considering the headphones covering his ears.

"Howdy." He turned off the machine and removed his earpieces.

"Good morning, Jeremiah. How's it going?"

"Nothing to complain about."

"Can I buy you breakfast?" I'd seen him Dumpster diving more than once. It broke my heart to witness his struggle to survive. Jeremiah had always been kind to me, and I didn't want to step on his pride.

He shook his head. "Much obliged, but I need to keep working."

"Don't go anywhere. I'll be right back." It was an easy walk to the parking lot, and I entered the pier diner. In less than ten minutes, I returned to Jeremiah with a breakfast burrito, coffee, and a hash brown patty. "Here you go."

His gaze was glued to the food but he backed away. "I don't take charity."

Men and their pride. "It's not charity. I actually have a favor to ask you."

The man crinkled his eyebrows.

"Plus, I like sharing coffee with other people. You can keep me company while I drink mine."

Jeremiah pointed to a log the length of a telephone pole that had washed up on the beach. "Let's sit."

We sat on the damp log, keeping a respectable distance between us. The older man lay the metal detector on the sand with the utmost care. "What's your favor?"

I handed him the bag of food and one cup of coffee, keeping the other for myself. "I think you know my friend Leroy Peck. He lives in the duplex next to Chip Johnson."

The man sniffed the burrito before taking his first bite. He ate slowly, as if savoring the food. "I know who you're talking about."

"He's new to your apartment complex, and I was wondering if you'd introduce him around."

Jeremiah met my gaze. "He ain't one of us."

"Do you mean he's not a local?"

"No. Most of us are barely surviving. Some people living at Piney Woods get arrested just so as they can get a decent meal. Your friend, he lives next to the manager. He can afford things."

"Leroy's not a rich man. Have you seen the rusty old clunker he drives?"

"At least he owns a vehicle. Most of us bum rides if we need to go farther than a bike can take us." He took another cautious bite of his burrito.

"Leroy fell off a roof and can't really work these days."

"Probably gets workers' compensation. Trust me, he's making out okay."

I watched the waves dance on the beach. Not a waltz, more like a doo-si-do. Kinda like our conversation. Jeremiah had a comeback for each point I tried to make. "I'm sorry for offending you."

"No offense taken."

"Did you ever meet Dirk Cutter? The man who lived in the blue beach house over there?" I pointed.

"Yes. He was a decent sort. One evening during spring vacation, I was here doing my thing, and we started up a conversation. He asked me if I had ever found something newsworthy. He talked to me like a real person."

Dirk Cutter continued to get mixed reviews. More positive than negative though. Even if the majority had hated Dirk, he didn't deserve to die viciously.

"I'd really like to apologize if I ever made you feel unworthy."

Jeremiah traded the empty burrito wrapper for the hash browns. "No, you've always been friendly."

"But not a friend." Again, was I a snob?

"Didn't mean it that way. You're good people, Andi Grace."

His polite words lessened my burden, but only by a fraction. "Thank you. I'm curious. How'd you answer Dirk's question?"

"If I ever found something newsworthy, it would be news to me." He chuckled before taking another bite.

I laughed with him. "Good one."

"I'll keep an eye on your friend."

"If you give him a chance, you'll probably become his friend. He loves to go fishing, and this pier is one of his favorite hangouts."

"Good to know."

I stood. "Jeremiah, if you ever need anything, I'd like you to know you can reach out to me. I've had hard times when I didn't know where the money would come from to buy groceries. So if you need groceries, shoes, a kidney, give me a shout."

"Yes, ma'am. If I ever need a kidney, I'll tell the docs to track you down. Thanks for the grub this morning. I don't often get a hot meal."

"You're welcome. Don't you have an oven in your apartment?"

"It doesn't work. My place is on the maintenance list. The new manager announced all the apartments would get updated. I ain't holding my breath though."

"I hope it happens soon. See you around." I left him on the log and crossed paths with Hannah and Georgia again. "How was your walk?"

"Good." The tension had disappeared from Hannah's neck and shoulders.

"Georgia, did you know Dirk Cutter?" I turned the paper cup in my hands. "He used to go by Don Caswell."

The woman's mouth dropped open.

Hannah stepped between us. "Leave my mother out of this."

Georgia tapped her daughter's shoulder. "It's okay. Hannah, I need to make a confession. Dirk and I dated in college."

Hannah slumped. "Mom, you don't have to say that."

"The truth will set us free, and you can go back to dating the nice sheriff."

Hannah pulled her phone from the pocket in her shorts. "Speaking of sheriff, this is Wade calling me now."

Chapter Twenty-four

HANNAH STEPPED AWAY to take the phone call from Wade, leaving me standing alone with her mother on the beach. A lonely seagull flew over us and headed toward the rising sun.

Georgia crossed her slender arms. "I never intended for Hannah to learn about my past. Dirk was around during the darkest days of my life. As you know, he went by Don Caswell back then. He was a lot of fun, and I needed some fun in my life. He could always make me laugh. At the time, I wondered if we were falling in love."

Love? In my opinion, she'd dodged a bullet by the name of Don. Asher was a much better catch. Decent, loving, and loyal to his family. "What happened to you and Don?"

"I was an utter mess in those days. My family was so poor. I earned scholarships to college, and modeled for extra money. It was challenging to juggle school and work. One weekend my sister Rose, the one with cancer, came to stay with me at college. I'd always tried to set a good example for my little sister. Rose is five years younger than me." Georgia closed her eyes for a moment. "Outsiders probably thought I was living the most amazing life, but I had to watch my weight, and a pimple would send me into crisis mode."

"I've heard that modeling can be stressful."

"There were good moments and bad. The shoots were always local, so I didn't get to travel unless it was on the weekend or during a school break. I'm not saying there weren't perks. For instance, I was allowed to keep some of the outfits. The money was good, and that's why I did it."

"What happened with you and Dirk, er, Don."

"He worked for the college radio station. His focus was sports and all things related to the teams. We met at a party. The athletic boosters paid models to attend." She raised a hand. "Before you ask, I only attended the parties. Nothing else."

"I'd never accuse you of anything bad."

Her eyebrows rose. "You say that, but I bet you wonder if I killed Don."

My face grew warm. "Well, yeah, but I consider lots of people. If you didn't do it, maybe Hannah killed Dirk to protect you."

"Now you're being ridiculous."

Hannah returned with a frown. "Wade's upset that I don't want to keep dating him. He's not buying my story about the campaign."

"Darling, the best way to handle my secret is to get on top of it. You should be the one to tell the story." She ran a hand down Hannah's arm. "Start with Wade."

"Did you tell Andi Grace what happened to you in college?" Hannah's voice was so low it was hard to hear over the waves.

Her mom grimaced. "We haven't gotten to the bad part yet."

"You may as well go ahead, otherwise she'll dig up the truth." She crossed her arms, and there was no denying she was her mother's daughter. Both were tall, slim, and elegant even on the beach, where wind tended to mess up one's appearance.

Georgia faced me. "The pressure of school and modeling got to me. By now Don and I were friends. He knew I was struggling to meet all the demands on my life, and he suggested he could hook me up with a drug dealer. I jumped at the idea because at the rate my life was spinning out of control, I couldn't continue to model and maintain my good grades. I bought 'study drugs.' When I took them, I could go for days without sleep or food."

"You mean like Ritalin?" My mouth dried.

"Yes. If I thought it would help, I tried it. But mostly cocaine. It was everywhere back then."

Wow. "What about crashing?" Depression also came to mind.

"Yes. It was part of the cycle. When Rose came to visit me and saw how thin I was, she became hysterical. Unfortunately, I'd crashed, and we had a huge argument. Rose told my parents, and they pulled me out of school, citing health reasons. Honestly, it was the truth. Mom and Dad forced me to go to a counselor, and I slowly got healthier. I finished my degree in marketing at a small school. We didn't have cell phones in those days, and I lost track of Don until a few weeks ago. Asher asked me to go to the radio station on an errand for our work. When I arrived, Don was in a conversation with another man. It was like seeing a ghost."

Chills rand down my neck and arms. "Did he remember you?"

"Yes. He carried a grudge because I never got in touch with him. His friend called me Mrs. Cummins, and Dirk Cutter, the podcaster, put the pieces together. The time arrived for him to exact his revenge."

"Revenge? For what?"

"Disappearing without a word. I would've explained to him, but my parents whisked me off campus so fast I didn't have a chance."

"You probably weren't in any shape to talk to him. So what did he do after you reconnected?"

"As you know, part of Hannah's platform is protecting our youth. Stop drug abuse, vaping, and human trafficking. He told me it'd be a shame if word got out I'd used illegal drugs."

"But he introduced you to the drug dealer."

"Yeah, but he met the dealer when doing a story on our basketball team. He claims he never did more than drink alcohol." Her shoulders drooped. "I'm the one who has a daughter with political ambitions. Dirk's the charismatic star. His philosophy is any publicity is good for his career. If he spilled the beans, it'd only help by bringing more attention to him."

Hannah shifted to her mother's side and held her hand. "It's okay, Momma."

"This is terrible. Which one of you was Dirk blackmailing?" Hannah to protect her mother or Georgia to prevent damaging her daughter's campaign?

Hannah said, "Both of us. He wanted me to verbally support his career, and he promised not to reveal my mother's secrets."

Georgia shook her head. "Dirk told me it'd be a shame if word got out and hurt Hannah's campaign. He wanted Asher and me to become a corporate sponsor of his podcast through Cummins Security Company."

The answer was worse than I'd suspected. Blackmailing both women and knowing they'd protect each other. If I'd had my journal, I would've written *Despicable Dirk*. "How can I help?"

"Will you take care of Gus today? I need to decide how to handle this situation." Hannah pushed a loose strand of dark hair behind her ear.

Georgia cupped her daughter's face with her hand. "Let's discuss it with your dad. He's always good in a crisis."

The tender moment between mother and daughter choked me up so bad, I turned to face the ocean until I corralled my emotions. I'd never get over missing my mom.

"You're right. Daddy always knows what to do. Andi Grace, what about Gus?"

"Since we live so close to each other, I'll walk home with you and pick him up." I hustled to keep up with their fast pace. They must've felt the urgency of the situation and walked briskly.

We reached Hannah's house in record time and walked up the outside stairs. "Has Gus eaten this morning?"

"Yes, and he's done all of his morning rituals. I hope this isn't too much trouble." Hannah unlocked the front door.

"Not at all." I followed Hannah and Georgia inside, where I harnessed and leashed the little mutt. "He looks healthier. You're doing a good job with him, Hannah."

Georgia disappeared, and a door slammed shut.

Hannah's smile wobbled. "Gus is good company."

The sound of an approaching car led me to glance out the window. "Wade's here, and I'm scooting. Do you mind if I take Gus to Stay and Play later? I've got a meeting with a photographer."

"Whatever you decide is fine. I know he's in good hands with you." She opened the door and nudged me out.

"Thanks. I'll bring him back to you when you're ready."

"Sounds good." She glanced over her shoulder from the doorway and called out, "Mom, I'll be right back."

My feet touched the ground as the sheriff approached dressed in his official uniform. "Hi, Wade."

He shook his head. "Andi Grace. Shoulda figured you'd be here."

I pointed to the little mutt. "Dog sitting, thank you very much. Oops, I didn't mean to sound ugly. Sorry."

A grin appeared. "No sweat."

"See you two later." I walked home, relieved Wade hadn't arrived to question me.

Chapter Twenty-five

WHEN WE ARRIVED AT STAY AND PLAY, I led Sunny and Gus into the play area. Sunny dwarfed the smaller dog, but what Gus lacked in size he made up for with energy. I couldn't help but laugh at his rambunctiousness and his attempt to lure Sunny into playing with him. My German shepherd participated in a tug-of-war with the little runt. Anybody watching would know Sunny held back because she could easily fling Gus across the barn.

Dylan appeared from the hallway that led to my office and his studio apartment. "Hey, boss. I didn't expect to see you today. Did the schedule change?"

"Don't worry, I still need you to handle the afternoon appointments."

He checked his phone. "I'm giving lessons to one dog, then playing with Captain and Pumpkin, and I even have a dog walk scheduled in the country. As if we weren't far enough from civilization."

I laughed. "This is country to me, but the more I drive out here the closer it seems to town. The first time I came to the farm to walk a dog, it felt like I'd arrived in the boonies."

A car arrived, and the driver honked.

Gus barked like crazy.

"I'll handle Gus, you see who's here. By the way, I've got an appointment with our wedding photographer for the business website. She may want to take pictures of you."

"Yes, ma'am." He waved and walked off.

"Gus. No barking." I entered the fenced-in area. "No. Barking." I kept my voice firm, and when he quieted down, I gave him a treat. "Good boy."

Sunny tilted her head and raised her ears.

"You're always a good girl, so you probably deserve a treat too." I pulled a bigger dog biscuit from my pocket. "You've spoiled me because I expect you to behave." I rubbed her head then strolled to my office humming one of Lincoln's tunes.

My phone buzzed, and I swiped it. "Zarina, are you here?"

"If you mean on the property, yes. I'm at the main house, and I'll join you in a minute."

"Great. See you in front of the barn. You should be able to see the signage for Stay and Play." There were multiple barns on the property, but this was the biggest. I stepped into the sunshine and pushed on my sunglasses. Because of the photo shoot, I'd worn a cute top, a nice pair of shorts, and my favorite sandals.

Zarina parked in the shade of a magnolia tree and rolled down her windows.

Under a big old oak with Spanish moss draping down, Dylan worked with Yoyo and his owners. The black Lab puppy had come a long way, and so had his people. Violet and Ethan Seitz had started out letting the dog control them. They were a perfect example of why owners needed to attend lessons with their pets.

"Sorry for running late." Zarina breathed hard.

My watch showed the girl was two minutes late. "I don't consider it late, especially when you drove out here on unfamiliar roads."

"Thanks for understanding." She took a deep breath and released it slowly.

"Listen, I've got a favor to ask. Would you take pictures of me before I begin to sweat?" I shrugged. "I don't mind if the others are perspiring, and I know it sounds vain, but it seems like the owner should look, well, you know, not hot. Pulled together. I even applied makeup this morning." Talk about rambling. I shut my mouth.

"Absolutely. You look beautiful. Let's get you in front of the barn and around this beautiful area. This place is so inviting. I mean, who wouldn't want their dog to stay here?"

"Zarina, we need to book you to take pictures of the B and B too. Maybe incorporate a few of the dog barn to entice people to bring their pets on vacation."

Her eyebrows rose. "I don't have another appointment until after school lets out, so we've got lots of time. Although, I don't want to be late for two clients in one day. Let's get started by taking your picture first."

After she photographed me outside, we entered the much cooler barn. I held Gus for some more photos then posed with Sunny. "We've got three more dogs staying with us this week, but I didn't get permission from their owners. Have you thought any more about Dirk's death?"

Zarina held the fancy camera to her side. "Did the cops declare it was officially a homicide?"

I placed a hand on her shoulder. "Yeah, I'm afraid so."

"If you truly want my opinion, I still believe it's the soon-to-be ex-wife. That woman is cra-cra. No doubt about it." Zarina pointed to the old kitchen. "Is that in use?"

"Yes. The building can be rented for a large family, or we can rent individual rooms with common areas. The back patio has been converted to a very small apartment. Why?"

"The sun is hitting it perfectly right this minute. Can we take pictures there before we lose the shot?"

"Go ahead." I walked beside her to the structure, and she chatted about never wanting to miss a good shot.

Zarina stopped talking long enough to snap pictures of the old kitchen. "I love this place. It's so peaceful out here, not like the noisy city."

"You're right about the quiet. I've wondered what it'd be like to live in a big city, but the beach is my favorite place. I can't imagine living anywhere else." I tried to imagine this place from her perspective. "You're brave to start a new life in Heyward Beach for you and your daughter."

"It hasn't happened yet, but I'm determined." Her eyes twinkled. "Have you listened to all Dirk's podcasts? In the beginning, he focused on what happened to retired superstar athletes. His radio show is about crime in the Carolinas. One day he discovered a retired baseball player who had been murdered. The case was never solved. At that point, Dirk began looking at cold cases for both the radio show and his podcast. The lines blurred between his programs. You get what I'm saying?"

"I get how that could happen. Only recently have I begun to listen to his podcast."

"His show helps me stay awake when I drive from here to my mother's home in Charleston. I can't be falling asleep behind the wheel and leaving my baby an orphan."

"I hope you can settle in Heyward Beach soon and quit driving back and forth. My fiancé was put in foster care after his parents died in a car crash. He was an only child and didn't have any family."

"Nobody adopted him?" Her voice rose like she couldn't imagine such a thing happening. "Man, that stinks."

"I think he was pretty closed off, and he wasn't a baby when it happened. It was a rough life. Take care of yourself, Zarina."

"I surely will. At least my baby has a grandma." She rubbed her arms.

"True, but she needs her mother. I know money's tight, but if you are ever too tired to drive back to Charleston, please stay with me."

Her eyes grew wide. "Really?"

"Yes." I pressed my lips together.

Zarina gave me a quick hug then stepped back. "Some nights I drive with my head hanging out the window just to stay awake."

"Don't ever do that again." My voice vibrated with emotion. Blame it on my big-sister tendencies. "You've always got a place to stay with me until you get settled here."

"Thanks." She blinked rapidly. "I'm not gonna get weepy on you. What were we discussing? Oh, yeah. Dirk. His podcast shows are about finding clues to cold cases and trying to solve them. The man had a knack for research and putting the pieces of a case together."

"He was able to help the police?" I couldn't get a handle on the man. Like plucking petals off a daisy—like him, don't like him. Either way, nobody deserved to be murdered.

"I wouldn't exactly say he solved a lot of murders, but he resurrected the old cases. Does that make sense?"

"His involvement got the cops looking at the cases again?"

"Exactly. He studies the murders, and he has a website with pictures to go along with the podcast." She hesitated. "I should be talking in the past tense. Dirk would give clues and ask if anybody knew anything about the murder. Lots of folks sent him messages, and he shared what they told him with the cops. He looked at cases all over the United States. Mostly in the South, but other states too."

"Do you know why he was so excited about the newest episode that never got made?" Seconds ticked by. "It was supposed to air the day of Dirk's murder."

"He had solved the crime, and he believed the case would take him to a whole new level."

I rubbed my forehead. "Well, I'll be."

"A monkey's uncle." Zarina snickered. "You can't just leave me hanging like that."

I laughed, and she took my picture. Several photos actually, if all the camera clicks were to be believed. "Zarina, can you think of anything else?"

"No, and you're the only person I've talked to about this. I don't want to tangle with his wife."

Why had she confided in me? "I knew you were smart, and in case the killer is somebody else, let's keep this conversation between the two of us."

"You got it, boss." She adjusted something on her camera.

"Dylan also calls me boss. He's the guy over there giving an obedience lesson. Go ask him and the Seitzes about including Yoyo in the pictures.

You wouldn't believe how lessons have improved the Lab's behavior. He was a good dog but out of control."

Her head jerked up. "You're not coming with me?"

"No, I want to check with Juliet Reed. She runs the bed-and-breakfast. You may have met her earlier. I'm sure the place is spotless, but she could be up to her elbows baking. I also want to find Melanie Bradshaw, my new dog groomer."

"You're giving me freedom to explore and take pictures?"

"Absolutely. Take pictures of whatever you like. I guess if you see guests, we'll need their permission and a waiver."

"Okay. If you need me, call my cell. I'll be around." Zarina gave me a lopsided smile.

"Make yourself at home. It's all good." I pulled my nice hairstyle into a ponytail and hurried to find my best friend. I stepped through the back door of the main house. The aroma of chocolate wafted to me. "Juliet, where fort art thou?"

"Shakespeare would not appreciate you butchering his words or the meaning. What's up?" She chuckled and slid a tray of cookies into the oven.

"I have a photographer here for Stay and Play. While we were talking, it occurred to me professional photos would make your website look better too. You know, professional."

Juliet nodded. "I'm all for it, my only question is when?"

"Today. Like soon."

"Watch the cookies, and I'll fix myself up."

Juliet was a natural beauty, but as a former hairstylist she had high standards. "You set the timer?"

"Of course. I'll be right back, and don't let them burn." She disappeared through the dining room, and her feet pattered up the stairs.

I sat on a bar stool and reached for an oatmeal raisin cookie with pecans. It was small enough to eat in two bites. Yum. Juliet never disappointed when it came to baked goods.

I tapped Melanie's number into my phone and called her.

"Hello."

"Melanie, this is Andi Grace. We have a photographer at Stay and Play today, and she'd like to take a picture of you for our website. Gus is in the barn with Sunny. After Zarina takes your picture, I want her to take a couple of you grooming one of the dogs."

"Okay. I'll be there in ten minutes."

"Great. I'm at the main house waiting on a batch of cookies to bake, but I'll be back soon." The timer displayed seven more minutes. Perfect amount of time to fix a cup of coffee.

Juliet always kept hot coffee for guests, and it didn't take long to find it. I filled a travel mug with coffee from the carafe and added sugar and cream.

"I predicted you couldn't resist coffee and probably a cookie." Juliet appeared, startling me.

I jumped. "Guilty. Boy, you sure can sneak up on a person."

"You look tired. We should do something fun."

"You're right. What do you have in mind?"

"We're both decently dressed today. Let's go to Charleston and look for wedding dresses."

I laughed. "Seriously. On the spur of the moment? That's so not like you."

"It took your brother long enough to pop the question. I'd marry him tomorrow if he suggested it. So, let's go shopping."

My brain whirled. I'd abandoned dreaming about wedding dresses years ago when my longtime boyfriend dumped me. Now I had a worthy fiancé, and history would not repeat itself. "Why in the world not? I need to make sure Dylan can handle everything at Stay and Play."

"Great. I'll get somebody to take care of the guests. Maybe we can leave after your photographer takes my picture."

It took about an hour to make all the arrangements, then I met Juliet and Zarina in the main house of Kennady Bed and Breakfast. "How's it going?"

"Almost finished." Zarina didn't even glance my way. Her focus was on Juliet and the baked goods.

I watched the rest of the photo session. After Zarina snapped the last picture, Juliet and I hightailed it to my SUV parked in the shade of an old magnolia tree.

"Wait a minute, Andi Grace." Juliet grabbed my arm. "You know the picture you sent me last night? The red car."

"Yeah, what about it?"

"It's a red Camry, and if I had to guess, I'd say it belongs to Melanie Bradshaw." She led me behind the old kitchen. "Act natural."

"I shouldn't have to sneak around my own property."

"Shh." Juliet stopped and pointed. "What do you think?"

Faded red sedan. Camry, to be exact. Dent. Chills covered my body. "That's the car." I reached for my phone and took a picture of Melanie's car. "Let's get out of here."

We hurried to my Highlander and left without confronting Melanie. The rest of the afternoon, I planned to focus on wedding preparations. Not mysteries and murder.

Juliet patted my arm. "I'm impressed you didn't leap into a confrontation."

"I doubt Melanie killed Dirk, and conflict would have eaten into our fun. The answer can wait."

"I couldn't be prouder of you." She reached for the radio control.

"Can we listen to Dirk's podcast?"

Juliet laughed. "That sounds more like it. Give me your phone, and I'll find the app."

I passed it to her. "I've been going in chronological order, and my journal is in the glove compartment."

"What am I supposed to do with it? Take notes?"

"Zarina explained to me that Dirk didn't always catch the killer by himself. He found interesting cold cases, researched them, then asked the public for help. He posted pictures of victims and suspects on his website and directed listeners to give them a look-see."

Juliet giggled. "Look-see?"

I glanced at her. "Yeah, it's a word Dirk used often."

"How did he come up with the cold cases?"

"Good question. Do you think Regina or Olivia is the best person to ask?" I turned onto River Road.

"Knowing you, we'll ask both of them."

"You're right. Would you mind looking on social media and see if anybody took pictures of the scene at Tuscan Tomato the other night? I've been meaning to check myself, but my days have been full."

"There's no crime in allowing yourself time to rest." Juliet removed her phone from her purse and tapped on it. "I can't get over you ditching work this afternoon. Have I mentioned how proud I am of you?"

I laughed and ignored the guilt niggling my conscience. "It's out of character and a little weird, but finding our dresses is so important. Where to first?"

"North Charleston and we'll work our way to downtown."

I remained quiet while my best friend searched the internet for pictures.

Pine trees lined both sides of Highway 17 except for the occasional house, restaurant, or roads leading to small towns.

"I've found a couple of blurry shots. They are fuzzy and dim."

"The confrontation was so fast, and I think most patrons were shocked. Can you take a screen shot of the pictures and forward them to me?"

"What do you hope to accomplish?"

"Not sure exactly." I gripped the steering wheel. "Within twelve hours of that scene, Dirk was murdered. What if the killer was following Dirk?"

"You're assuming it's not Regina or Olivia." Her phone made a slight click as she copied the photos.

"Yeah. Regina asked me to help, but I can't quite figure out Olivia. If they are innocent, the killer could have been lurking in the shadows of the restaurant watching for the perfect moment to strike."

"I'll keep looking then."

It wouldn't be the first time I followed a misleading clue. I'd either find something useful or fail, but I had to try.

Chapter Twenty-six

ONCE WE ARRIVED IN NORTH CHARLESTON, we found an app for bridal shops and bopped from one to another. Most had openings for appointments for both of us. One clerk confirmed Wednesdays were slow days. Only two boutiques turned us away. Still, we tried on numerous dresses, but nothing hit my fancy. On the other hand, Juliet loved everything she slipped into. The more lace, the better.

The process confused me. Juliet was the picky person when it came to looks and style. I wore shorts and T-shirts to work. I should've been the easier person to please. What prevented me from saying yes to even one dress?

Shop number six was in downtown Charleston. My energy waned, and thoughts of eloping began to appeal to me. I walked out of a dressing room wearing another selection the saleslady had suggested. Juliet and I met in the open space with white carpet on the dark hardwood floor. We studied each other, and I couldn't stop smiling. "Juliet, that dress is perfect on you." The delicate gown with floral appliqués fit Juliet's personality.

"Look at this." She stepped into her dressing room and reappeared. "A matching cape. It'll be perfect in the fall."

My heart swelled with sisterly love for my best friend. "You're exactly right."

"I know. There were gowns I could've been happy with, but this seems like me." She twirled and looked at herself in the three-way mirror. "I'm so glad I waited before choosing."

"Exactly, and now you can pick a wedding date." I circled my best friend and future sister-in-law. "I don't think you'll need any alterations. It's flawless. The next question is a veil or a hat?"

"I'd like to do a fancy braid with little white flowers."

"I can't imagine anything more appropriate for you. You're a magician with hair."

"Thanks." She quit looking at herself in the mirror, and the smile dimmed. "What do you think about your dress?"

I whispered, "It's still too froufrou."

We heard the saleslady clip-clopping our way before we saw her. "How is everybody doing?" She appeared with a bottle of champagne and fancy glasses.

Juliet beamed. "I'm going to take this one."

The fifty-something woman studied Juliet. "It's rare to sell a dress that doesn't require alterations, but it appears as if this was created just for you."

"I'll change before anything happens to it." Juliet opened the door to her dressing area.

Soft jazz played over the sound system.

"How do you feel about the dress you're wearing?" The woman set the bottle and champagne flutes on a glass table.

I looked down at the sequins and lace puffing out. "It's not quite right. I'm more of a simple girl than my friend."

"A tomboy, perhaps?" The woman whose fancy name tag read *Peggy* ran her hand along the back of her updo.

"No." I tried to picture elegant women without overly dramatic flair in order to explain what I was looking for. "I lean to more of a minimalist elegance. Maybe I should keep looking."

"You change, and let me see what I can find. Are you sure you want to go with white?"

"Of course. While my taste is minimalist, I'm also a traditionalist." Definitely a white gown, and I wanted it to be long.

Juliet exited wearing her regular clothes, and she handed her dress to the woman, who hadn't gone to look for another gown for me yet. "Would you be so kind as to prepare my dress and cape in one of those nice bags so I can take them with me tonight? I'd really appreciate it. Meanwhile, I'll look around for a dress for Andi Grace."

The woman smiled. "I'd be delighted to get this ready for you. What about a veil?"

"Just the dress and cape, please."

The woman's smile remained as she left us.

"I overheard the conversation." Juliet patted my shoulder. "Don't give up. I know your taste better than Peggy does."

"I'm starting to have doubts we'll find one to suit me."

"Never fear. Don't forget we watched Prince William marry Kate and Prince Harry marry Meghan. I know how you felt about Kate's and Meghan's gowns." She left me alone, and I wandered around the elegant dressing area. Gold-framed photos of women in wedding gowns hung on walls.

I studied each one hoping for inspiration. Elimination was easier. I didn't want a long train in case we got married on the beach. Strapless wasn't my style and probably not the best idea for a fall wedding. Low-cut would make me uncomfortable.

One photo stopped me in my tracks. Olivia Caswell. She'd been gorgeous on her wedding day. Deep down I had felt like Dirk's widow was tacky and enjoyed flaunting her womanly curves, but her wedding dress made me question my earlier assumption. Beautiful and tasteful.

Juliet appeared. "I thought you were going to change."

"Look here. It's Olivia on her wedding day."

My friend's mouth dropped open. "She looks younger and happier."

"I know. It makes me think she truly loved Dirk."

"Don't they say there's a thin line between love and hate? Will she remain on your suspect list?"

I leaned closer to the picture. "Yeah, but what leads a person who is so happy one day to murder her husband another day? I mean, if she really did the deed. She was plenty angry Thursday night, and I'm sure most of the patrons in the restaurant can picture her killing Dirk."

"It's baffling, but can we think about it later? Get out of that dress."

I turned to Juliet. "What'd you find?"

"It's a surprise. I'll show you when you're prepared to try it on."

"If you're hopeful, then so am I. Give me a minute." I stepped into my private dressing area. After removing the exquisite gown and hanging it on a pillow hanger, I slumped onto the metal stool, wearing the lightweight robe the salon provided. What was wrong with me? Had the saleslady assessed me correctly? Was I a tomboy? No. I was more practical than anything. I admired other women in fancy frocks, but as for me, I felt like a little girl playing dress-up.

A memory of wearing my mother's wedding dress flitted through my mind. She'd been bustier than I was, and she sometimes wore low-cut dresses, but they weren't over-the-top extravagant. Whether I remembered the exact dress my mother had worn or not, there was an image in my mind. I knew deep in my soul what dress I wanted to wear when I married Marc. It wouldn't be my mother's dress, because it'd been destroyed in a fire. Still, my dress could be like her wedding gown, if only I could find it.

Juliet tapped on the door. "What are you doing? I can't wait much longer."

I opened the door. "Let's see what you've got."

She held out a white frock. "Ta-da."

One look at the amazing wedding dress and I burst into tears. The white traditional gown was so much like the image I'd dreamed of. Simple. Timeless. Elegant. Bateau neckline.

"It's silk crepe." Juliet lifted one of the sleeves. "Three-quarter sleeves. Perfect for a fall wedding."

"How'd you know?" I blubbered.

Juliet plucked a tissue from a box on a shelf by the mirror. "I remembered you describing your mom's dress back in high school. You always got a starry-eyed look when you talked about it. You also mentioned it when Prince Harry married Meghan Markle. This gown seems to combine what you told me that day with what you remembered about your mother's dress."

I took the quintessential wedding gown and hung it on the nearest hook right before hugging my friend with all my might. I wasn't a freak or a tomboy. Deep down I'd known the perfect dress for me, and Juliet had plucked it from a rack in the front of the wedding boutique.

Without wasting another second, I tried it on. Floating out to the three-way mirror, I twirled.

None of the women who'd been trying to help us had come close. My best friend nailed it. I'd have worn anything in order to marry Marc, but this suited me. No, it made me deliriously happy. "Thank you so much, Juliet."

Chapter Twenty-seven

MARC AND LINCOLN HAD COME TO CHARLESTON to meet with a local attorney about a lawsuit between a national tabloid and Lincoln. The trashy magazine had accused the country star of having a torrid affair with one of his band members. Lincoln had given Marc permission to tell me about the lawsuit, but he requested I keep it a secret along with the story about Thomas. The tabloid was only focused on Lincoln's relationship with his wife.

My parents had worked through their marital issues. From my perspective, Dad had been the person doing the hard work. Olivia and Dirk had struggled. Lincoln's career had put a strain on his marriage, but he'd always been faithful to his wife. How would Marc and I make it as a married couple? I loved him deeply, and a fifty-fifty partnership was our goal. I'd meant it when I promised to stand by him no matter what.

Juliet and I met Marc and Lincoln at a downtown restaurant for dinner. We chatted about the weather until we'd been seated and ordered.

Marc laced his fingers together and leaned forward. "I'm dying to know. Did y'all find dresses?"

"Yes." My throat tightened, so I pointed to Juliet. I couldn't burst into tears again, especially with Lincoln at our table. It'd embarrass me and draw unwanted attention to our group and the country music singer.

"I found an amazing dress that fits like a dream." Her gaze bounced from Marc to me then to Lincoln and back to Marc. "Your girl was under enormous pressure to buy many dresses at different stores by multiple women. Not all of the salesladies were kind. They tried to convince her they know more than she does about wedding gowns. In general, they do."

Marc's eyes widened. "But?"

"But Andi Grace stuck to her guns, even when the mean one called her the *t* word."

Marc's mouth dropped open. "What's the *t* word?"

Lincoln said, "It sounds like you're going to need to whoop someone's—"

"Hey, man, ladies are present." Marc shook his head and wore a *what am I going to do with him* expression.

"Sorry, ladies." Lincoln raised his hands. "After the day we had, I'm ready to punch a wall, or, well, you get the idea."

Marc squeezed the bridge of his nose. "Can somebody please explain the *t* word?"

Juliet rested her arms on the table, and we all leaned forward. "Tomboy."

Marc and Lincoln looked at each other, and both burst into laughter.

Juliet slapped her hand on the linen tablecloth. "Gentlemen, evidently you do *not* understand the nature of the insult. No lady wants to go look for the dress of her dreams, her wedding gown, and be called a tomboy."

I said, "Even if she is one, you don't discuss it while preparing for your wedding."

Marc took my hand in his and rubbed his thumb over my knuckles. "Oh, baby. I'd never call you the *t* word. I love the fact you'd rather wear fun clothes and tennis shoes to work with dogs. I also love the fact you enjoy going out on a boat with me. You've never once complained about getting wet. Even more, you touched my heart more deeply than you'll ever know by offering to go to Maine for our honeymoon so we can go kayaking. I love you, Andi Grace."

Lincoln pulled his phone out and started typing. "Keep going. This could be your wedding song. We'll title it something along the lines of, 'She Ain't No Tomboy,' or 'I'm in Love with a Tomboy.' What do you think?"

"Cut it out, Linc." Marc turned back to me. "Did you end up finding a dress, or do you need to keep looking?"

"I sat alone in the last dressing room, reflecting on why all of the salesladies had acted frustrated with me. Then it hit me. I had a memory of playing in my mother's wedding dress, and that's what I'd been looking for without realizing it. And just then, it was like Mom looked down on me from heaven, and Juliet walked in with the exact dress I'd dreamed of."

Lincoln sang, "Halleluiah."

Marc scooted out of his chair and hugged me from a kneeling position. "I love you."

"I love you too, and I can't wait to be Mrs. Marc Williams."

Lincoln pounded his fist on his chest. "You guys are killing me. I need to call my wife, but y'all start eating if our food arrives before I get back."

Marc returned to his seat but continued to hold my hand. "I'm glad today was a success for you two. Lincoln and I haven't been as fortunate."

"What's wrong?" Juliet looked up from her phone. "Pardon my rudeness. Nate just texted me. Is Lincoln having trouble with the press?"

"I can't share any details, but our meeting didn't go well. In fact, we're spending the night here because Lincoln and I have an early morning meeting tomorrow. I called Dylan earlier. He ran by my place and picked up Chubb."

My shoulders drooped. Poor Lincoln. And poor me. I'd looked forward to spending more time with Marc, but pouting would be selfish. "I'm sorry for Lincoln and his family. I guess being a celebrity isn't all it's cracked up to be."

Juliet said, "Next week a politician booked all of the rooms at the B and B so his family could have time away from the spotlight. He's paying extra for me to prepare all of the meals. Thank goodness I convinced him to have some catered to offer more variety. Even so, his privacy will be protected. The other restaurants will never know who the food is for."

"Will it be more, or less, work for you to meet their needs?" I wondered if I should pitch in and help.

Juliet drummed her fingers on the table. "I'll have fewer rooms to clean, but keeping the family fed will be more labor-intensive. Nate's going to help me plan outdoor activities so nobody gets bored."

"My brother always has good ideas on recreation."

"Yeah, and Nate's strong, handsome, and fun." Juliet giggled. "Do I sound like a woman in love?"

I nodded. "Which is good since you're about to marry my brother."

The waiter appeared with our drinks and appetizers. "Sorry for the delay. One of the waitresses thought she spotted Lincoln Zane. Evidently, he's a big-shot country singer. So, all the girls in the restaurant are trying to get his picture. When I say all, I'm including the employees too. It's a zoo in the kitchen."

Marc frowned.

I patted his hand but addressed our waiter. "Will you box up our meals and bring the bill? The faster you can do this and get us out of here, the bigger your tip will be."

The young man about tripped, backing away from our table. "Yes, ma'am. You can count on me. Food, discretion, and speed."

Juliet gathered her purse. "I'll find Lincoln and try to sneak him out of here. This incident makes me understand better why our politician rented out the entire bed-and-breakfast. Where should we meet you?"

Marc said, "Let's try to find a quiet area at the Battery. Tell Lincoln to wear a hat or something. There are plenty of gift shops, so it shouldn't be hard to buy some kind of disguise."

"No problem. See you there." Juliet left the two of us alone.

The only appetizer our waiter had placed on the table was stuffed mushrooms. I popped one in my mouth. "Sorry, I'm starved."

"Shouldn't let them go to waste." Marc ate one too.

"You know how the waiter said people were trying to take pictures of Lincoln?" At his nod, I continued. "Juliet found a couple of pictures on social media of Dirk, Olivia, and Regina on Thursday night. Of course, Dirk wasn't a big celebrity like Lincoln."

"Not many people are." He ate another mushroom.

"Dirk wanted to be famous. Craved it, actually. He had a story on Lincoln, which convinces me his murder could be related to his radio show or podcast. A solid motive would help find the killer."

"It wasn't Lincoln." The anger in Marc's tone surprised me.

"Agreed, but what if Dirk's murder is related to his shows instead of a person he knew personally?"

"Love and money are often the motive for murder." Marc met my gaze. The anger had disappeared. "Sorry about my outburst. It's been a rough day."

"I never believed Lincoln was the killer, and you're right. Love and money are big motives, but what if the culprit killed Dirk to protect his loved ones? Again, I'm not talking about Lincoln. Or if it was a financial secret that led to the murder?"

"Protect the secret by killing Dirk?"

"Exactly, and the secret would cost the killer dearly whether it's related to money or love for another person." It seemed like a logical motive to me, but what would Marc and the authorities think?

The waiter returned with our food bagged up and the bill. He placed them on the table near Marc.

Marc lifted a hand to stop the waiter. "Don't go anywhere. Please."

The young man looked at the empty chairs. "I guess your friend is Lincoln Zane. Hope I didn't offend you, but I'm into rap and just never heard of him before tonight."

"No offense taken. We appreciate your help." Marc placed some bills into the leather folder holding the ticket and handed it to our waiter.

"Actually, if you want to follow me, I can take you to a side door. It'll save you pushing through the crowd forming."

We followed him to the side door, and Marc handed him a business card. "If you ever need legal assistance, or if you're in Heyward Beach, give me a call. You're going to go far in life if you're this nice to others."

"Thanks, Mr. Williams."

I wrapped my hand in the crook of Marc's arm. "You are one of the nicest people in the world. How'd I get so lucky to be your fiancée?"

"I'm the lucky one." He pointed across the street. "There's my truck. Let's get out of here."

Chapter Twenty-eight

NATE HAD BEEN WORKING ON A RESTORATION PROJECT in Charleston with Griffin Reed, Juliet's brother. Griffin had moved to Heyward Beach but still did some contracting work in Charleston. His current project was a home on the historical register. Griffin had hired Nate to help design the garden to match the time period of when the house had been built.

Before we finished eating our dinner on a bench in Battery Park, Nate appeared and whisked Juliet away for a stroll along the waterfront. He assured us she'd get home safely, meaning I'd drive home alone. No problem. More time to think about the case.

I stuffed the empty containers into the restaurant's paper bag and disposed of it in a nearby garbage can. "I should go and let you two discuss your case."

Marc stood and reached for my hand. "We'll drive you to your vehicle."

"I don't mind the walk, but if you have time it'll be nice to spend a few more minutes together."

"Su-weet."

I rode up front with Marc in his red Silverado, and Lincoln settled into the backseat. Marc slowed the truck in front of the restaurant, where a crowd spilled into the street.

Marc whistled. "It's not that I didn't believe you, man, but it's ridiculous how you can't even take time to eat a meal in public."

"Told you. Hey, why don't you talk some of that mushy stuff to your girl? I'll sit back and take notes." He chuckled.

I glanced back at Lincoln. A regular guy cutting up with his friends. "Very funny."

"The best song for your big day will be from the heart. Marc, you're up."

Marc came to a complete stop for two girls dashing across the street. "Um, I can't just, uh, you know."

I laughed. "It's rare for romantic words to gush out of Marc. We both got lucky earlier."

"Fine." Lincoln's melodic voice floated through the truck, and he pointed at me. "Then you say something romantic."

My face grew hot. "Well, uh, it's not easy with you listening."

"That's the point." He laughed so hard, he snorted.

Time to change the subject. "Let's talk about Dirk. Have any of your famous friends discussed him? Stars of the past maybe? Newcomers?"

Lincoln sobered and swiped a hand across his face. "His podcast covered cold cases and people who disappeared from the limelight. Me and most of my friends are more concerned with tabloids spreading lies and twisting the truth. I could ask around if you'd like, but I don't want to attract attention to Thomas."

I turned around and faced Lincoln. "No, I don't want that either. Just let it rest."

Marc pulled into the parking lot and idled behind my Highlander. "We'll make sure your truck starts. Call me when you get home, so I know you're safe. I hate that Juliet's not riding with you."

"I'll listen to Dirk's podcasts. They should keep me awake."

Marc leaned toward me, cradled my jaw in his hand and kissed me. "Call me."

Nice goose bumps popped up on my arms. "I will."

Lincoln opened the door for me, and I walked to my SUV. As soon as it started, I headed home. Once I'd gotten out of the downtown traffic, I played the next episode of *Where Are They Now?*

Through the podcast Dirk took me to Atlanta, where he'd asked for assistance with a cold case involving a Vietnam veteran. At the end of the original episode, Dirk came back and announced that with help from volunteers at a food bank, the veteran's killer was arrested.

The road to Heyward Beach was dark and lonely. Dirk had helped find justice for the veteran. The man's killer had been arrested. Were there other killers afraid Dirk would find them? Was his death related to the podcast or something closer to home?

What about Jeremiah? He was a veteran. Chip worked at the apartment complex and claimed he wanted to improve conditions for the people who lived there. Jeremiah had confessed his disbelief, but he'd lived at Piney Woods for years and probably had no plans to move. The poor man had no doubt heard empty promises about the living conditions there more than once.

Chip appeared to stand for a noble cause. Decent housing for the poor was his goal. Nothing to do with Dirk. I needed to keep an open mind.

Regina and Leroy each thought Chip was a decent guy. If I ruled out Regina, Lincoln, and Chip, I was back to Olivia on my suspect list, along with Hannah and Georgia. My thoughts drifted. It'd been a long day, starting with my time on the beach.

Georgia Cummins had known Dirk in college. How scared was Georgia? Had she confronted Dirk before his death? Would actions from thirty years earlier be enough for Dirk to hold over Georgia's head? How far would Georgia go to protect her daughter's dream of becoming our next state representative?

Zarina knew Dirk had plans to meet somebody from his past. It could've been Georgia. Maybe she'd wanted to discuss the situation privately. It made sense they'd meet at his beach house. Perhaps the meeting started calmly, but emotions escalated and got out of hand to the point Dirk had been accidently killed. To protect Hannah, had Georgia tried to cover up the situation? Was Georgia strong enough to drag Dirk's body to the pool to make it look like a drowning?

I tried to picture the scene in my head. Dirk was a big man. Not obese by my definition, but big. Probably two hundred fifty pounds, give or take a few. Georgia was slender, and I couldn't imagine her dragging his body out of the house, down the steps, and across the pool deck to dump him into the water. Unless the woman was stronger than she appeared. Was it possible she'd had some kind of hysterical strength kick in?

What about Hannah? Would she have confronted Dirk to protect her mom? Again, I couldn't visualize her lugging his body from the house to the swimming pool.

Could they have teamed up and killed Dirk together? If their motives were to protect each other from Dirk's blackmail, it didn't make sense they'd work with each other to kill the man. When caught, they'd both serve time.

Back to Olivia. She was much bigger than either Hannah or her mom, but could she have moved the body? I shook my head. I didn't see how it was possible, unless there'd been an argument. If it started in the house and ended up near the pool. The neighbor had heard arguing. If Dirk was killed near the pool, then rolling his body into the water was more believable than dragging him from the house.

Three women. Three motives. Two I couldn't imagine, but it wouldn't be the first time I'd been fooled.

A deer darted out from the woods and onto the highway. I slammed on my brakes and swerved into the emergency lane. The car behind me zipped around my vehicle in the other lane and honked.

"What a moron." I gritted my teeth and took a deep breath before steering myself back onto the road.

If I'd hit the deer, my Highlander might have been totaled. People died in car crashes involving deer. Or the driver behind me could've rear-ended me. How soon before anyone would've gotten worried?

Dirk's body was found because of the town scavenger hunt. If Olivia hadn't returned to the beach house, how long might it have been before the body was discovered? Of course, this assumed Olivia was innocent.

I increased my speed to the appropriate fifty-five miles per hour. My thoughts returned to Dirk's death. I'd continue nosing around until the killer was caught. It didn't seem fair that a man devoted to solving cold cases might end up a cold case himself.

Chapter Twenty-nine

I SWUNG BY THE PLANTATION TO PICK UP SUNNY, Chubb, Peanut, and Gus. Dylan was at the main house with his girlfriend, Kylie Black. She was helping Juliet by taking care of the guests.

Many good things had happened throughout the day, but I was exhausted and went directly to the dog barn instead of going into the main house to chat.

Melanie popped into the barn. "Who's there? What do you want?"

"It's me, Andi Grace." The girl liked to have scared me to death. What was she doing out here at this hour?

"Sorry for startling you. How are you tonight?" Her voice grew louder.

"Fine." I leashed the dogs and stepped out of the shadows. "What are you doing?"

"I'm still getting used to how dark and quiet it is in the country. When I heard you, I thought I should investigate." She stuffed her hands into the pockets of her tight jeans.

"Aw, yeah, you're a city girl. In fact, I think I saw your car last night near Paula's Pickings."

"I only went into the store the day I got here. You know, to find linens. Uh, like you suggested."

Chubb pulled on his leash, and I moved to the door. "I know, but why were you there last night? In the dark. In the rain." I motioned for her to follow me.

"It's not like I planned to rob the shop or anything bad." She reached for Sunny's leash, and I let her have it. "I'm trying to get to know the town. The more people I meet, the more grooming appointments I can get."

I didn't believe her story, and I was too tired to dance around the truth. "Melanie, don't lie to me."

"Please, don't push this. I told you there were private reasons for my moving to Heyward Beach. It's too soon to explain, but I'd really appreciate it if you'd trust me."

No logical explanation for why she'd been sitting in the parking lot that night came to me.

Chubb headed for a tree, and all three dogs sniffed around.

"Melanie, I won't push you for answers tonight, but you can't be sitting alone in parking lots at night. It looks bad."

"How?"

Was she that naïve? "How about you could be waiting to make a drug deal? Or what about prostitution? You know, bad things."

Melanie gasped and pushed up her glasses. "I'd never do either one of those."

I reached for the leash in her hand. "Then you need to quit hanging out in dark parking lots when no businesses are open."

"Are you firing me?" Her nostrils flared.

"Not now, but I need to know you're trustworthy."

Her posture straightened. "I promise. You won't be sorry for hiring me."

"Two-week trial, remember." My stomach rolled. What was Melanie up to?

"Yes, and I won't disappoint you again."

I got the dogs into the Highlander and drove away. All the way to the island I considered potential reasons for Melanie to sit alone in Regina's parking lot. Nothing made sense.

I swung by Hannah's house and led Gus to the front door.

Hannah met me on the porch. "Hey, thanks for taking care of Gus." She picked up the little mutt and held him to her chest. "Can you send me a bill?"

"No problem. How'd your conversation go with Wade?"

"I told him the truth about everything." She leaned against the white porch railing. "He's not going to arrest my mother or me, but there's a huge strain between us. I doubt we'll ever go back to dating."

"I'm sorry to hear that. You two seemed like a great couple."

"It's my fault, and I own it. Wade feels like he can't trust me, and I did hold something back. So, there you go. He needs to be able to count on me being honest. I thought he was the one until Dirk died."

"Trust is a huge hurdle. I just went through this same conversation with one of my employees. I mean, we literally just talked about it before I came over here." I hugged my friend.

Gus gave a squeaky bark, and Hannah pulled back. "What am I going to do?"

"Give Wade time. Let him see he can count on you." Wade had history with Hannah. Although he'd probably let her into his heart, which might make him feel worse that she hadn't revealed the truth about her mother to begin with. Nobody would win if they didn't find a way to make up.

My issue with Melanie was completely different. We barely knew each other. If she was going to be my permanent dog groomer and handle people's beloved pets, I had to be able to trust her. The only way to do that was to give her the opportunity to prove herself. I'd keep my eyes open.

Hannah and I talked a few more minutes, then I headed home with Sunny, Peanut, and Chubb. I carried in the wedding gowns Juliet and I had bought and hung them in a guest room. All three dogs were familiar with my house, and they headed to the water bowls. I slipped off my sandals and plopped on the couch.

Ever so slowly, this was beginning to look like my home instead of the crisp environment from when Tabby Malkin owned the place. Her decorating style had been minimalistic. When it came to my home, I was all about coziness. Plants, throw pillows, afghans, and extra rugs added color and warmed the place up.

I picked up a French decorating magazine from the coffee table. A dream of visiting Paris one day had led me to buy French magazines. I'd also discovered my decorating style leaned toward French country combined with beach casualness. The walls remained white in my home. I kept the basic pieces of furniture that had come with the house, but the pops of various blue hues made a huge difference. Two French bistro side chairs had been added to the ends of the big kitchen table. All in all I was pleased with the effect.

I yawned and let the dogs into the backyard. Relaxing in a wicker chair on the porch, I watched as they wandered in the yard. Stars filled the sky, and waves crashed onto the beach. The sound never failed to soothe me, and I couldn't stop yawning. As much as I wanted to do more research on Dirk, it didn't seem physically possible tonight. Tomorrow would be soon enough to come up with a plan of action to find the killer. Once the mystery was solved, I'd put my full attention on my upcoming nuptials. Maybe Hannah and Wade would work out their problems, and with some luck there wouldn't be any murders to solve for a long time. Forever would be better.

Chubb and Peanut ran up the porch stairs, and Sunny came at a more sedate pace.

"Let's go to bed." Once we were all inside, I locked the door and set the alarm. All three dogs followed me to my bedroom, and I wasn't sure which one of us fell asleep first.

Chapter Thirty

SIX DAYS AFTER DIRK CUTTER HAD BEEN MURDERED, and where were we on catching the villain? Villainess? I returned to my original notes. Both men and women had landed on my suspect list. Olivia, Regina, Lincoln, Georgia, Hannah, Chip, and a person I'd yet to identify.

The radio station's website had old episodes of *Cut to the Truth*, Dirk's radio program. He'd been a stickler for stating that the first forty-eight hours were the best time to catch the killer. Surely six days wasn't impossible. If so, Dirk wouldn't have started the radio show covering regional cold cases.

I checked my morning schedule. Rain had rolled in during the early morning hours, and last-minute calls for appointments had completely changed my plans for the day. Clients who didn't want to deal with inclement weather were always a nice boost to my business.

While Sunny, Chubb, and Peanut went out in the yard, I got dressed and fixed my first cup of coffee for the day. The dogs didn't spend much time out back. I dried them off and got them settled before taking off to conquer my schedule.

First stop was Phyllis Mays. Pumpkin and Captain were always entertaining, and I never wanted to miss an opportunity to squeeze in a bit of training. On our walk around the neighborhood, I received a message from Olivia for help with Copper. I texted her an estimated time, and she agreed.

Less than an hour later, I called Wade as I drove to Cutter's Landing.

"Morning, Andi Grace. What's up?" His voice came out like a croak.

"Oh, Wade. You sound terrible. Are you getting any sleep?"

"Resting isn't my top priority while we have a killer on the loose. Why'd you call?"

"Two things. I'd like to discuss Dirk's case, but as your friend I want to encourage you to forgive Hannah." Please.

His sigh carried over the line. "She hid potential evidence from me."

"And she feels terrible about it. Hannah's instinct was to protect her mother."

"I get it, but she should've trusted me with the truth." Another sigh. "Let's stick to the case."

I turned onto the causeway leading to the island. "I'm heading over to see Olivia Caswell."

"Don't interfere with my investigation." His aggravated tone carried over the line.

"Olivia called me about her dog. I don't know what she wants exactly."

"Are you scared to go by yourself?"

"No, should I be?" Ahead of me, Jeremiah rode his bike in my lane. A fountain of rainwater sprayed behind his tire. I slowed until the other lane was clear.

"The coroner confirmed Dirk was strangled then placed in the pool. No water in his lungs, and there are bruises on his neck. You get the picture."

Exactly like I'd imagined. "Here's what I had in mind, but you need to approve it. Copper is a shih tzu, and he's Olivia's baby, if you know what I mean. Peanut was Dirk's beagle."

"I remember, and you've got the beagle."

"For now, yes. Leroy Peck tried to foster him." When there was no oncoming traffic, I eased into the other lane so I could safely pass my friend riding his bike. I waved, and he returned the gesture.

"Okay, so what's the problem."

"Peanut goes crazy when he's around Chip Johnson, but so far he's been fine around other men. Do you know Chip?"

"Andi Grace, I am the sheriff. Of course I've met Chip." He growled. "He seems like a good guy. Are you accusing him of murdering Dirk? Why? What would be his motive?"

He jumped on me so fast, it made me wonder if he'd already considered Chip to be a suspect and ruled him out. "Sorry, I didn't mean to step on your toes. I just found it interesting."

"Is that all you've got?"

I turned onto Main Street. "No. If you approve, I thought about asking Olivia if I could take Peanut back to Dirk's house and see if he'd sniff out any clues. I can do it without your permission, but I thought you, or one of your deputies, might like to be there."

My proposition was met with a long silence.

I swallowed hard. "Wade, did I lose you?"

"Just thinking. Go ahead and ask Olivia, then let me know what she says."

"I'll be in touch." I took a deep breath. "Wade, you're a good sheriff. I'm not trying to step on your toes or anything."

"I know, but you have the gift of getting people to blab. Call me later."

He disconnected the call. Wade seemed grumpier than usual. Was it because of the dustup with Hannah? I hadn't gotten far with him concerning their relationship, but he'd agreed to allowing me to return to Cutter's Landing with Peanut. I counted it a win.

Wade's words rang true about my so-called gift. I believed people weren't afraid of me and tended to open up more. They were inclined to be more cautious around law enforcement, giving me an edge on gathering information.

I pulled into Dirk's driveway and parked. Olivia was a firecracker, and I never knew what to expect. I took a calming breath and counted to ten in French. One day I'd visit Paris, but today Olivia awaited. I stepped out of the car, climbed the stairs of Cutter's Landing, and rang the doorbell.

The door flew open, and Olivia stood there wild-eyed. Her long bleached blonde hair looked like it had tangled with a hurricane and lost. "I thought you'd never get here." She snagged my arm and pulled me into the house.

Ouch. Her strength gave me the impression she could've strangled Dirk and dragged his body to the swimming pool. Good thing Wade knew where I was. "What in the world has got you so upset? I told you it'd take me a little while to get here."

Olivia slammed the door behind us, and I hurried to keep up with her steps so she didn't drag me. "Copper's sick. He's throwing up and shaking."

The little dog lay on his side on the kitchen floor. I dropped to the ground beside him.

"This is bad, Olivia. Did you call the vet?" Had the poor thing gotten into some kind of poison? Insecticide or rat poison? "Please tell me you didn't give him more of your anxiety medicine."

"No, I didn't give him diazepam, and I don't remember the vet's name." She wailed so loud my ears hurt.

"Dr. Hewitt. He's the best around. We need to take Copper to his clinic. They will do blood work, and I'm sure they'll put him on an IV."

"What kind of IV?" She rubbed her neck.

"Copper's probably dehydrated, so they'll give him fluids. Maybe antibiotics if there's an infection. I'm not a vet, but your dog needs help. You need to get real clothes on, and I can drive you."

"No, you take him."

I glared at the woman. "He's your dog. I don't know Copper's history except for him taking your diazepam the other day. Are you positive he didn't take any more diazepam? It's better to tell me the truth."

"No. We learned our lesson the first time. I don't know what's wrong with my baby today. I can't handle it if he dies too. First Dirk then Copper. It's too much to bear."

I flinched at her words. "At least ride over with me and hold him in your lap. He'll be more comfortable with you."

"Give me five minutes." She disappeared faster than I'd ever seen her move, but her five minutes turned into ten. It would've been a perfect opportunity to look for more clues, but the dog's survival was more important.

I gave Copper tiny ice chips from the freezer door and patted his side. "It's okay, boy. We're going to get you help." My anxiety rose the longer it took Olivia to get ready, making me wish I'd taken her shih tzu by myself. At last, she reappeared, and I breathed easier. "Let's go."

Olivia arranged a towel on her arms, and I placed the sick dog on it. The drive to the vet clinic was quiet, and true to her word, Olivia insisted on me taking her beloved pooch inside.

Chapter Thirty-one

"THIS IS CRIMINAL. Nobody should allow their pet to get in such bad shape," Doc Hewitt's gravelly voice rumbled. "And the owner didn't have the decency to bring Copper in herself. Why, I've got a right mind to report her to Animal Control."

I patted the older man's arm. He'd given me a job years ago, and I'd discovered my love of animals at his vet clinic. Working for him had led to pet sitting on the side and eventually my dog-walking business. "I'm keeping my eye on her. I believe she loves him, but in my opinion she's too self-absorbed to know the best way to care for Copper."

"Depending on what the test results reveal, I may still report her." Despite his anger, he remained gentle in how he handled Copper.

"Please let me know what you find out."

"Sure thing." His eyes remained on the dog, and I slipped out of the exam room.

I returned to my SUV and pulled out of the parking lot before speaking. "Doc Hewitt is keeping your dog for tests. Copper couldn't be in any better hands."

"What about a specialist in Charleston or Wilmington?"

My heart pounded hard. "I don't think he'd be alive if we'd made the drive to either of those places."

The woman whimpered.

I didn't say another word to Olivia on the way back to the beach house.

"What am I going to do?" Olivia's voice wobbled, but no tears appeared.

People needed to quit asking me that question. "I know you're upset, but can I offer a suggestion?"

"Sure." The flatness of her tone told me how upset she was about the dog.

"Get books on how to take care of your dog. Shih tzu, specifically. Copper's not a little person, he's a dog. No matter how much you love him, you can't treat him like a human being."

She nodded and remained in the passenger seat.

"Now I've got a favor to ask you." I bit my lip and hoped she'd agree.

"What?"

I explained my plan to come back with Peanut and the sheriff. "Maybe we can find a clue to who killed Dirk. What do you think?"

She met my gaze. "May as well, although I can't imagine what a dog can do to help catch a killer."

"You'd be amazed, and you told me Dirk had many hiding places. Peanut may find a clue by following Dirk's scent."

"When do you want to do it?"

"The sooner the better, like today."

"Fine. If I don't answer the door when you return, I'll be by the pool." She exited my SUV and walked up the outside staircase of Cutter's Landing.

I backed out of the driveway and called Wade's cell. My phone was synched to my SUV, making it easy to talk while driving.

"Yes?"

"Olivia agreed, and I'm heading home right now. When can you meet us?"

"Thirty minutes."

Faster than I'd predicted. "Awesome. See you soon."

At the house, I played with all three dogs before getting ready to leave with Peanut. Sunny napped more these days and didn't seem to mind. Chubb barked, but I gave him a safe chewy bone. It satisfied him, and I left with the beagle.

Wade had parked his official Sheriff's SUV in the pier parking lot, so I pulled in beside him and lowered my window. "Hey, Wade. Thanks for meeting me."

"Thank you for including me." His grouchy tone confused me.

"What's wrong?"

"Nothing really. We're here on official business. No need to discuss my personal problems."

My guess was the sheriff's mood was connected to Hannah. I attached a leash to Peanut's harness and joined Wade standing at the front of his vehicle. "Olivia's other dog was sick, and that's why she called me earlier. Copper's with Doc Hewitt now."

"What kind of sick? You don't think he was poisoned, do you?"

"Olivia hovers over her dog like a mother hen, so I can't imagine how he'd get poisoned on purpose. Doc's running bloodwork, so we should have answers soon."

"On purpose?"

"If I was a betting person, I'd suspect Olivia of neglect if anything. It's definitely more likely than believing she'd intentionally allow her dog to get into something harmful." Peanut tugged on the leash, as if anxious to get in the house and find Dirk. Poor thing. "I hope my plan doesn't backfire."

"What do you mean?"

"Peanut's still recovering from Dirk's death. It's possible he believes we're here to reunite him with his owner." I followed the dog to the house. Instead of going to the front door, he led me to the open parking area under the beach house. "I never really considered finding a clue in this open space."

Wade kept up with me. "I can't believe I agreed to this."

"It's worth a shot." I loosened the leash and allowed Peanut to explore as much as he wanted. "Wade, I'm sorry for opening my big mouth on your relationship with Hannah. You're both important to me, but I should mind my own business."

"I understand you meant well, but let's not discuss it." He pressed his lips together.

"Message received."

Peanut sniffed around a six-foot vertical storage unit in the carport.

Wade slipped on gloves and opened the doors of the plastic shed. Beach chairs, umbrellas, and floats filled the space.

I scrunched down and reached for my phone. "Wait a second, what's in the back of the blue beach chair?" I turned on the flashlight app and held it closer.

Wade reached for the item and bumped my shoulder in the process. "Sorry." He pulled a spiral notebook out of a pouch on the back of the chair. The pages had yellowed and begun to curl. "What do we have here?"

I leaned closer.

Wade squinted at me. "By we, I mean me."

"Hey, you would've closed the door if I hadn't seen it."

"If I had an aggravating sister, I imagine she'd be like you." He shook his head. "Anything you see here is off the record. You can't go blabbing all over town about this."

"Thanks for the vote of confidence." Peanut tugged on the leash, and I followed him around the corner and up the back stairs leading to the swimming pool.

Wade scooted around me and opened the gate. "Gee, at least give me some credit for offering to allow you to see it." He came to a dead stop so fast, I walked into his back.

"Wade. What in the world?"

He faced me and with his thumb directed my attention toward the pool. "Can you tell Mrs. Caswell that I'm here and would appreciate it if she put on more clothing?"

Olivia laid on a lounge chair wearing nothing but a skimpy bikini.

I handed the leash to Wade and pointed to the grassy area. "Why don't you take Peanut down there while I talk to Olivia?"

"Gladly." He walked the dog down the appropriate set of steps. There was no telling how much money Dirk's builder had spent on outdoor stairs and decks. They went in all directions.

"Olivia, we're here." I walked to where she lay.

She propped herself up on elbows. "I thought you were bringing the sheriff."

"Right. Sheriff Stone is here, but he'd be more comfortable if you wore a few more clothes."

She stood and slipped a blue V-neck cover-up on. "Better?"

"Yes. Should we talk inside?"

She ran a hand through her long hair. "The back deck is better. I don't want to get sunscreen on the furniture inside."

"Lead the way. Sheriff Stone will catch up with us."

We sat at a raised metal and rattan glass-top bar table. Wade joined us, handing me the leash in the process of sitting in the seat with the best view of the yard. "Mrs. Caswell, thank you for your time. Have you thought of anybody else who might have wanted to hurt your husband?"

"Nobody specific, but he frequented cold case websites under his real name, Don Caswell. You might see if he left messages on them." She propped her rhinestone-studded sunglasses on top of her head.

Peanut whined, and I picked him up. "What's wrong, boy?"

He panted and turned his head right and left.

Wade focused on Olivia, and I spoke soft soothing words to the beagle in hopes he'd calm down.

Wade said, "Mrs. Caswell, do you know any of the specific websites?"

"No, it's been a long time since we discussed Dirk's research. He was a passionate man, and people were drawn to him. I'm a passionate woman, and when we were together it was like fireworks going off on a steamy summer night."

Whoa, what was she insinuating? My face grew warm, and I avoided eye contact with both of them.

Wade opened his notepad and clicked his pen. "You mean women were drawn to your husband?"

"Yes. The more his fame grew, the more women were interested in him." She faced the beach. "Men clamored for his attention, too. Dirk was just a likeable guy."

"Were the other women what brought your marriage to an end?"

"Pretty much." Olivia studied her manicure. "I didn't moon all over my husband. I treated him as an equal, and other women adored him. It's hard to compete with younger, more beautiful ladies flaunting themselves in his face. Did you look into Regina Houp's alibi for Friday morning? If I had to guess, she'd be at the top of my suspect list."

"Ms. Houp has been questioned." Wade's tone remained neutral.

Olivia's nostrils flared. "Then why haven't you arrested her?"

"Little thing known as lack of evidence." That was the kind of smart-aleck response I was used to from the sheriff. Wade continued, "When we can prove our case, we'll arrest the guilty party. Anything else you care to share, Mrs. Caswell?"

"Not at this time."

I did a double take. Did she mean to be so rude?

Wade stood. "May we take your husband's dog into the house?"

"Yes, but I plan to go inside too." She flung her long hair back.

Olivia had just told me she didn't want to go inside and risk getting sunscreen on the furniture. Why had she changed her mind?

Wade opened the back door. "After you, Mrs. Caswell."

I followed Olivia inside and placed Peanut on the floor. He sniffed around, and I trailed behind him.

Wade entered the room and stood at the kitchen island. "Mrs. Caswell, we found this notebook in the carport. Have you seen it before?"

I glanced toward them to gauge her reaction.

Olivia took it from Wade before he could object. Sand spilled out of the pages. "It's Dirk's handwriting, but I don't remember this specific notebook. He was always taking notes when the mood struck. If he didn't have a notepad, he'd write on a napkin, index cards, or his hand if it was the only option. He always feared forgetting a key piece of information."

Wade held out his hand. "I'd like to keep it and read through the notes."

Olivia shrugged and passed it to him. "Sure."

I followed Peanut around the room. He paused near a half-eaten chocolate candy bar.

"No, Peanut. Drop it." I snatched away the candy. "Olivia, did you give

Copper chocolate? You do know dogs can't handle it, right?" My pulse pounded in my neck.

"It always helps me feel better." She batted her eyes and stuck out her lower lip.

I didn't cave to her attempt to manipulate me by acting pitiful. "That's probably why Copper is so sick. Dogs cannot eat chocolate, and he's so tiny it probably didn't take much."

"I didn't realize." She dropped onto a bar stool at the kitchen counter.

I longed to go off on the woman for not taking better care of her little shih tzu. Instead, I counted to ten in French before speaking. "Now you know. Right?"

"Yes," she mumbled.

"No drugs and no chocolate for your dog. Don't forget to order the dog books."

Wade walked between us and followed Peanut to the stairs. "Ladies, he's going up, and I plan to follow him."

Olivia dropped her arms and head onto the counter. "Go with him, Andi Grace. I can't take much more."

I stomped out my frustration climbing the stairs and joined Wade and the beagle in the playroom.

He met my gaze and chuckled. "Thanks for not punching her. I'd hate to arrest you for assaulting a grieving widow."

I kept my voice low like he'd done. "I'm not convinced she's grieving. If she could mistreat her beloved pooch, no telling what she did to her soon-to-be ex-husband."

"I get it." He passed me an extra pair of latex gloves and the notebook. "Here's your shot."

I pulled on the gloves before he could change his mind and sat in a cushioned chair. Once I opened it and adjusted to Dirk's messy script, I got lost in his words. While his handwriting was sloppy, his notes were orderly.

A quick glance showed most of the victims he featured were women. The majority of the cases were in the Carolinas, probably for his radio show. None of these pages were related to the celebrities for his *Where Are They Now?* podcast.

I continued reading Dirk's notes. The last page involved a cold case in California. A twenty-eight-year-old woman had been murdered. Three men had been questioned and released. Two were now dead. One died in a motorcycle accident, and the other had a heart attack. Dirk hadn't listed their names. Maybe because they wouldn't be able to provide answers to the California woman's murder. These notes must be what he'd referred to as his Triple C threat. Regina had mentioned it to me, and I'd seen it written in his other notes.

I gazed out the window toward the beach. So where was the third suspect? How long ago had this murder taken place? "Wade, have you listened to Dirk's podcast?"

"Yep." He crossed his arms but continued to watch the dog.

"In the beginning, his episodes were more lighthearted. Dirk focused on athletes and movie stars that had disappeared from the limelight. Most were doing good things, but a couple had fallen on hard times. Bad investments and mismanaging their wealth had been detrimental to their lives."

"Your point?"

"Dirk's focus turned darker. Crimes and murder." I shivered.

Wade nodded. "Keep going."

I glanced toward the stairs to make sure Olivia wasn't about to join us. No sign of her but I kept my voice soft. "Like the way Dirk wanted to expose the story about Thomas Zane."

"It's in line with the other shows, but I agree it's a little darker. Meaner."

"You're right. On the other hand, his radio show revolved around cold cases in the Carolinas." Some of the pieces weren't fitting together, and it was driving me crazy.

"True." Wade's clipped answers were getting on my nerves.

"Then can you explain why the theme of his radio show was Carolina crimes, but the last entry in here is about a cold case in California? Regina heard him mention this case and even called it a Triple C threat. In fact, it's referenced in some other notes Olivia gave me after the police searched the house."

Chapter Thirty-two

WADE'S JAW DROPPED. "California? I don't know anybody from California related to Dirk's case. I also expect you to turn the other notes over to me immediately."

"No problem." I handed the notebook to the sheriff. "If you've not come across anybody from California, it's probably not related to Dirk's murder."

"We shouldn't dismiss it. Yet." He looked down at the page I referenced.

"We?" My pulse leapt.

Wade frowned. "We as in me and my deputies."

"I understand. Where's Peanut?"

"No sign of him." Wade kept the notebook in his gloved hand and walked around the room. "Maybe he's in one of the bedrooms."

"I'll check the office." I entered the room Dirk had used to produce his podcast. He'd probably spent many hours here researching websites for his show. "Wade, was the laptop ever found?"

"No." He joined me in the tidy blue room with white trim. "I imagine there was information on it that would lead us to the motive and killer."

"It makes sense the killer would take it with him or her." I looked under the desk and came up empty.

"Um, what are you doing?"

"Olivia told me that Dirk had quirky hiding spaces." I moved to the acrylic bookshelf. "If there was proof on the laptop, it could be a will or notes for a radio episode or his podcast."

"Deputy Sawyer is scanning cold case blogs looking for comments from Don Caswell. He says it's tedious and interesting at the same time." He opened a closet door. "Now, where'd that little rascal get off to?"

"Did Regina tell you Dirk owned a storage unit and has at least one safe behind a picture in this house?"

"No. I'll look into it."

"You know, Regina claims she and Dirk were just beginning a relationship. Do you think it's odd she is aware of the safes and storage unit?"

He smirked. "There are valid reasons for why we questioned her."

I fisted my hands on my hips. "Wade, don't you think it'd be hard to get Dirk's body into the pool? He'd be dead weight. Literally."

"I've thought about it. The coroner said there was damage on the back of the skull. You know, like if his head bounced on the steps."

"The steps outside are the fancy wood composite stuff. It's not as hard and wouldn't do as much damage as concrete. At my house there are steps from the back porch down to the yard. It's also made of composite decking."

Wade's stiff posture relaxed. "Andi Grace, it's your home, and it's a nice one. You almost act embarrassed to own it."

"All those years of scrimping and worrying about taking care of Nate and Lacey Jane may have affected me." I sat on the fancy office chair and shrugged. "If Tabby was still alive, I wouldn't be living there."

"I get it. A woman died, and your—"

My nostrils began to sting like right before I started to cry. "I'm sorry, Wade, but can we focus on Dirk?"

Peanut barked from another room.

"Sure thing, Andi Grace." Wade followed the sound.

Taking a moment to compose myself, I studied the awards and pictures around Dirk's office.

Wade reappeared holding the beagle. "Found him in the bathroom, barking at the linen closet."

"Olivia claims Dirk was paranoid about his research. Maybe there's something important sandwiched between the towels."

He handed the dog to me and disappeared.

"You're all right now." I held Peanut close. His body shook, and he panted. "It's hard to lose a loved one, but I promise to find you a good home."

I walked to the bathroom and leaned against the doorframe while cuddling the beagle. "Have you found anything yet?"

"Men's slippers. Maybe the dog smelled his master."

On the floor near the toilet sat a basket of what looked like *Sports Illustrated* magazines. "Wade, I doubt Dirk used this toilet often, but if he provided something for his company to read—"

"One step ahead of you. He's probably got the same thing in the big bathroom off the owner's suite." He brushed past me. "I doubt most people keep important information by their throne, but I'm beginning to learn that Dirk's not most people."

As much as I longed to follow Wade and see if he found any evidence, Peanut struggled to leap out of my arms. "I'll be out back."

"Don't leave without me."

I snagged the sandy notebook and carried Peanut to the main floor so he wouldn't disappear again. At the back door, I attached his leash before stepping outside.

Olivia lay on the lounge chair, but I took the dog down to the yard.

How could she sunbathe when her husband was dead and her beloved shih tzu was sick due to her complete lack of knowing how to care for a dog? I gave Peanut more than enough time to sniff around because the anger at Olivia's careless actions hadn't dissipated.

At last, I took a deep breath. Time to face the grieving widow. Our conversation required more than counting to ten in French, so I said a little prayer.

Peanut and I weren't quiet as we approached Dirk's widow. She sat up and adjusted her big white hat. "Any luck?"

"Peanut found Dirk's bedroom slippers, but I didn't notice anything else." My palms grew damp. "Listen, Olivia, you really need to take better care of Copper. If he survives, don't let him eat chocolate. If you're not sure how to take care of him, call me. And for crying out loud, order a book so you can be a responsible dog owner."

"Where's the sheriff?" She didn't act a bit concerned.

Wade jogged down the steps and joined us. "Mrs. Caswell, thank you for allowing us to look through the house again. To be clear, you gave permission for me to take the spiral notebook with your husband's notes."

I passed the notebook to him and kept my mouth shut.

"Yes. You can keep anything you found related to the case as long as there's no monetary value to it. Sheriff Stone, I hope this proves my innocence. If I was guilty of harming my husband, wouldn't I have kept you away?"

I studied the woman. How conniving was she?

"I see your point. We'll get out of your way. Thanks again." He met my gaze and motioned with his head. "Let's go."

Weird vibes rolled off the sheriff, but I didn't question him. Instead, I forced myself to smile at Olivia. "See you later. I hope Copper's going to be okay."

"I'm going to have faith he'll pull through." She reclined in the chair without speaking another word.

Wade and I took off, and I didn't say anything until we reached our vehicles at the pier parking lot. "Wade, what'd you find?"

He held up a jump drive. "You're my witness. Olivia gave me permission to keep anything related to the murder."

I high-fived him because the news deserved more than a fist bump in my opinion. "Way to go, Sheriff Stone."

"See you later, Andi Grace." He drove away with a smile.

I got Peanut settled into the backseat and started my SUV.

A flash caught my eye, and I looked toward Dirk's house. Olivia stood on the upper back deck and looked straight at me. Goose bumps popped out on my arms, and I drove away wondering if she'd overheard any of my conversation with Wade.

Chapter Thirty-three

SAFE AT HOME, I lost myself in researching cold case blogs. Almost every site agreed that roughly thirty percent of murder cases were never solved.

If I'd known about these websites years earlier, would I have spent time searching for the hit-and-run driver who'd killed my parents? Maybe, but it would've taken away from helping my siblings heal and grow. Only recently had the driver been discovered, so I wouldn't need to spend time searching for answers. Still, I could easily imagine becoming consumed with such a search.

Dirk appeared on various blogs as Don Caswell. He often left comments. Sometimes he made observations, and other times he asked insightful questions. Bottom line was once you looked beyond Dirk's desire to schmooze and become a star, he'd been a smart man.

I better understood Deputy Sawyer's comment to Wade about the investigation being boring and interesting. Many of the blogs I discovered had no comments from Don. On sites with search bars, I started by looking for cases in California.

The doorbell rang, interrupting my research. The dogs barked and took off to the front hall. I closed my laptop and waded through the dogs to answer the door.

Marc stood there holding a large brown paper bag.

I opened the door and threw my arms around him before he could walk in the door. "Oh, Marc. I'm so glad you're here."

Chubb ran circles around us, but Sunny and Peanut wandered back to the family room.

Marc embraced me, and the bag crinkled when it touched my back. "Are you okay?"

"Yeah, I'm fine. It's been a thought-provoking day, and I need to talk it over with you." I quit hugging him. "How'd it go with Lincoln?"

"You know I can't say, but I brought dinner."

"It smells wonderful. What time is it?" I waved him in.

"Six." The familiar tap of his footsteps on the wood floor was a distinct sound. Blindfolded, I could pick Marc out by the unique sound of his walk. Chubb remained at his side.

"I lost track of time. The dogs probably need to go out back. Peanut had a stressful day, and the three of them have been hanging out together this afternoon." I opened the door, and all the dogs rushed outside.

Marc put the bag on the counter and leaned his hip against it. "I missed you."

"Aw, honey. I missed you too." I wrapped my arms around him again, and he kissed me. Our romantic moment lasted until the dogs barked.

Marc chuckled and strode to the back door. "Guess they want in."

I reached for the food bag. "What's for dinner? Can I open the sack?"

"I picked salads up on my way here from Tony's Pizzeria. There are also breadsticks and a small vegetarian pizza."

"Uh-oh. I bet I'm in trouble." Tony had been a good friend to me for years. I loved his restaurant, but it'd been a while since I'd eaten there.

"He's not happy that it's been so long since you've been to see him." Marc moved to the sink and washed his hands. "He worries you don't get enough to eat and all that jazz."

"It's just so hard to go in and only order salad. Once I smell his pizzas and spaghetti, I'm a goner."

"Me too. That's why we've got more than salads tonight."

I filled two glasses with water. "Do you want to eat on the back porch or inside?"

"Outside sounds wonderful after sitting in offices the past couple of days."

We got settled at the patio table, and the dogs lay near our feet. Tony's house salad included mixed spring greens, red onion, cherry tomatoes, black olives, croutons, pepperoncini, and Parmesan cheese. Topped with his secret Italian dressing, it was one of my favorite salads. "I love Tony's homemade salad dressing."

"It's the best." Marc speared a tomato with his fork. "Have you thought about a wedding date?"

"October seventeenth."

His warm laugh filled the night. "I'm impressed you had time to look at your calendar. Why that date?"

"The weather in October is lovely, and it'll still be nice enough for a honeymoon in Maine. Not too hot and not too cold."

"I hope you're right. It could be chilly that late in the fall."

I toyed with my salad. "Yeah, which means we'll be able to snuggle in front of a fire. Don't you think the leaves will be beautiful then?"

"Probably, but I haven't studied Maine's weather enough to know for sure. Still, I like the sound of snuggling." He chewed a bite. "Big or small wedding?"

"Small. Neither one of us has much family, and I don't want to stress over planning a big wedding. I want us to enjoy the time leading up to our nuptials, which leads me to a question. Do you want me to sign a prenuptial?"

He shook his head. "I'm planning on forever. Why would you ask about a prenup?"

"Olivia warned me to get one. Would the divorce be motive for her to kill her husband?"

"Dirk was smart. Money wasn't a problem for him, so it's possible he wanted to protect it in case the marriage didn't work. Having a prenup would make it more enticing for Olivia to murder her husband in order to inherit his wealth."

"You're saying Dirk would want one to protect himself from Olivia taking him to the cleaners. The whole situation is just so sad." I took a bite of pizza.

"Yeah, I'd say there are two sides to a prenup." Marc finished eating and leaned back in the wicker chair. "You have a good bit of property. Do you want me to sign a prenup?"

I laughed even though he spoke the truth. "No way, but I'd like to run something by you."

"Shoot."

"My favorite part of the plantation is Stay and Play." My palms grew damp. "How would you feel about us giving part of the land to Nate and Juliet for a wedding gift?"

"It's up to you, but I like the idea. What about your sister?"

"Can we give her a parcel of the property? She might want to build a little place on it or sell it for college money." My heart raced, and I couldn't for the life of me decide why I was so nervous voicing my desire. Marc knew how much my family meant to me, but I didn't want him to think I was reckless with my belongings.

"One of the first things I learned about you is that you'll always want the best for your siblings." He looked off in the distance.

The sound of waves hitting the beach soothed my bad case of nerves. "Well?"

"You still hope to add a dog shelter out there, and that'll require some of the land. I think we should give Lacey Jane my house. I was going to sell it anyway, and she'll still have the option to live there or sell it."

I gasped. "Marc, I can't let you do that."

He leaned forward and propped his arms on the long outdoor table. "I don't want us to be a family with his and her checking accounts. If our mentality is always yours and mine, what's the point of getting married? To me, marriage means becoming one in every way, including financially. It's important to you to give property to your siblings, so it's important to me. Simple as that."

It took a moment before I could speak. "When my parents died, I assumed the role of head of the family. I've asked a few select people for advice over the years, but I've never had one person to always turn to. Not even Juliet." Could I relax into Marc's love and always turn to him? I met his gaze and knew it was possible.

Marc folded his fingers together. "Nate and Lacey Jane are adults now. Nate's a man about to get married. Your sister has Ike Gage in her life."

"I know, but Lacey Jane and Ike are still getting to know each other." My snappy reply surprised me. "Oh, I'm sorry."

"It makes sense you'd feel a little left out."

"I've only got myself to blame, because I'm the one who introduced them. I really am happy for Lacey Jane, but you're right. I feel excluded. When she has free time, Ike's usually hanging around. If it's not her biological father, it's David Wayne. I miss my baby sister."

"As far as Ike goes, you sacrificed your feelings for Lacey Jane's benefit. It's one of the many things I love about you. Dating a good man was inevitable. My guess is David isn't going anywhere. You need to make peace with both of these relationships. As for us, it sounds like we're in agreement. No prenuptials."

"Agreed. It's terrible that people like Dirk and Olivia go into a marriage worried the other will take advantage of their material possessions."

"I've got a feeling Olivia will be very rich soon."

"I'm not confident about anything regarding this case. For instance, the will hasn't appeared. Was it on Dirk's laptop, or is it hidden in the house? I forgot to tell you. Olivia let Wade and me take Peanut into Cutter's Landing today."

"You don't say?" Marc leaned back in the wicker chair and stretched his long legs.

I updated him on the situation. "Olivia even left us alone while she laid out at the pool. She's either innocent or very crafty."

"If she's hiding anything, it could be at her place in Wilmington." Marc yawned. "Sorry, we had an early morning."

"Why don't you go home? We can talk tomorrow."

"Naw, I want to spend more time with my best girl." He winked. "Any more thoughts on Olivia as a legitimate suspect?"

"Her motives would probably be freedom from Dirk and getting his money. The beach house alone is bound to be worth over a million dollars." Living on the island could only be topped by living on the actual beach. "Can you imagine waking up every morning and seeing the ocean from your window?"

"It's a legitimate option for you." Marc rubbed his large hands together.

"How?" The tempo of my heart picked up.

"Sell my place, sell the part of your land not related to your business, and sell this house. It should be enough to make a legitimate offer on a beachfront home."

It didn't take two seconds for the dream to fizzle. "I don't want it that much. I'd rather stay here and gift the land to my family."

Marc said, "I figured as much."

Peanut nudged my leg.

"If I can't find a place for this little one, how do you feel about becoming a three-dog family when we get married?"

"No problem, but I have been wondering about a home office for me. Do you suppose you can squeeze me into your office?"

"It's possible, but I'm just starting to organize it to get my personality in there." I picked up our dirty dishes. "Let's give it a look, though, at making it work for both of us."

Marc gathered the leftover food, and the dogs followed us inside.

"Go in there and see what you think." I threw away what couldn't be recycled, placed what we hadn't eaten into the refrigerator, then joined Marc in my office.

He stood behind me and wrapped both arms around my shoulders. "It's not going to work." He kissed my neck.

Chills danced up my spine, making me think October seventeenth was too far away. "We'll find a solution."

"Yes, we will."

Despite my attempts to put my touch on the space, it still looked like the previous owner's office. "We can move out the couch and armchairs. Two desks can be arranged to face each other."

Marc chuckled. "Sitting across from you will be too much of a distraction to accomplish any work."

He made a good point. "Let me talk to Griffin. Not only is he a contractor, but he designed the updates on the old kitchen. Griffin should be able to come up with some ideas for us." Juliet's brother Griffin had handled various projects at Kennady Plantation to improve the B and B. He'd also been the one to build the studio apartment where Melanie was staying.

"Let me mention it to him. After all, he still crashes at my place when he's in town."

"Is he close to finishing the project in Charleston?"

"Yeah, that's why your brother was there working on the gardens. They should be done in the next few days, but Griffin made a bid on a project up in Southport and got it."

"I'd hoped he'd only work around Heyward Beach."

"It's still his goal, but this project was evidently too good not to bid on it." Marc walked around the office. "We've got time to make plans for this room before we get married. October seventeenth gives us five months to plan a wedding, a honeymoon, and living arrangements. Do you want me to take charge of the honeymoon?"

Originally, I'd intended to plan our trip as a surprise for Marc, but maybe turning the front room into an office for my future husband would be a nicer gift. "As long as you pick a place with a water view in Maine. And we'll need a fireplace. I want us to kayak, hike, eat fresh lobster, and relax."

"Trust me to handle it." He yawned. "And you better believe it'll have a working fireplace so we can snuggle."

"Awesome." My heart warmed. "You need to rest. Go home."

"I won't miss the drive from your place to mine once we're married. Do you want to go for a run in the morning?"

"I'll meet you at the pier." We kissed at the front door, and Chubb followed his owner out.

I locked up and returned to the office to search more blogs focused on cold cases. I couldn't ignore the feeling Dirk's death was related to his radio show or podcast. I kept at it until my eyes closed and my head dropped. Jerking awake, I looked at my faithful German shepherd. "Let's go to bed, Sunny."

She led the way upstairs, and we found Peanut sleeping on the fuzzy rug at the end of my bed. I gave him a pat then fell asleep in my comfy bed.

Chapter Thirty-four

EARLY FRIDAY MORNING Marc and I finished our run and walked toward the pier. "What's on your agenda today?" He used his shoulder to swipe at perspiration on his face.

He was in much better shape than me, but eating healthier and running more often had helped me catch up to him. In the old days I'd still be trying to catch my breath. "I plan to head to Stay and Play and check on Melanie. If she's doing a good job, I'll schedule more grooming appointments for her to handle. Most of my day will be out there."

"No dog-walking appointments?"

Ike Gage jogged toward us, but he gazed straight ahead. He still carried himself like a military man.

I waved. "Hi, Ike."

The retired marine circled back to us. "Morning, Andi Grace. Marc. How's it going?"

"Good." Marc shook his hand. "Is the rumor true? You bought HOSE?" The business had been our local outdoor equipment store, but the owner lost it because of some nefarious dealings.

"It's true, but I plan to change the name." He adjusted his hat.

"So you're moving to Heyward Beach?" I focused on Lacey Jane's biological father.

He removed his sunglasses and met my gaze straight on. "My original plan was to find my daughter, settle down where she lived, and start a relationship with her."

His intensity made me glad I'd never been under his command. "Yes, sir."

"Your sister has enough room in her big heart for all of us. I believe you voiced the same opinion in the past."

I nodded. "You're exactly right, and I'm glad you're in her life."

"Good to know we're on the same page. You two have a good day."

I stepped toward him. "Wait, Ike. I didn't mean to offend you. Really, it's good to have you around."

His stance relaxed. "Lacey Jane is related to both of us, and it'd be nice if you'd consider me family. We can't avoid each other without hurting your sister."

"I agree. We'll be one of those modern blended families." I didn't know whether to shake his hand or hug him. In the end, I did neither. "Let us know if we can do anything to make your move smoother."

"That means a lot. I'll keep your offer in mind." He pushed his sunglasses on, waved, and ran north.

I glared at Marc. "You weren't much help."

He lifted his hands in surrender. "You had the situation under control. I'll always have your back, but don't expect me to butt in if you've got things handled."

I almost argued, but if he'd interrupted, I probably would've gotten upset with him. "Thanks. You know my siblings will be your family too once we're married."

"Lacey Jane and I have grown close from working together. It'll be nice having her for a sister. I'm looking forward to getting to know Nate better."

His words made me happy. "Do you have time for breakfast?"

"Afraid not. I need to shower and get to the office."

In the distance, a familiar figure waved his metal detector back and forth.

"Come with me to say hi to Jeremiah. It won't take long."

"Do you have any idea how hard it is to say no to you? Let's go." Marc held my hand as we crossed the sand and stopped beside the man intent on finding a treasure.

I waved to get his attention. "Hey, Jeremiah."

He removed his headphones and stopped work. "Morning."

"Good morning. I'd like you to meet the man I'm going to marry. This is Marc Williams."

Marc held out his hand. "Nice to meet you, sir."

"Likewise." Jeremiah shook Marc's hand.

The three of us carried on a brief discussion about the weather before Marc announced his need to get ready for work.

I kissed Marc's cheek. "Have a good day."

"Stay out of trouble." He gave me a quick kiss then ran to the parking lot.

Jeremiah said, "Seems like a right nice fellow."

"Yeah, he is. Are you having any luck today?" I pointed to the metal detector.

He looked right then left. "This is my usual sweet spot. It's where people lay out when it's nice. The towel line, so to say."

"That's a new phrase to me." What kind of island girl didn't know all the beach lingo?

"It's where the people lay their towels. It's above the tide line, and you can usually tell by the seaweed, shells, and bits of driftwood left from the tide."

"Makes sense. Do you have other favorite spots?"

"The path from the parking lot to this area is where I often find goodies. If it's what I consider a sentimental notion, I notify the diner." He pointed to the building in front of the pier. "You know, just in case anybody reports it missing. I always return necklaces, rings and stuff like that."

"What's the best item you returned?"

"Car keys. They belonged to a family with four kiddos. The parents were frantic. As soon as I noticed the ruckus, I had a hunch the keys belonged to them. Man, they were so grateful, it was almost embarrassing. They offered me a reward, but it wouldn't have been right." He shrugged.

If anybody could've used extra money, it would be Jeremiah. "Have you had breakfast?"

He shook his head. "Too busy."

"Let's take a break. My treat."

"No, thanks. I best keep at it."

"Please. You're helping me by watching out for Leroy. I'd like to return the kindness. Besides that, my fiancé had to go to work. Don't make me eat alone."

He scratched his scraggly beard. "As a matter of fact, I do want to talk to you about your friend."

"Great. I'll be right back." I hurried and ordered breakfast burritos, two coffees, and a bottle of water for Jeremiah in case he planned to stay on the beach long.

We sat on the sand and shared breakfast in silence. Two pelicans flew low over the waves. A few people walked their dogs. Incoming waves broke on the shore before washing back to the vastness of the Atlantic.

At last, I asked, "Have you found any treasures recently?"

Without speaking, Jeremiah pulled a faded red bandana from his pocket and opened it. "Coins are my favorite thing to find. No need to feel guilty about them, and they spend real good."

His words made me want to come out early one morning and spread a bunch of quarters around his favorite area. "What else do you have?"

"Earrings. Women always lose jewelry in the sand. You'd be amazed how many times I find one earring. See this gold ring?"

"It looks like a man's ring because it's thick and chunky."

"Yep. My eyes ain't as good as they used to be, but I think it's a college ring. Maybe a fraternity or some club. The people at the diner know about it and will contact me if a man comes looking for it. If nobody asks about the ring, I plan to take it to the pawn shop on Seventeen."

Highway Seventeen had many pawn shops going in both directions. "Do you ever check with the police?"

"Nope. Once I was arrested. Mistaken identity, and they eventually let me go, but it only takes one time to get sideways with the cops to scar you for life. I avoid them as much as possible."

"I'd probably feel the same way in your shoes." I leaned closer to his treasure and pointed. "What's that?"

"Key ring with no keys. Just one of them drive things you use in computers." He scratched his jaw. "I may be poor, but I'm not stupid."

"Of course you're not stupid." My heart beat faster. "A person isn't smart just because they have money or earthly stuff. You're smart and a survivor, Jeremiah."

He stared at the key ring. "Appreciate you saying that."

I imagined he wasn't used to words of affirmation, so I changed the subject. No need to make him feel uncomfortable. "Did you find all of these items this morning?"

"Most of them, but I've been carrying the drive around for at least a week." He gave me a knowing look. "Do you think it's important?"

"Possibly. Can I buy it from you?" We were close to Dirk's beach house. Did it possibly belong to the dead man? What secrets did it hold?

"It's yours." He handed it to me.

"Thank you so much." I accepted the jump drive and held it tight in my hand. "What's going on with Leroy?"

Jeremiah looked right and left. I wasn't sure if it was a habit from the war, or just a Jeremiah thing. "He's a good guy, and I've introduced him to some of the men. His friend, the apartment manager, is another story. I can't quite figure him out."

My palms grew damp. "What's going on?"

He shook his head. "Might be best if I keep it to myself."

"Please don't hold back. Is Leroy in danger? What's going on?"

"I'm only gonna tell you because of your friend. You asked me to watch out for him, and I'd hate to hold back then have something happen."

I understood Jeremiah was a man of few words. A retired veteran who minded his own business and kept a low profile. "I appreciate you."

The older Black man watched the waves before speaking. "Chip acts like he's your friend, but if you watch the man close there's a darkness in his eyes. I might be reading the situation wrong, but something just don't feel right. You and your friend need to be careful around him."

"Yes, sir." I trusted Jeremiah's gut instinct. "I was only worried because Peanut, Dirk Cutter's beagle, doesn't like Chip. I don't guess Chip has shared much about his family."

"Not to me." He stood and brushed the sand from his raggedy jeans.

"Do you need a ride anywhere?"

"I plan to keep working the beach. Thanks for the grub."

"See you later." While walking home, I shook the jump drive in an effort to get the sand out. As much as I longed to see what it held, it didn't seem worth ruining my laptop.

Once again, my plans changed. Good thing flexibility was my middle name. When I got home, I showered quickly and then took the dogs with me to see Leroy. Jeremiah's words had released a tidal wave of anxiety in me for my friend, and it wouldn't rest until I saw him for myself.

Chapter Thirty-five

I DROVE THROUGH THE FRONT ENTRANCE of Piney Woods Apartment Complex. Two brick columns with black outdoor lights on top welcomed visitors to the property. Too bad chunks had fallen out of the columns. One of the vintage lanterns tilted to the side. It wasn't for me to judge the condition of the neglected entrance. More than likely, Chip had inherited the problem.

Pine trees bordered the property. I headed for Leroy's duplex and heaved a sigh of relief at the sight of my friend.

Leroy sat on his front porch with Frank Hoffman, another retired military man. It did my heart good to see the widower out and about. Both of the men had become dear to me, and I was happy they'd become friends with each other.

I hopped out of the Highlander but left the dogs inside with the windows down. "How are two of my favorite people?"

Frank stood and grinned. "You must be hurting if we're at the top of your list."

Leroy was slower rising, but his smile was just as big.

"I'm blessed to know you both." I hugged each one. "What are you up to?"

Leroy pointed his thumb at Frank. "We were discussing baits and hooks. Fishing stuff."

Frank shrugged. "You know I'm more of a gardener, but Leroy convinced me to give fishing a try."

"Nice." I glanced around the area. Chip wasn't anywhere to be seen. "Where's Chip?"

Leroy said, "Not sure. Maybe the hardware store."

"Okay." Made sense with all the work the apartment complex needed. "Would y'all like to meet me at Stay and Play? You can help with the dogs then go fishing at the river. Marc's place has a nice dock, and Juliet can fix a to-go lunch for you."

Leroy grinned. "You don't have to ask me twice."

Frank nodded. "I'll drive."

The men followed me to Stay and Play, and I walked back to the dog-grooming station.

Melanie was bathing one of my regulars, Heinz. He was an older Westie who hadn't lost his spunk. She spoke to him softly, and her gentle manner with the dog suggested she was a good fit for the job.

"Hey, Melanie. I've got a couple of friends with me."

The perky blonde stepped away from the small stainless-steel tub. After drying her hands, she looked at Leroy. "It's good to see you again."

"You, too. This is Frank Hoffman."

Melanie shook hands with Frank. "Nice to meet you. Do you have a pet?"

"No pets. My wife was allergic, and since she passed I just haven't put any thought into adopting one. Have we met before?" Frank squinted. "You kinda look familiar."

Melanie stepped back into the shadows. "I'm from Charleston. Just moved here. I must have one of those faces everybody recognizes."

"Probably so. How can we help you today?" Frank didn't appear to be fazed by her negative response.

I looked at Melanie. "The guys are here to volunteer."

"Melanie, that's a coded message." Leroy chuckled. "Andi Grace is trying to make sure we behave."

"Hey now." I'd invited them to help them stay active and involved in life. Each one had withdrawn from society not so long ago, and each had lots to offer. I didn't want my two older friends to be sitting around lonely and miserable.

"Dylan probably could use help more than me." Melanie's voice squeaked. "There are a few dogs boarding with us, and they might like to go for a walk or play fetch."

Leroy said, "We know Dylan. We'll find him, and you ladies can focus on getting the animals all gussied up."

I patted the men on their shoulders. "Juliet will have lunch for you on the back patio in a couple of hours. I'll meet you there, then drive you over to Marc's dock."

We each went our separate ways. In my office, I scheduled grooming appointments for Melanie. In the past, many clients had requested the service, and it was exciting to meet their needs. Once the next week was booked, I searched social media in hopes of finding information on Melanie. It didn't sit well, knowing she had a secret. If she was into something dangerous, I'd let her go.

Chills danced up my spine, and I shivered. What if she killed Dirk? She had a secret, and she was living on my property. No. It was a total coincidence she arrived in town the same time Dirk was murdered. With an open mind, I returned to social media.

There were lots of old pictures of Melanie with friends but none with family, and no recent posts. I pulled out her application and looked for clues to why she wanted to live in Heyward Beach. Under emergency contact, a friend had been listed. Again, no family.

Marc and I had both lost our parents in car accidents at different points in our lives. Did Melanie have family in our little town? Why had she been in the parking lot of Paula's Pickings in the dark?

Had she come across a family heirloom in the store on her previous visit? Regina was also from Charleston, and it was possible she had something for sale in her shop that Melanie recognized. Still, it'd be a stretch to imagine I sent Melanie to Regina's store for linens and she'd found something belonging to her family.

The alarm on my phone buzzed. "Time for Yoyo's next obedience lesson."

Violet Seitz stood under an oak tree with Yoyo pulling on the leash trying to go after a barn cat. "Yoyo, stop."

The Lab didn't obey at first, then Violet stood firm and commanded the dog to stop. He did a double take then submitted with a whimper.

I clapped. "Way to go, Violet. Do you have a treat for Yoyo?"

With a confident smile, she pulled a dog biscuit out of her shorts. "Yes. Aren't you proud of me? We're both learning."

"I'm delighted. What do you want to work on today?" From where we stood, it was easy to see Dylan, Frank, and Leroy walking dogs in the wooded area of the property.

"Sometimes he acts weird around strangers." She gazed at her Lab.

"Weird how?"

"Maybe shy and fearful." She tapped her jaw. "He's never tried to bite anybody, which is good. He often hides behind Ethan or me at first. Once he warms up to a person, I become worried he'll knock them over from excitement."

"Peanut is one of my rescue dogs, and there's one man in town he doesn't like. I'm trying to decide why. Does Yoyo only get upset around one particular person?"

"No, it's pretty random." Her thick red ponytail drooped.

"Let's try an experiment." I grabbed my phone and texted Dylan. "Three different men are going to come over here. Two are older, and one is younger. I want to see how your dog reacts with them."

Violet pointed at Dylan. "Yoyo's worked with him before."

"Okay, but let's still try my experiment."

Dylan was the first to reach us, and Yoyo was fine. Next came Frank with Sunny. No negative reaction. In fact, Yoyo was so focused on Sunny, he didn't seem to care about Frank. Leroy was the last to approach Yoyo. Peanut trotted at his side. The two dogs sniffed each other, and Peanut barked once, but there was no negative reaction from Yoyo.

"I don't understand. Why is he behaving now?" Violet shook her head.

I smiled at the guys. "Thanks, y'all."

"So weird." Violet knelt and rubbed her dog. "Why are you good today but not other times?"

The three men walked to the barn with the dogs, and I faced Violet. "Think back. Does Yoyo react to big men? Men who smell like they've been fishing, hunting, or smoking? Is there a common denominator between the people he reacts to?"

"I'll pay better attention." She hugged the dog then stood. "What's the story with Peanut? Why does he get upset with the man?"

No way I'd share my silly theory about Chip being involved in Dirk's death. "Peanut's owner died recently, and I wonder if the two guys had an argument or something that the dog witnessed."

Violet nodded. "It makes sense, especially if they had a disagreement recently. Peanut remembers the altercation. His master is gone. He wonders if the fellow you're thinking about is involved. Maybe he's aggressive toward the man in hopes he'll bring his owner back."

I stared at her. "What an interesting theory." If her assessment was correct, I'd need to scratch Chip off my suspect list. Although, I'd never come up with a legit motive for him to kill Dirk. "You're here for a lesson, so let's refocus. If you come up with a pattern for men who upset Yoyo, maybe we can work on his attitude."

"I would love that, and I'll start taking notes."

An hour later, we finished our lesson, and I returned to my office in the barn.

"Knock knock," Dylan tapped the doorframe while speaking.

"What's up?"

"I went ahead and took the guys to Marc's place. They've got lunch and are set up to spend the afternoon fishing." He sat in a chair on the other side of my desk. "Peanut went with them, and Leroy says he'd like to have another shot at fostering the dog."

I leaned back in my chair. "They're a good match, but his neighbor is the problem."

"Yeah, Leroy told me all about it." The young man pushed away a tuft of dark hair falling in his face. "I didn't know whether to encourage him or not."

"I don't know what the right answer is, but Peanut is comfortable with Leroy and will get lots of love and attention from the man."

"That's what everybody wants, isn't it?" Dylan's mother had left him years earlier, and his dad was currently out of the picture.

"How are things with you and Kylie?" They'd become friends earlier in the year. Maybe more.

"She's pretty focused on getting her nursing degree, but we hang out when we can." His face reddened, but he didn't elaborate.

"Dylan, will you close the door?" My door usually remained open, but I didn't want our conversation to be heard by Melanie.

He closed it and returned to his seat. "Is something wrong?"

"No, but I'd like your feedback on Melanie." I turned on my radio as an extra precaution.

"She stays busy. When she's not grooming, she's cleaning her workstation, washing towels, and playing with the pets we're boarding. I'd say Melanie's better with animals than people."

"Has she mentioned her family?"

Dylan's gaze dropped to the floor. "She was put up for adoption when she was born, and she'd like to meet her mother one day."

Interesting she'd arrived in town around the time of Dirk's murder. "Does she know her mother's identity?"

"She thinks so, and she's trying to get up the guts to talk to her."

"Do you know who her mom is?"

Dylan jerked back in his chair. "I shouldn't say anything else. If you want to know, ask Melanie yourself."

"You're right, Dylan. I'm sorry for putting you in the middle. Let's talk about you."

He laughed and tugged at the collar of his faded plaid shirt. "Uh, can we go back to discussing Melanie?"

I joined his laughter. "Seriously, how is the job going? Are you happy working here?"

"It's good, but I miss the construction projects."

"I'm not surprised. Building is your background, and if you find a different job, I'll understand. I'll miss you like crazy, but I'll understand." I'd given Dylan a job working for me in order to turn his life around. He'd been a model employee, and he did an amazing job with the animals. "What about working for Griffin?"

"I'm not sure he's ready to hire permanent employees yet." Dylan rubbed his hands together. "I don't want to be disloyal to you, but is it okay for me to talk to Griffin next time I see him?"

"Absolutely, and I understand you probably need a better-paying job. All I ask is that you give me at least a two-week notice before you leave."

"You've been good to me, Andi Grace. Good like a big sister. I'd never leave you in the lurch."

"Thanks, and I feel like you're family too."

Dylan stood. "If you have time, I think there's a good spot for your future dog shelter on the property."

"Lead the way." I turned off the radio.

Crash.

Something hit the ground on the other side of the door. My heart leapt. The music may have hidden my conversation with Dylan, but it'd also prevented me from hearing somebody approach.

Dylan opened the office door, and Melanie was on her knees picking up bottles of shampoo, grooming blades, and hair clips.

"I'm so clumsy. Sorry about dropping all this stuff."

Dylan hurried to help her pick up the mess. "Don't worry about it, Melanie."

I watched her nervous movements. Her voice shook. Was it from the accident or a guilty conscience? One thing was for certain. When I caught Melanie at a time when she wasn't as nervous as a long-tail cat in a room full of rocking chairs, I'd ask about her mother.

Chapter Thirty-six

SUNNY AND I SETTLED INTO MY OFFICE at Stay and Play. Peanut was still with Leroy and Frank at Marc's dock. Having Sunny all to myself was like old times. A girl and her dog. Nice. I needed to carve out one-on-one time with Sunny. Today was business, but we needed to spend time having fun.

Juliet brought me her old laptop, knowing full well inserting the sandy jump drive could ruin it. She also gave me a new soft toothbrush from the emergency supply she kept for guests. We plugged in her old computer, and while it began charging, I turned my attention to the key chain jump drive Jeremiah had given me earlier. "It's probably a long shot that this used to belong to Dirk."

"I need to prepare tea for the guests. Good luck with getting anything useful." Juliet waved and walked out the door.

"Have fun." I shook and brushed the little device until not another grain of sand landed on my desk. The time had arrived to boot up the computer. Once it came to life, I inserted the data stick with shaky hands and held my breath.

Sunny napped at my feet, oblivious to my anxiety.

At last, the drive opened. No password was requested. I explored options until coming to a list of files. I began to speed-read my way through the list of documents. Most were related to sports. There were others about family, friends, and genealogy. It appeared that the owner of this drive had children. I searched through photos.

There were many pictures of a couple with two children. Baby photos, toddlers, and grade school. In each one, the dad's hair looked progressively grayer.

I didn't want to give up, but it didn't seem possible this was Dirk's drive.

"Andi Grace," Leroy's cheerful voice called out.

Sunny roused and left my office with a spark in her step.

I ended my research and joined the others near the play area. "Were the fish biting?"

Frank pointed to a cooler. "It was glorious. I never caught so many fish in such a short time. The company was good too."

Leroy's face beamed. "We're heading to my place to clean and cook what we can eat. The rest we'll freeze for another day. Do you want to join us?"

Tail wagging, Peanut stood at the older man's side.

"Did he go swimming?"

"Yeah, I'll take him home for a bath."

I shook my head. "No need. Let's do it here."

Peanut barked.

"Problem solved. A simple bath won't take long. Why don't y'all wait in my office? There are drinks in the little fridge. Help yourself." I led the beagle to the grooming area.

No sign of Melanie.

"Okay, boy. It looks like it's you and me." I led the beagle up the stairs and into the tub. "Let's get your collar off. We'll get you a new one from the office after you're clean."

I lay the faded orange collar to the side with a thunk. It didn't take long for me to bathe and towel-dry Peanut. I snatched the collar and carried Peanut to my office. "One nice and clean beagle almost ready to leave with you."

Leroy sniffed. "He definitely smells better, and we won't get Frank's vehicle dirty."

I opened a cabinet of supplies and removed a collar and temporary name tag. "Leroy, why don't you put your contact information there? You know. Just in case."

His eyes widened. "Emergency contact for Peanut? I like it."

Frank stood and tugged on the straps of his overalls. "We should let Andi Grace get back to work."

I secured the name tag onto the new collar and fastened it onto the beagle. "Looking good, boy. Now if only—"

Leroy raised his hand to stop my flow of words. "You never answered our dinner invitation."

"I'd love to join you guys, but there are a few dogs needing to be walked soon. Thanks for the invite though."

"Yes, ma'am." He removed his hat and rubbed his head. "Frank and I were talking about the dog. It could be I panicked, when he barked at Chip."

"It's up to you."

Leroy nodded. "He's going home with me tonight."

"Don't hesitate to call me if you have any trouble. Peanut is still traumatized from losing Dirk."

"Don't you worry. Frank offered to take him home if we have a problem."

"Ah, so the gardener may become a dog man." I walked with the men and beagle to Frank's vehicle and waved them off. Peanut would be safe with Leroy and Frank.

I strolled back to my office and reached for Peanut's old dog collar. It'd slickened over time. My thoughts drifted to Dirk, wondering what kind of a dog owner he was. The man had been a people person. It made sense dogs would like him too. He'd probably spent time playing with Peanut. I ran my hand over the purple embroidered letters on the collar. *Peanut.* The gap where the buckle was located had been sewn closed.

I sat straighter. Was that normal? I pulled another collar from the supply cabinet and compared the two collars. There was a gap big enough to see light through on the new collar. It allowed you to adjust the collar for a better fit.

I reached for the scissors on my desk and tried to cut through the stitches. They were tight, and the scissor blades were too big. I ran to the grooming station.

Melanie stood at the dryer, folding towels.

"Where are the straight shearers?" Not all dogs liked the noise or vibration of clippers, so we kept shearers on hand.

Melanie opened the cabinet and brought me a selection. "Here."

"They need to be strong but small enough to get in a tight spot." I reached for a black-handled pair of scissors. "This should work. Hopefully."

"Those belong to me." She stepped forward.

"Do you mind if I use them? I'll be very careful." I gave her time to answer.

"It's just that I don't have a lot of money."

"If there's any damage, I'll pay for you to replace them. As in, I won't exchange them for something cheap. You can pick the replacement, and I won't question your selection."

Melanie nodded. "Okay, then. Sorry if I overreacted."

"You need to trust that I won't take advantage of you. I'm sorry if it came across that way." I wandered back to my office and shut the door. No need to drag Melanie into my experiment.

Unlike the random jump drive Jeremiah had found on the beach, if there was something hidden in the collar, it definitely belonged to Dirk Cutter.

Chapter Thirty-seven

WITH SLOW PRECISE MOVEMENTS, I clipped at the thread and removed the stitching. The buckle clinked onto my desk first. Two more snips, and my finger touched plastic. "Bingo."

"Woof." Sunny paced in front of my desk.

"It's okay, girl. Better than okay." I tugged out the tiny plastic bag. It was like what a coin collector might use for quarters. The single-track zipper was easy to open, and the folded piece of paper fell onto my desk.

My heart raced. I was entering dangerous territory if my actions altered evidence in Dirk's murder. I hustled back to Melanie and handed the scissors to her. "Good as new. May I have a pair of rubber gloves?"

"What are you doing to Sunny?" She pointed to my German shepherd at my side.

I glanced at my faithful companion. "She's fine, and to put your mind at ease, I'll leave her with you for a few minutes."

Melanie plucked two medium-size gloves from a box and handed them to me.

"Thanks." I jogged back to my office, locking the door behind me this time.

Gloves securely on my hands, I unfolded the index card. Dirk's messy scrawl filled both sides.

California cold case.

Goose bumps covered my body. California. Not Carolina. Triple C. Why had it intrigued Dirk?

Twenty-eight-year-old Roxy Starr was the victim of murder twenty years ago. Stan Koch, Juan Perez, and Charlie Jones were the three main suspects. Police questioned each man, but there'd never been enough evidence for an arrest and conviction. Also not enough evidence to prove their innocence.

Roxy had an affair with a famous television producer, and the police suspected the producer's wife of being involved in the murder. An iron-tight alibi kept her out of prison.

In the past two decades, Juan Perez died in a car accident. Stan Koch was on a waiting list for a heart transplant. Charlie Jones vanished into thin air. Roxy had been strangled, and her body was discovered in an almond orchard.

All three men had worked construction, but it's unclear if they knew each other.

I shivered. Dirk probably never imagined he'd die of strangulation. Coincidence or not?

Dirk ended his notes with a description of Charlie Jones. *Six-foot-two. Long, narrow face. Bulbous nose.*

I took pictures of the index card with my phone, then sealed it in the plastic bag. Next, I opened my laptop and searched for the mysterious contractor, Charlie Jones. Pages of people appeared with the same name. There were golfers, bakers, marketing gurus, and health care professionals. Shifting gears, I looked on social media for Chip Johnson. There were too many accounts to mention.

Charlie Jones. Chip Johnson. Same initials. I shivered again despite the humid afternoon. It was a leap to believe they were the same person.

If, and it was a big if, Charlie Jones had killed a woman in California twenty years earlier, how had he ended up in Heyward Beach?

The timing was another issue if Chip was really Charlie. It couldn't be a fluke Dirk planned to air an episode solving the cold case soon after Chip moved to Heyward Beach. How long had Chip been in town? Long enough to work as the apartment manager of Piney Woods.

If Dirk and Chip had become friends, how had Dirk stumbled upon the other man's murky history? It didn't make sense for Chip to reveal his secret to a well-known radio personality. Dirk liked to drink and could hold his liquor. Was it possible the men had met each other at a bar? It could've even been a golf outing or fishing trip. People were known to drink when participating in sports or watching others play. What if Chip had too much to drink and spilled the secret that he'd kept for two decades? It didn't make sense. Why keep the deadly secret for two decades then get careless?

Dirk had been ambitious, and he had a desire to help solve cold cases. If he'd discovered Chip was part of an unsolved murder in California, nothing would've stopped Dirk from revealing the truth.

The uneasy feeling I'd experienced around Chip morphed into me placing him solidly at the top of my suspect list. I wrote Chip's name in bold letters and emphasized it with a blue highlighter.

Before I pursued Chip full-throttle, I'd rule out Olivia Caswell, Georgia Cummins, Regina Houp and Hannah Cummins. Regina would be first on my list because the police had questioned her, and I wanted to make sure she wasn't playing me for a fool. I grabbed my keys, the index card, and my list and ran out of the office. "Sunny, where are you?"

She appeared with ears perked and tilted her head.

"Let's go, girl."

Dylan entered the barn. "Is everything okay? Why are you hollering?"

"Just in a hurry to get moving." My hands shook so hard, my keys rattled. I didn't stop to chat though.

"You look kinda pale. Sure you're alright?" He walked with me to my SUV.

"Yeah, thanks for asking." I opened the door and allowed Sunny to hop inside first. "See you later, Dylan."

"Be careful." He stood there staring at me as we drove away.

If Dylan had guessed my thoughts, he might have tried to stop me. It was one of the reasons I needed to get back to town fast.

Chapter Thirty-eight

ON MY DRIVE TO THE ISLAND, I left messages with Hannah and Olivia. Not knowing Georgia's number, I'd decided to find a way to contact her later. Mothers would go to great lengths to protect their children, but Georgia didn't seem like a killer to me. As far as Hannah was concerned, I imagined she'd give up her dream of politics if it'd protect her mother.

My phone rang. "Hello."

"What do you need?" Olivia's voice sounded bored.

"Hi, is it possible for us to meet this afternoon? I can spend a little time working with Copper, and I have a couple more questions about Dirk."

She sighed. "Today won't work. I'll call you tomorrow."

"Okay. Thanks." I parked at Paula's Pickings then entered the store. I wandered around the antique shop while Regina finished ringing up a customer. My knees shook, and I struggled to look casual. A cracked white crock caught my eye.

"Hi, Andi Grace. Did you find something you like?"

"This would look nice in my home office, especially if I filled it with flowers." My voice cracked, and I cleared my throat.

"Aunt Paula found it at an estate sale. It's not my taste, but I see how the piece works for you."

I gaped at the woman. Had she insulted me or complimented me?

"Be sure to register here before your wedding."

"All right." Now I was committed, but what did Regina have in stock to fit my taste? There was plenty of time to figure it out.

Regina picked up the crock and held it in front of her chest. "Where are you on proving my innocence?"

"I'm getting closer." I kept my most recent thoughts to myself. Loose lips could sink more than ships. They could get you killed.

"Good, because Sheriff Stone showed up yesterday afternoon with a few more questions. Do I need to hire an attorney?" Her nostrils flared.

"That's up to you, Regina, but I think if they had enough evidence you'd be sitting in jail."

"Good point. What about Dirk's wife?"

"She's got plenty of motives to have killed her husband, and I plan to talk to her again soon."

"Who else is a suspect?" Regina's grip on my pottery caused her knuckles to whiten.

"I don't plan to start any rumors about who I suspect. Just trust me. I'm working on proving you're innocent." My heart beat faster. This was my opportunity to quiz her on Chip. "Focus on something fun. Your love life. for instance. Have you been out with Chip again? Maybe you'll be registering for your own wedding soon."

"We've been enjoying each other's company." Her face flushed. "The man sure knows how to treat a lady. Champagne, nice dinners, walks along the beach. He has interesting stories, but he's also a great listener. Dirk was fun, but he was mostly interested in talking about himself and his career. Dirk enjoyed entertaining people. Chip's easier to spend time with because he's attentive to my answers."

I tried not to stare at Regina. What would the odds be she had not only dated the victim, but now she was dating the potential killer? "When did Chip move to Heyward Beach?"

"About three months ago. He left Atlanta to take over the apartment complex."

My mind flew back to Dirk's episode on the Vietnam vet in Atlanta. "It'd be funny if Dirk had met Chip in Atlanta, wouldn't it?"

"Not really." Regina's chin lifted. "Why would you suggest such a thing?"

I shrugged in an effort to appear nonchalant. "Dirk helped solve a cold case in Atlanta involving a Vietnam vet. Did you hear the episode?"

"No, but I never got around to listening to all of the podcasts before his—" She took a deep breath. "Are you suggesting Chip and Dirk met in Atlanta, and became friends here? You do realize there are half a million people living in Atlanta?"

The derision in her tone hit a nerve. My heartbeat pounded in my hot ears. "You asked for my help to prove your innocence. When I'm looking into a murder, I create and discard thoughts all the time. Questions fill my brain night and day. Life would be less complicated if I wasn't helping you. I agreed to your request to be nice, not to have you hurl insults at me. Why don't you hire a private investigator and attorney? I have no problem walking away from all this."

"No, I still need your help." She sounded like she was doing a favor for me. "Trying to draw a connection between Chip and Dirk confused me."

"It's probably nothing." I studied the vintage crock in her hands. "I've changed my mind on that."

"Take it as my way of apologizing." Regina held it out to me. "Are you still willing to help prove I'm innocent?"

I counted to ten in French. Nothing would make me happier than to stay out of Regina's line of fire, but I'd made a promise. "I rarely back down from a person in need, or a challenge. Let's continue to keep this between us. There's no need to upset the sheriff."

The shopkeeper bell tinkled, and heavy footsteps sounded. "I agree."

Chip appeared around the corner and joined us. "You agree to what?"

"Uh, you know, Andi Grace is, uh—"

I clutched the heavy pottery to my chest. It was white with a faded blue crown, and the thing was heavy as all get-out. "Hi, Chip. I'm getting married later this year, and Regina agreed to keep her eyes open for gifts I might like to put on my registry. The items she carries in the store are exquisite, but I prefer a beachy French theme."

"That's my woman. She loves nice things." Chip slipped his arm around Regina's shoulders.

"Yes, she sure does. I better go. Sunny's waiting for me in the car." I turned and beat a hasty retreat, not even remembering to thank Regina for the crock.

I took Sunny home then stopped at Marc's office. Once I was inside, the place was quiet as a cemetery at midnight. No sign of his overprotective office manager. "Hello."

"Sis, is that you?" Lacey Jane appeared from the conference room. Her complexion was pale, and there were dark circles under her eyes.

I hugged her. "What are you doing here? Shouldn't you be studying?"

"My roommates already finished their finals, and they've been celebrating the end of the semester. I needed a place to hunker down and focus where there were no disturbances."

"You could've gone to my house. Even though it's not the home you grew up in, I don't want you to feel like a visitor."

"Okay." She avoided eye contact.

"Honey, is there something wrong?"

Lacey Jane shrugged. "I'm just stressed over this exam."

Now wasn't the time to push my sister, but it seemed as if she was mad at me. Actually, I hadn't spent time with her in ages. I put my feelings on hold so she could study. "Where are Marc and Rylee?"

"Marc's in court, and Rylee took the afternoon off." She smiled. "I've got the whole place to myself. I've got a few minutes to catch up. Dad said he saw you on the beach this morning."

She'd talked to Ike but not me. If our family was going to survive, there was no room for hurt feelings or jealousy. "It sounds like you two are making progress on your relationship if you're calling him Dad."

"Do you mind? It doesn't take away from how much I loved our dad."

"I'm happy for you, Lacey Jane, and we'll catch up later. Right now, I'll run by Daily Java and get you a boost for your afternoon."

"Thanks, but can you get me something with no caffeine?"

I did a double take. "No caffeine?"

"Yeah. I've heard natural fruit drinks help you think clearly. There's evidence they help you stay awake without getting jittery."

"Really? Okay then, a natural drink it is. Lock up after me, and if Chip Johnson shows up, don't let him inside."

"I don't know who that is, so I just won't let anybody inside except for you."

"Great." I left her in the quiet office and walked to Daily Java, keeping alert for Chip. Once I entered the crowded coffee shop, I ordered something for myself too and waited at an empty table.

"May I?" A man's hand touched the empty chair.

I swallowed hard and met Chip's gaze. "Sure."

"You should know that Regina confided in me." His frown emphasized his bulbous nose. Like Dirk's notes on the California killer.

"She did?" My voice squeaked.

"Yes. I've noticed you're a good friend to practically everyone in these parts."

"But?" My breathing hitched in my chest. Where oh where was my order?

"A person should only go so far to help out a friend." He fisted his hands. "There can be a dangerous line to cross, and for the sake of self-preservation, you don't want to step over it."

"Andi Grace, here's your order." Erin placed two fruit smoothies on the table and a brown bakery bag. "The cookies are for Lacey Jane. I know she's going to pass her tests with flying colors."

"Thanks, Erin." I watched her walk away, but the shop was busy. Chip couldn't harm me in the middle of the day with so many people around.

Chip pointed to my order. "You better get those to your sister. I'll see you around."

Was he threatening me through my sister? Perspiration broke out along my hairline. Forget the others on my suspect list. Chip's aggressive behavior terrified me. I texted the one person who might treasure my sister more than Nate and me. Ike Gage.

Chapter Thirty-nine

IKE MET ME IN FRONT OF MARC'S OFFICE. "I'm glad you contacted me. What's going on?"

"Thanks for hurrying. I'm worried about my sister." I caught him up on my investigation. "When Chip mentioned Lacey Jane, I almost vomited. She doesn't need to worry about anything except passing her classes. Will you hang out with her?"

"Yes, but David should be aware of the situation."

David. My sister's boyfriend. He'd protect Lacey Jane. Maybe I should've called him first. "You're right. I plan to update Deputy Wayne and Sheriff Stone before the end of the day."

"The sooner the better."

I handed Ike both drinks and the cookies and pointed to the office. "She's expecting the smoothie, the cookies are a gift from Erin." I texted my sister and asked her to open the door.

"Two drinks?"

I hadn't taken a sip of either one. "It's for you. Thanks for looking out for my sister."

"She'll be safe with me, but Andi Grace, be careful. I don't like the idea of you putting yourself in harm's way."

"Count on it." I waited until he was inside before walking to my Highlander. It wasn't just my imagination. Chip had delivered a veiled threat. I jumped into the driver's seat and turned on the air conditioner full blast.

Ike had responded to my request right away. He'd listened to my fears and jumped in to watch over Lacey Jane. His love for my sister warmed my heart, and he'd even sounded concerned about me. That's what family did.

My phone vibrated, and Hannah's name appeared. Good. Maybe she wasn't upset with me. "Hey, what's up?"

"Wade wants to meet me. Like now. Will you go with me?"

"Sure. Where?"

"His place. He suggested we could walk our dogs and talk."

"I'll meet you there." I drove the short distance to the sheriff's house.

Hannah stood in the driveway holding Gus, and I parked behind her.

Wade walked out of his house wearing his hot-weather uniform of khakis and a brown short-sleeve polo shirt. His faithful dog trotted beside him. Once Wade and I made eye contact, the man stopped moving. "Why do I feel like you two are teaming up against me?"

"It's my fault, Wade." Hannah set Gus on the ground.

The little runt and Duke, Wade's black and white rescue dog, sniffed each other.

"Care to explain a little more?" His gaze darted from Hannah to me.

Hannah said, "I need you to eliminate my mother from your suspect list."

"I'm not sharing my list with either one of you. Do you want us to date again so I won't arrest your mom?"

"No, Wade. The reason I broke up with you was to not put you in a bad spot."

"I don't know what to think, Hannah." Wade's nostrils flared. "Protecting your mother is noble. Going behind my back is where we've got a problem. Concealing evidence is even worse."

"I understand." Seconds ticked by with the two of them staring at each other and me watching.

"Why don't I walk the dogs and you two talk?" I took Gus and Duke and left the two of them. Something told me if they were going to work out their issues, it'd happen faster without my interference.

If Hannah convinced Wade her mother was innocent, who would be left on his suspect list? Did he still believe Regina was guilty? What were his thoughts about Chip? Had the jump drive he found at Dirk's house provided any clues?

I really needed to tell him about the index card with notes on the California cold case. He should also be aware of Chip's threat.

I circled the block as slowly as possible. Hannah and Wade needed time to work out their problems, but I didn't want to get too far away in case Chip showed up.

Both dogs sniffed around a stop sign, giving me time to call David.

"This is Deputy Wayne."

"It's Andi Grace. Why don't you have me in your list of contacts?"

"You're there, but the sun's in my eyes. What's up?"

"I need to talk to you and Wade about Dirk's death. Can you meet me at his place?"

"It's my day off, I'm running, and I planned to surprise your sister with dinner from Tony's Pizzeria. Can it wait until tomorrow? Or can you just tell him?"

"Lacey Jane might be in danger."

"I'm on the way." He didn't sound angry, more like resigned.

When we returned to Wade's place, he and Hannah sat on the front porch. Wade met me on the sidewalk and took the leashes. "Thanks."

"You're welcome. I'm sure you'd enjoy a little time alone with Hannah, but David's on his way over."

His shoulders drooped. "Why?"

At the rate I was blocking men from romantic gestures, I'd lose my unofficial title of local matchmaker.

"Andi Grace, what do you need to share?"

"Something happened today, and I want to tell y'all about it. Actually, there are two things I need to tell you. I'm going to text Marc. He's in court now, but he'll want to know too." I pulled the phone out of my pocket and sent him a message. "There."

David joined us wearing shorts and a sweat-wicking shirt. "I'm here. What's the deal?"

I looked both ways to verify Chip wasn't in the area. "I don't mean to sound paranoid, but can we take the conversation inside? You know, somewhere private?"

Wade led us inside to his kitchen table, and Hannah joined us. Three sets of eyes stared at me.

"I'm wondering if Chip Johnson is the killer responsible for Dirk's death. I also believe he could have killed before." I stated my suspicions, including the index card.

David walked to the sink, ripped a paper towel off a roll, wet it, and ran it over his face. "How does Lacey Jane fit into your theory?" He pulled a plastic glass from the cabinet and filled it with tap water.

"A little while ago, I went to Daily Java and got her something to drink."

David's eyes widened. "She's drinking coffee?"

"A strawberry smoothie. Why can't she drink coffee?"

His face reddened. "Oh, uh, we're trying to give up caffeine for the summer. You know, it can lead to dehydration."

"Something doesn't sound right about that." If he tried to brainwash my sister into giving up things she loved, I'd be all over him like white on rice.

David turned on the faucet and refilled his glass with water.

Wade frowned. "Can we get back to the case?"

My thoughts raced. "Okay, so after placing my order for fruit smoothies, I sat at a table to wait for Erin. Chip appeared and sat by me. He said it wasn't smart to help a friend if it put me in danger. Or something like that. Then he mentioned Lacey Jane."

David shut off the tap and drank the water until the glass was empty. "Where's Lacey Jane now? Why aren't you protecting her? We could've come to you instead of meeting here."

"She's at Marc's office with Ike, but I'd feel better if you were watching her too."

"Call and tell her I'm on the way." He pivoted on his toe.

Wade stood and placed a hand on David's chest. "Wait just one second. I'll go over there. Let's try not to alarm anybody. David, you take a shower, get the dinner, and whatever else you'd planned. I'll keep her and Mr. Gage at the law firm. When you arrive, I'll mosey over to the apartment complex and poke around."

David glanced down and tugged on his shirt. "Thanks."

I stood. "I'll drive you home. It'll save time."

Hannah said, "I'll order your dinner and have it delivered to Marc's office."

The four of us skedaddled, intent on accomplishing our missions. The main goal had transitioned from catching the killer to protecting Lacey Jane. However, if Chip was Charlie Jones, he'd already killed two people. One more murder victim on his list wouldn't add much time to his prison sentence. The man had little to lose by going after me or my sister.

Chapter Forty

AFTER DROPPING DAVID AT HIS PLACE, I stopped by my house to check on Sunny. A brief phone conversation with Dylan assured me he had work under control. My stomach growled, and I plucked a banana from a bowl and drove back to Marc's office.

Marc pulled into the parking area behind me. Before we could hug, Ike walked out of the building and joined us. "You people sure know how to call out the calvary."

I crossed my arms. "Yeah, that's what we do around here, especially if it involves family. How'd Lacey Jane take the news?"

"David's kept it low-key so far. The sheriff said he dropped by to speak to Marc. He and I shot the breeze in the waiting room and allowed Lacey Jane to study. David arrived, then Wade got word about a pileup on Highway 17. After Wade took off, Hannah showed up with food from Tony's, which is where we are at the moment. There's enough story spinning in there to make a person dizzy. But the motive is to protect Lacey Jane, so I'm fully on board."

My phone vibrated. "Oh, dear. It's Leroy. Peanut's missing."

Ike cleared his throat. "You should definitely go, but do you need my help?"

"As long as you and David protect Lacey Jane, that's all I need."

"On it." Ike returned to the office.

"I'll drive." Marc opened the passenger door of his Silverado for me and tossed his tie in the backseat. He jogged around the hood, hopped behind the wheel, and gunned the truck. "Piney Woods?"

"Yes." I held on to the console with my left arm as Marc took a curve faster than he normally did.

"What did Leroy say?" Both of Marc's hands clenched the steering wheel.

"Not much. Let me call him." I looked for his name in my contact list and hit the call button. No luck. "He's not answering."

"He could be in the woods looking for Peanut. I doubt he has reception."

"You're probably right." I prayed for Leroy's safety.

Marc slowed when we approached the entrance.

"Wait." I pointed to a bicycle laying abandoned in the grass along the edge of the woods. "It looks like Jeremiah's bike." I lowered my window and leaned out.

Marc shifted into Park and walked to the bike. "If I was a betting man, I'd agree. There's his boom box, a paper sack, and red bandana. I don't want to contaminate the scene if he came to harm."

"Hurry, Marc." My heart hammered against my ribs.

My fiancé hopped back in but studied his phone. "I'm going to drop a pin so we can find this spot if it turns dark before we return."

"Jeremiah warned me to be careful around Chip. What if something happened to him? And what about Leroy and Peanut?" I took a deep breath. "You should've seen Leroy and Frank earlier. They were so happy fishing on your dock. Leroy was convinced he could handle the dog. I mean, he wanted to make it work so bad."

Marc drove onto the property with low-income apartments. "Let's check Leroy's duplex first."

"Man, I wish we had a gun." Wait, I didn't know the first thing about shooting a gun. "Scratch that. I'd probably shoot myself."

"It's going to be okay. We'll keep our eyes open and stay alert." He turned and parked in the grass area beside the duplex.

"There's Leroy's truck, but no sign of Frank's vehicle."

"The door to Leroy's place is wide open."

My feet hit the ground with a thump. "Leroy, where are you?" I darted through the open door. The duplex was neat and organized, but there was no sign of my friend or the beagle.

I returned to the driveway. "Marc, where'd you go?"

My phone vibrated. It was a message from Marc. *Come to the back and try to be quiet.*

Good point. If the older men were in danger, we needed to be cautious. I joined Marc by the grill. There was a patio table, two chairs, and coolers. "Leroy and Frank had planned to clean and grill the fish they caught earlier. Let me give Frank a call."

"Be right back. Don't go anywhere." With stealthy motions, Marc walked to the wooded area bordering Leroy's backyard.

I paced, keeping my eyes open for any sign of Peanut, Leroy, or danger. Frank's phone rolled to voicemail. "Hi, Frank, this is Andi Grace. I'm trying to find Leroy and was wondering if he might be with you. Call me when you get this message. Please. Thanks."

A dog barked in the distance.

I hurried across the small yard and joined Marc in the woods. "Did you hear the barking?"

"Shh, let's see if we can follow the sound." Marc led the way.

I tried to calm my breathing to make it easier to determine which direction to go. Peanut's life—and Leroy's—might depend on us. My ears tingled from the effort to listen.

"Woof. Woof."

I angled right, seeking Peanut.

The dog whined.

I turned on my phone's flashlight app to see better in the shadows. Sunset approached, making visibility challenging. "Peanut, where are you?"

"Woof."

I was closing in on the beagle. There. A flash of white and black. "Marc, I see him."

Marc trampled through the brush, and we reached the dog at the same time.

"Hi, Peanut. Try to stay calm." I dropped to the damp, sandy dirt. "He's tangled up in this honeysuckle bush."

"I'll try to cut some of the branches." Marc removed his key chain and opened the little knife on it. "By the time this is over, we'll all probably be covered with poison ivy, but it'll be worth it to save the little guy."

"Good boy. It's going to be okay. We've got you now." I spoke soothing words over and over while Marc snipped away the vines tangled around Peanut's legs.

Marc paused, breathing hard. "I think this is the last one. Have you got him in case he tries to run off?"

I adjusted my body to securely hold the dog when he was freed. "Yes."

One more snip, then Marc stepped back. "There."

I held the beagle tight, but he didn't fight me. "Poor thing may be exhausted. Let's get him some water in case he's dehydrated too."

"Lead the way."

We trudged through the woods, and I carried Peanut. When we reached Leroy's patio, I set the dog down by the plastic bowl of water.

Peanut lapped it up, and I collapsed in one of the chairs. "He's heavier than you'd think. Now we need to find Leroy."

"And possibly Frank."

"Exactly. Leroy reached out to tell me Peanut was missing. At that point, he was alive and well." I tried calling my friend. "He's still not answering, but I'll text him. Maybe if he's in and out of service, he'll see we found the dog."

Marc raised his hand. "Wait. Try to call him again."

I hit the button to redial his number.

Marc walked away, barely making a sound.

The call rolled to voicemail.

Marc reappeared. "Would you keep calling his number until I tell you to quit? I'm sure I heard a phone's ring tone. I'm going to wander around this area."

"Absolutely."

Peanut followed Marc.

I didn't stop him in case he could sniff out the man. In fact, I trailed a good distance behind the two of them. I called Leroy's number three more times before Marc and Peanut rejoined me near the edge of the woods.

Marc said, "I found the phone but nobody, as in no body."

"That means he may still be alive." I bit my lip. Crying wouldn't find Leroy, so I raced to Chip's patio and pounded on his door.

Marc caught up and reached for my hand, preventing me from beating the door down. "Andi Grace, what're you doing?"

"Looking for my friend. He may be hurt or in trouble at Chip's place."

"Please, don't wander away from me again. We need to stick together." Marc sat in one of the Adirondack chairs. "Give me a minute. I want to see if I can find a clue on this phone."

Peanut stood beside Marc with his ears up and looking around.

I turned my attention to the two homes connected by a wall. No lights came on in Chip's half of the duplex, nor did he answer the door. I refilled the dog's water bowl and touched the doorknob of Chip's back door. It turned in my hand. Chills covered my body but I pushed it open and stepped inside. "Hello, is anybody home? Leroy, are you here?"

Fingers wrapped around my arm, and a hand covered my mouth. Marc had told me to stick with him, but I'd traipsed in here alone. I couldn't scream to warn him about the danger. The desire to faint hit hard, but weakness could lead to death. Maybe even multiple deaths. I needed to find a way to escape if we were going to survive.

Chapter Forty-one

My muffled scream didn't go anywhere.

"Andi Grace, it's me." Marc's voice sent a waterfall of relief through me, and I sagged against him. After taking a deep breath, I turned and threw my arms around his neck. "Shh."

I whispered, "What's wrong?"

"Somebody's behind the azalea bushes near the edge of the trees. I feel like I can sneak around and get the jump on them. I just needed to make sure you were safe. Keep Peanut with you."

My breathing quickened to the point I was afraid of hyperventilating. "Don't go."

Marc placed his hands on my shoulders. "Calm down."

"You said it's better to stick together."

"True, but if something happens to me, I need you to call Wade. I'll be back."

"You better come back."

Marc kissed me before walking out the front door.

I sent a text to the sheriff. *We're at Leroy's duplex. Need backup. ASAP. Please hurry.*

The sound of a scuffle alarmed me. A thud led me to scurry around and look for a weapon. The items in Chip's kitchen were useless. I raced out the front door and into Leroy's place. He fished and cooked, so he must have something I could use for a weapon. There. On the kitchen counter. Leroy's butcher block knife holder. I grabbed the largest knife.

Peanut barked.

"Shh, we've got to help Marc." I raced out the door, through the woods, and toward the sound of the scuffle. My flashlight helped me avoid falling. At last, I reached Marc and a smaller man. Instead of lunging with my knife, I turned the light's beam on him. "Jeremiah! What are you doing?"

Peanut growled.

The man's eyes widened, but he didn't speak.

"It's me, Andi Grace Scott, and that's Marc Williams. My fiancé. You met him earlier." I turned the beam of the light on my face in order for him to identify me. "See?"

Jeremiah dropped his arms. "I thought you were after me."

Marc stepped back. "No, man. Sorry for the scare. We're looking for

Leroy Peck."

"Well, good luck with that." Jeremiah ran a hand over his face. "Did you take time to wonder why your friend's phone is here, amongst the trees? You didn't find it near his truck or his place."

I stepped closer. "Do you know where Leroy is?"

"Yep. I warned you about Chip Johnson. He ran me off the road and took your friend. They're holed up in one of the empty apartment buildings."

"The sheriff should be on his way."

"It won't be soon enough." Jeremiah shook his head. "Saving your friend will be up to us."

"Let me shoot off one more text for help." I sent a message to David and Wade. *Chip has Leroy hostage in one of the apartments. Hurry.*

Marc said, "Do you know exactly which apartment they're in?"

"Sure do. I'll take you there, but the mutt needs to stay back. If he barks, we'll lose the advantage of surprise."

"Makes sense. Let's take him to my pickup then drive to where you tell us. No need to waste energy when it's not necessary."

Counting Peanut, the four of us hurried back to Marc's truck and piled in.

Jeremiah pointed to the road. "Last building on the left. They're getting renovated. Perfect place to hide. Far enough away that ain't nobody gonna hear a person scream." The tone of his voice painted a picture of his glory days. I imagined Jeremiah analyzing war situations and taking action in Operation Desert Storm.

"Park over there." Jeremiah pointed to a shadowy spot. "He'll hear us if we drive too close to the building."

Marc followed the older man's directions, no questions asked. When he drew to a stop, the three of us hopped out without making a sound.

Peanut tried to follow me, but I gave him a treat and closed the door. His nose pressed against the window, and he howled. I shook my finger at the beagle. "Be quiet. I'll be right back."

I backed away from the truck while maintaining eye contact with the dog. He stopped howling and climbed into the front seat. He placed his paws on the dash and looked both ways. The interior light dimmed, then went out.

I joined the men. "We should be good to go. Peanut's keeping watch."

Jeremiah said, "Are you sure the cops know where to find us?"

"Actually, I could be more specific. It'd be terrible for Wade and David to get here and not know where to look." I texted them directions to the exact building we planned to search and also dropped a pin. "Ready."

Jeremiah rubbed his large hands together, making a scratchy sound. "Here's my plan. We're going to circle to the back of the building. It'll be an easier entry because of the scaffolding at the front. If I held a hostage, I'd go for one of the ground-floor apartments. Easier to escape if the situation goes south. The building has four apartments on each of the two floors. Eight total. All of them are being renovated."

At least a dozen questions needed answers, but out of respect I didn't voice any. "You're in charge, Jeremiah."

"I agree." Marc waved for the man to take the lead.

The veteran may have appeared scrawny, but he had never breathed hard on our trek through the woods. We maneuvered in the shadows and under trees until we reached the last building. "I'll run up and try the door. If Chip's smart, he'll be watching for us while planning his next move."

Marc held out his keys. "Use the knife if you need."

Jeremiah nodded and accepted the key ring with a Swiss Army knife. "Stay here unless I wave for you. If the situation goes sideways, get help. No sense in all three of us getting captured."

I circled Jeremiah's wrist with my fingers. "If Chip is who I suspect, he's murdered two people that I know of. There's no need for you to put yourself in harm's way."

"It's what I was trained for." He turned and ran in a crouched position to the back door of the apartment building.

A flicker of light appeared from the bottom left apartment.

Marc pushed me to the ground and lay at my side. "Keep your head down."

I turned and faced him. "We should've given Jeremiah one of our phones. He needs to know."

Jeremiah flattened himself against the building.

Marc whispered, "It looks like he knows how to handle himself."

The beam of a flashlight scanned the grassy area before extinguishing.

I counted to ten in French, never taking my eyes off Jeremiah. If our mission wasn't about saving Leroy, I might have yelled for Jeremiah to run to safety.

At last, the veteran squatted and worked on the door.

"He's the very definition of patience, isn't he?" I pushed back a strand of hair that fell in my face.

"I'd wager patience saved his life more than once. He's a real American hero."

Jeremiah pushed the door open. He waited for what felt like ten minutes but was probably two, then signaled us to join him.

"Be sure to crouch." Marc reached for my hand, and we ran.

Once we joined Jeremiah, the three of us stood with our backs against the wall. Why, I didn't know. Probably to make sure Chip didn't come looking for us, but I trusted Jeremiah's sense of caution. This wasn't the time to get impatient. Leroy's and possibly Frank's lives might depend on our actions.

Finally, the veteran opened the door and went through first. I was second, and Marc brought up the rear.

Light blinded us, and my heart sank. Despite all of our precautions, somebody had caught us.

Chapter Forty-two

"THIS NIGHT KEEPS GETTING BETTER." Chip greeted us from behind the blinding light. "Andi Grace, my gut told me you wouldn't give up. Thanks to you, three men will die tonight."

"If I'm the one you want, please let them go. I'll tell you where I kept my murder notes."

"I'm afraid none of you will survive the night." He turned off the professional dual lights. A work crew had probably used them for remodeling the place. Chip's action threw me off-kilter.

I blinked hard and tried to get my bearings.

Chip grabbed my shirt and held the gun to my head. "Gentlemen, you should take my advice. Don't try to be a hero. Go on into the apartment."

Jeremiah went first. Marc held back. "Let her go. No, let us all go. I promise to defend you."

The killer shoved Marc. "You don't have the time to defend my crimes, and I can't afford you. Go."

Marc stumbled into the empty apartment.

Leroy sat on a bar stool with his hands zip-tied behind his body. Duct tape covered his mouth. Leroy's eyebrows rose, but the rest of his body appeared to shrink.

I said, "Leroy, don't you worry one bit about Peanut. He's safe."

The man closed his eyes.

Jeremiah crossed his arms and spread his feet apart. "Now what?"

"You're in no position to question me, old man." Chip pointed the gun at Jeremiah.

Marc said, "Let's all stay calm. Chip, you don't want the cops to come. We don't want to die. We should be able to resolve this situation to everyone's satisfaction."

The cold gun against the right side of my head had me trying to inch away to the left and away from Chip. "Marc's right. You could bind us all and escape."

"I don't think so." Chip tightened his grip on my arm. "You two. On the floor."

Marc and Jeremiah sat on the chipped tile floor.

"Old man, secure the lawyer's hands." He tossed plastic fasteners to him.

Jeremiah did as commanded. "Now what?"

Chip pointed the gun at him. "Andi Grace will bind you." He pushed me toward the men.

My knee hit the hard floor, but the relief of not having the gun against my head trumped the pain. I took the zip ties and sat beside Jeremiah. "I'm sorry to do this." I used one around his wrists and fastened the other around his ankles.

"Ain't no thing."

"Whatever happens tonight, you're a hero."

"Shut up." Chip yanked my arm, pulling me to my feet.

"Why'd you kill Dirk?"

"He was going public with what happened. I'd kept the secret over twenty years and couldn't let him destroy me."

"What secret?" I forced my body to relax in hopes he wouldn't feel threatened by me. Loose as a goose.

Chip glanced around the room. Like an actor on a stage, he began his story. "Years ago, I had the opportunity to make a lot, and I mean a lot, of money. I didn't think twice about my actions. Unfortunately, Dirk discovered what I'd done, and he planned to reveal my secret to the world."

"How did he learn the truth?"

"One of his talents is to be able to drink most people under the table. I got soused and for some reason told him about my past. It's the biggest regret of my life." He sat on the empty bar stool. "There's a song about regrets. Maybe it was playing in the bar. Who knows why I told him? But I did."

"Was your secret connected to California?"

"Yeah. I worked with a team of men to build an outdoor oasis for a family. While we worked on the project, the wife discovered her husband was having an affair. It was a big project, and she'd been flirting with me for days. She asked me to stay late one afternoon when the others knocked off work. I was surprised but decided to let whatever was about to happen play itself out. Never in my wildest dreams could I have predicted the turn of events. The wife offered me fifty thousand dollars to kill her husband's mistress. The first time she asked, I said no. Then she started crying—well, you get the picture. She wore me down, and I killed the other woman." Chip showed no remorse for his actions. In fact, he'd just stated his biggest regret in life was telling Dirk the truth. The man was a monster.

My knees shook. If I kept him talking, it'd give Wade and David a better chance to rescue us. "How'd you hide the truth so long?"

"Hey, I'm a likeable guy with skills. I traveled all over the country, changing my name and picking up different jobs along the way. You'd be amazed how many people will pay you cash for a job and never report it on their taxes." Chip rubbed his jaw with the hand holding the gun.

Marc and Jeremiah sat on the floor between Chip and the door. Marc moved his head in a circular motion, trying to give me some signal.

With small steps, I inched toward the far wall, hoping it was what he wanted me to do.

Marc's nod was almost imperceptible.

"Chip, if that was twenty years ago, maybe you can get a lenient sentence. You've been running from your past for a long time."

Chip turned the gun on me. "Murder cases don't just go away."

I gulped. "I know, but what if the cops don't have their case files anymore? According to Dirk's notes there were only three suspects, and I believe the other two are dead."

He looked at the ceiling. "It's too much to hope they'd drop the case."

"I bet a really good attorney could get the charges dropped. You've learned your lesson. It doesn't pay to kill a person for money."

"Even if I didn't go to prison for killing Roxy Starr, there's the little matter of Dirk."

I needed to get him back to talking about events in California. "Her name was Roxy Starr? How pretty."

Chip swiveled on the stool, putting his back to the door. "She was beautiful. After she died, I learned she'd moved to California to become a movie star."

I struggled to think up an appropriate response. "How sad."

"Yeah, and you know what the really sad thing is? The woman who hired me had a rock-solid alibi. She was with friends in San Diego the night I killed the girl. Her husband was there too. Ironically, they were attending another couple's anniversary party."

I nodded. "You're right. That's sad."

Using his legs, Marc scooted backward until he reached the far wall then he inched his way up until he stood.

"Why'd you decide to run instead of taking your chances?"

"The cops had questioned me because I made the stupid mistake of meeting the mistress. She liked to work out. I followed her to a popular gym and pretended to be a producer. I didn't imagine she was as wicked as the wife described. Turned out she was. She'd do anything to become a big star."

Cold. Still, she didn't deserve to be murdered.

The sound of an approaching vehicle ended the conversation.

Chip cursed and lunged toward the door. At the sight of Marc on his feet, he cursed again. Chip hit my fiancé in the head with the gun and turned off the lights.

I dropped to the floor and crawled in Marc's direction.

Chip lifted the blackout curtains at the front window. "The cops are coming."

"Marc, are you okay?" Running my hands over his face, I felt dampness. There was a sticky wet spot near his eye.

Marc moaned. "Get Leroy on the floor in case bullets start flying."

I scurried to Leroy and whispered, "We need to get you on the ground."

"Once I'm down, I'll need help getting back up with my trick knee."

"No problem." I wrapped my arm around his shoulder, led him to the wall by Marc, and eased his body to the floor.

Jeremiah bumped into me. "Andi Grace, I've still got Marc's key chain. It's in my shirt pocket."

"Everybody shut up," Chip screamed before ripping down the metallic curtain rod. It hit the tile floor with a crash and echoed in the apartment devoid of furniture.

Vehicles screeched to a stop in front of the building. Blue, white, and red lights flashed in the darkness.

I felt for Jeremiah's shirt pocket and removed the keys. With a click the knife opened, and I cut the plastic ties on each man.

Glass broke, and Chip fired a shot toward the people here to rescue us.

My heart leapt.

Jeremiah whispered, "I think we'll be safer upstairs. We can barricade ourselves in one of the apartments so Chip can't get to us. If we try to make a run for it outside, there's a chance the cops will accidently shoot us. No need to get taken out by friendly fire."

"Good idea. Can you help Leroy? Marc's bleeding but conscious. I'll help him."

"See you up there."

Poor Leroy groaned and wobbled, but the commotion outside masked the sounds. The two men made it out the door without Chip noticing.

Wade's voice came over a megaphone. "This is Sheriff Stone. Chip Johnson, we've got you surrounded. Come out with your hands up."

"I've got hostages, and I won't hesitate to kill them all."

I leaned over Marc and spoke softly in his ear. "Let's sit you up."

He turned onto his side but nothing more.

I lay on the cold floor facing him and wiggled one arm under his body. Now what? How could I leverage his weight and mine off the ground?

Chip yelled, "I want a cabin cruiser waiting at the pier, a million dollars in small bills, and a cooler of water, snacks, and beer."

Wade didn't reply.

Chip banged the gun on the window frame. "You've got one hour. After that, I'll shoot one hostage at a time."

The megaphone squawked. "Release one hostage in good faith. We'll work on finding a boat, but the cash will take more time."

Chip fired his gun toward the sheriff. "Those are my terms."

"We'll do the best we can." Wade kept his voice calm.

I held my phone between my body and Marc's and texted Wade. *Leroy and Jeremiah are upstairs. Marc is hurt. We're in same apartment as Chip.*

Chip stomped across the apartment and yanked me up by the arm. My phone fell and hit Marc's shoulder before slipping onto the floor. "Where are the old men?"

"I don't know, but you injured Marc. Please let him go. He can be your good-faith hostage, and the cops will work harder to meet your demands."

"Not a chance." Chip flipped the light switch, and light flooded the room. He dragged me to the large busted-out window but kept his body shielded by the wall. "Andi Grace will be the first to die. Fifty-seven minutes, man."

Wade answered, "Stay cool. We're working on it. Nobody needs to die tonight."

Chip dragged me back to the door and turned off the lights. "Now, where did the old geezers get to?"

"I don't know."

"You're lying." He punched the door and growled.

I froze in place, unsure what to do or say that wouldn't make the situation worse. Marc was bleeding and could've lost consciousness. The men had escaped upstairs. Help was outside, but Chip was furious and freaking out.

Lord help us. It'd take a miracle to survive.

Chapter Forty-three

CHIP STUFFED THE GUN IN THE WAISTBAND of his pants, then clamped his hand on my shoulder. I tried to shrug away from Dirk's killer, but his viselike force didn't allow me to escape. At least I remained upright, giving me a better shot of escaping if the opportunity presented itself.

He dragged me away from Marc, down the hall, and toward the dark rooms in the back of the apartment. The tightness of Chip's grip would probably leave bruises. One hand on my shoulder, and the other on my wrist. I tried to ignore the pain. When it grew too dark to see from the light of the main room, Chip released my shoulder and pulled a small flashlight from the pocket of his jeans. We entered every room, and he shone the light toward each corner. Both bathrooms, two bedrooms, and the tiny laundry room. No sign of the other hostages.

Chip stomped back to the main room, which was lit only by the street-lights, cop car lights, and the moon. Somehow, I managed to match his pace without tripping.

Chip kicked my phone. It whizzed across the slick floor until it hit the door.

Chills slithered up my spine.

"What do we have here?" He snatched it up with his free hand. "What's your code?"

If he saw my text messages to Wade, Chip would flip. I sealed my lips.

"Andi Grace, I won't hesitate to force it out of you." His hot breath flamed over my face.

I didn't budge. If he discovered the truth, we'd be in more danger than we were in now.

Chip twisted my hand and pressed each finger on the circle near the bottom of the screen. My pointer finger landed on the perfect spot, and the phone came to life.

Text messages appeared, and he shoved me away.

I stumbled sideways. My ribs grazed the kitchen counter, and I planted my hands on the laminated countertop to keep from falling.

Lifting the phone closer to his eyes, Chip shook his head. "Looks like you've been texting the sheriff. Shame, shame, shame. You lied to me." His eyes narrowed to dark slits.

"When?" Yeah, I'd lied in the name of saving our lives.

"The men are hiding upstairs. It says so right here." He stepped back and hurled my phone against the cabinets, and it landed on the laminate.

I tried to get to my cell. Before I reached it, Chip closed the gap between us.

Forgetting the phone, I backed away. Too bad Chip was faster. His fingers circled my throat. The pressure tightened.

I caught a flash of movement in my peripheral vision. Marc stood and placed his hand on the nearest wall, dizzy and trying to steady himself after Chip's attack on him.

I clawed at Chip's hands. When his grip loosened, I gasped for air. "Chip, I'm sorry. They're old, and I felt sorry for them. Don't forget, Leroy's your friend. But you can still count them as hostages."

"You're like a punch in the gut. Everybody thinks you're so nice, but you're one big pain in the rear." He squeezed my throat again.

I reached up and scraped any body part I could with my fingernails. My vision grew fuzzy. I worked to pull Chip's hands off my throat.

Marc moved. If I could only hold on a little longer. I scratched Chip's face and tried to poke his eyes. It was hard to aim while gasping for air. My strength waned, but I attempted to free myself.

Marc plowed into Chip from behind like a linebacker tackling an unsuspecting quarterback.

Chip hit the tile floor. "Umph."

I fell against the wall and gasped for air. Sweet, beautiful air. My vision cleared, but my legs wobbled.

Marc landed on the killer. Two shadows wrestled on the floor.

The gun slid across the floor with a metallic sound.

I ran for the weapon with spaghetti legs. "Wade, help." Would he hear my shaky voice outside? I took a big gulp of air and screamed, "Help."

Marc continued fighting Chip.

With shaky hands, I grabbed the gun.

Men with riot shields jumped through the broken window. Scaffolding clattered in the common hall of the building. A floodlight shone into the room from outside. Three deputies dressed in military vests pulled Marc and Chip apart. When standing, the men panted and glared at each other.

Wade appeared and pointed at Chip. "Arrest him."

The deputies released my fiancé and two other men walked away with Chip in handcuffs, reading him his rights.

Wade gazed at us. "Are y'all okay?"

"Here's the gun." My voice came out a whisper. I held out the weapon with the barrel pointed at the floor and approached the sheriff.

With easy motions, Wade took the revolver from me. "You didn't answer my question. Are you all right, Andi Grace?"

"Yes." I hugged the sheriff. "Thank you so much for rescuing us."

"All in a day's work." He patted my back the way my brother would.

I stepped away and met Wade's gaze. "I need to check on Marc."

"We'll talk soon."

I turned and joined Marc, elbowing Deputy Sawyer out of the way. "Oh, Marc. You saved the day. I was almost Chip's third victim." The words burned my throat, but I was alive.

"You fought back, but we're better together." He kissed me, and Deputy Sawyer scooted to the side.

• • •

Hours later, after we'd given our story to Wade and Marc had been checked out by the paramedics, we found ourselves sitting in my family room.

Marc and I sat on the couch and went over our stories with Wade again. I drank chamomile tea with honey and lemon to help my throat.

Lacey Jane and David pushed two sitting chairs next to each other. They held hands and listened to the details.

The sheriff shook his head. "Let's review one more time before I contact the police in California. I've never experienced anything like this, and I want to be sure of the facts. Chip is Charlie Jones, who murdered a woman in California for money twenty years ago. He's been running ever since. There's also Regina. She dated both Dirk, the victim, and Chip, the killer."

I shivered. There'd been some close calls with Chip. "Right. She was close to both men, but she claims Dirk misled her about his marriage. That's a line she won't cross, or so she says."

Marc nudged me. "You're getting off track. Regina wasn't involved in either murder."

"You're right." I leaned into my fiancé. "Go ahead, Wade."

"I'll send the police our mug shot of Chip and his fingerprints. We'll let them determine if it matches their man."

"Why? He confessed to the California murder. The victim wanted to be a movie star, and her last name was Starr. A woman paid him fifty thousand dollars to kill her husband's mistress."

"Andi Grace, please quit interrupting." Wade ran a hand through his hair. "Roxy Starr is the victim's name. Chip strangled her and Dirk."

Lacey Jane leaned forward. "Don't forget, he strangled Andi Grace."

David said, "It appears to be his MO."

I met my sister's gaze but kept my mouth closed.

Wade continued, "Dirk discovered the truth and planned to expose Chip on the podcast the day he was killed."

I nodded.

Wade covered a few minor details and looked up. "Anything else?"

Marc propped his arms on his thighs. "There's one thing I'm curious about. Did Chip date Regina to find out if she knew about the podcast or was he interested in her?"

I leaned forward. "What about my new dog groomer, Melanie Bradshaw? Remember, she was sitting in her car late one night watching Regina's shop?"

Wade added to his notes. "Regina was one of our first suspects because of the scene at Tuscan Tomato, but we ruled her out. I don't know the deal with Melanie. As far as Chip goes, he could've dated Regina for multiple reasons."

"I plan to question Melanie again, as long as it doesn't hurt your case." I reached for my mug of tea to ease my sore throat.

"I doubt she was spying on Regina for Chip." Wade rubbed his chin. "Although as far-fetched as this case is, it's possible. I'll question the girl."

"Don't let her size fool you. She's tiny, but she can be feisty. She's twenty-four. And she can handle the big dogs, so she's stronger than you'd imagine."

Wade chuckled and stood. "Sounds like I need to take backup."

"It couldn't hurt." I walked him to the door. "Thanks again for coming to our rescue tonight."

"It's my job, but you and Marc seemed to have the situation under control."

"Not by a long shot. Good night, Wade." I locked the door and returned to the family room.

Marc's feet were propped on the coffee table, and he'd closed his eyes. Sunny lay beside him on the couch with her head on his thighs.

I plucked an afghan out of a large wicker basket and covered Marc before grabbing my mug of tea and cozying up next to him.

Lacey Jane was crying, and David rubbed her shoulders.

I pointed at them. "What's going on with you two?"

Marc reached for my hand and sat straighter. "Give them a chance to explain."

"Uh, explain what? How do you know what's going on and I don't?"

"Shh. Give them a chance."

I turned my attention to Lacey Jane. "Well? What's the big secret?"

Chapter Forty-four

"DAVID AND I GOT MARRIED." My sister's eyes shone.

Tears sprang to my eyes. "You what?" My voice croaked.

David leaned forward. "I should've asked for your blessing, but it happened so fast. I'm sorry."

My throat burned. "Did you ask Ike for his blessing?"

David stood. "No. We applied for the marriage license, and I truly meant to speak to you."

Lacey Jane stood next to David. "I'm the one to blame. David really wanted to speak to you, but I worried you'd try to talk us into waiting."

There was no arguing her point. "Why were you in such a hurry?"

My sister's face grew pale. Now that I thought about it, she had looked peaked the last few times I'd seen her. "Are you—"

Marc rubbed his thumb over my knuckles.

Lacey Jane nodded. "I'm pregnant, but I love David with my whole heart."

I didn't understand how they'd fallen in love so fast, but it hadn't taken me long to fall for Marc. I rose to my feet. "Congratulations. I'm happy for you two." I hugged both of them.

Lacey Jane held me tight and whispered, "You're not mad?"

"No, sweetie." I kept any regrets to myself, regrets like wishing she'd talked to me earlier.

Marc stood and swayed.

David reached out and steadied him. "You okay?"

"I'm a tad dizzy, but the medic said to expect that. Maybe I should sit." He returned to his spot on the couch. "Where are you two living?"

Lacey Jane motioned for us to sit. "We're in David's apartment, but it's only one bedroom. We're going to look for a bigger place, but it's also got to be affordable."

David smiled. "Not Piney Woods Apartment Complex though."

Marc elbowed me and raised his eyebrows.

I nodded. "You tell them."

Marc said, "Lacey Jane, we were going to give you my house after we got married. My only request is you allow us to use the fishing dock."

My sister gasped. "Why? I mean, why would you give me your house? Not why do you want to use the dock."

"Marc and I will live here. The plantation is too much for us, and we'll give Nate and Juliet part of it."

Marc ran his hands over his thighs. "If you don't want to live in my house, you can sell it and buy another place. Again, I want the dock. If you sell, we'll adjust the property lines so I can keep the dock and boat shed."

Lacey Jane laughed. "I'm sensing a theme here."

David smiled. "Me, too. The man wants his boat dock."

Marc lifted his hands. "What can I say? I'm a boat man."

My sister dabbed at tears. "I can't believe you're giving us a home."

Marc said, "It's small, but bigger than a one-bedroom apartment. There are plenty of ways to expand it. Griffin can help if that's what you want to do."

David shook Marc's hand and gave me another hug. "Words can't express how thankful we are. I want Lacey Jane to finish her education. Not having a house payment will make it much easier."

We made plans for Lacey Jane and David to go through the house and walk the property. I walked the couple to the door. "You better tell Nate about the marriage. Sooner rather than later. And Ike needs to know."

"My last final is in the morning, so I'll tell them both tomorrow."

"We need to plan a reception for you two, but we can discuss it later. Y'all have a good night." I hugged them again and waved when they drove off.

When I returned to the family room, Marc was stretched out on the couch. I covered him with the afghan and settled into an easy chair.

Marc and I had assisted in catching another killer, and we'd survived another close call. I was still curious about Melanie, but the mystery of her could wait.

My eyes grew heavy.

No more catching killers for me. I had a wedding to plan, and our family would have a new baby soon.

Marc's gentle breathing shifted into a light snore, and I smiled. Life with Marc would be my greatest adventure.

Chapter Forty-five

THE NEXT MORNING, Lacey Jane, David, Ike, Nate, and Juliet showed up at my door with a coffee cake. Juliet had hired Kylie to be in charge of the bed-and-breakfast so she could join my posse in an intervention.

Knowing it wouldn't be a quick conversation, I stepped outside with Sunny and called Dylan.

"Hey, boss. What's happening?"

"Morning, Dylan. Can I text you my morning schedule? The gang's all here to confront me about Dirk's death."

"I'll handle it. Say, the sheriff showed up asking to speak to Melanie. Do you know anything about it?"

"I really can't say." Not a lie because I couldn't comment.

"Yeah, yeah, yeah. You know, but you can't tell me."

I laughed. "Exactly. Let me know if they take her away in handcuffs though."

Dylan's inhale came over the line. "Is that a possibility?"

"I doubt it, but just in case, I'd like to know."

"Yes, ma'am."

"Thanks. I'm going to text you my schedule now." We ended the call, and I sent Dylan what he needed. Sunny returned and looked up at me. "I hear you. No more stalling. Time to face the music."

We entered my house, and all conversation ceased.

I lifted my hands in surrender. "Is there any chance Marc got y'all up to speed."

Marc's wide-eyed gaze met mine. "It appears that we're both in hot water, so I waited for you."

I met Lacey Jane's gaze and quirked an eyebrow. Had she announced her marriage and pregnancy?

My sister shook her head.

I sat beside Marc at the large table. "Lacey Jane and David heard most of this last night, so we'll try to be concise."

David said, "I don't mind if you want to start from the beginning."

"I think you all know it began last Thursday night at Tuscan Tomato." I launched into the story of Dirk's murder. Marc added some of his thoughts, and together we shared everything we knew about Chip and the killings. "To sum it up, Chip killed a woman in California and ran. For twenty years he kept his identity a secret. Then after a night of drinking, his secret came out. When Dirk discovered the truth, he wanted to reveal it on the podcast. Chip killed Dirk in an effort to protect his deadly secret."

Nate shook his head. "Sis, you can't keep putting yourself at risk. You've got to quit solving murders."

I pointed at him. "Don't forget you're one of the people I proved was innocent."

"Yeah, but I didn't want you to get involved then either." He leaned back and crossed his arms.

Ike said, "I love how you kids stick together. I also know Andi Grace's first concern yesterday was for Lacey Jane's safety. David and I took care of her. Why don't we just all be thankful we're sitting here this fine morning? I know how much I appreciate you welcoming me to the family."

My sister patted his hand. "You are family."

The marine pursed his lips and stared at his coffee.

My mouth dried up. I wasn't sure how Ike would take what I was about to say, but if nothing else, it would show my acceptance of him into the family. "Lacey Jane's right, and I have another request for you, Ike."

He looked up. "Name it."

So far, so good. My hands grew clammy, and my face heated. This was ridiculous. He wouldn't agree. The man was Lacey Jane's family. No, we'd just said he was our family. "Would you consider, and uh, there's no pressure, but I'd be honored to have you walk me down the aisle."

"Yes." He didn't hesitate to answer, but his voice croaked. "It'll be my privilege to walk you down the aisle at your wedding."

Tears filled my eyes, and I walked over and hugged the man.

Lacey Jane wrapped her arms around both of us. "I'm so happy."

Ike patted our backs. "I've actually got a little announcement."

"What is it?" Lacey Jane's eyes sparkled.

I returned to my seat and held Marc's hand.

"My offer to buy HOSE was officially accepted. I'm considering turning it into a general store with the ability to rent bikes. I've also found a place to live."

"Where? Will you be close to me?" Lacey Jane leaned forward.

"No, but there's an extra bedroom if you want to stay with me. I hope to move in next month. There's a little cottage on the same property as the business. It's a mess, and it's small, but it will be livable once I finish working on it."

I stared at my sister. She was about to move. There was no way Ike could know if they'd be close to each other.

David cleared his throat. "Sir, I can round up some of my friends. We'll help."

Juliet nodded. "I can provide food for you and the crew. Oh my stars, Griffin can pitch in too. Once you get the place cleared out, he can handle any remodeling plans."

"I'm staying in a long-term hotel rental and can extend it." He shrugged. "It'll be worth it to have a nicer home."

"It sounds like you've put a lot of thought into your future." I stared at my sister. "Anything you want to add?"

She stood and placed her hands on her belly. "I'm not quite sure how to announce this. Maybe blurting it out is the best way, like pulling a bandage off quickly."

David joined my sister and slid his arm around her shoulders.

Their eyes met, and the difference in my sister was immediately visible. Her shoulders relaxed, and she smiled. "We're married, and we're going to have a baby."

Pandemonium broke out for the next few minutes. Laughter filled the room, and I leaned into Marc. "Isn't it wonderful? Not long ago, it was just Nate, Lacey Jane, and me. Now we've got a room full of family and love."

He kissed my temple. "I can't wait until we're married. Don't suppose you want to elope too?"

"No, we've got a honeymoon to plan."

"I like the sound of our honeymoon in a cozy cabin in Maine." He gave me a slow, lingering kiss, and I almost reconsidered his suggestion to elope.

Lacey Jane squealed. "Look at the time. My political science final is in forty-five minutes. I'll see y'all later." She hightailed it out of my house, bringing an end to the conversation. The others left soon after her.

Marc lingered on the front porch. "Your request of Ike surprised me."

I shrugged. "It seemed like the perfect way to make him feel like part of the family. When Dad died, it grieved me he'd never be able to walk me down the aisle. Lacey Jane worries about being disloyal to Dad by loving Ike. Including him in our wedding seemed perfect. Do you mind?"

"No, as an orphan I believe the more family the better." He kissed me. "I need to pick up Chubb from Stay and Play. It seems like a great afternoon to work from home. See you tonight?"

"How about I go with you? I need to check things out."

"Sounds good, but what exactly do you mean? Did you miss the point of this morning's intervention?"

I ignored his question. "There's still something about Melanie that's not adding up."

"Let's roll." Marc got Sunny and Peanut settled in the back of his truck, and I gathered my cross-body bag and tattered backpack full of work notes and schedules.

In less than an hour I sat in the dog barn office, waiting for Melanie to appear. She'd been a good employee so far. Before she continued working for me, though, I needed to clear up the mystery she was hiding. If I'd learned nothing else from my experience with Chip, it was that secrets could be deadly.

Chapter Forty-six

WHILE WAITING ON MELANIE, my phone rang. Zarina's name appeared. "Hello."

"Andi Grace, the pictures look amazing. I sent the announcements you wrote and the photographs to the *Tide News*, the *Coastal Observer*, and the *Post and Courier* in Charleston."

"Thanks so much, Zarina. Text me the exact amount I owe you."

"Sure thing, and Andi Grace, what about the wedding? Did you pick a date?"

"October seventeenth. Can we schedule you for the night before and the entire day of my wedding?"

A shadow crossed my desk, and I looked up. Melanie had walked into my office and I pointed to the chair. She sat quietly.

Zarina said, "Perfect. I'm adding you to my calendar now."

"Thanks. Let's discuss it more later." I hung up then looked at my dog groomer. "Melanie, thanks for coming by."

"Is there a problem?"

"You tell me." I counted to ten in French to calm my nerves. I didn't want my tone to sound accusatory, but I needed an answer. "Why are you so interested in Regina Houp?"

Melanie adjusted her glasses. "I think she might be my birth mother."

Not the answer I'd expected. "Oh, okay. Then I suggest you quit spying on her and just ask. Do you want me to help?"

Her eyes widened. "You're right. I need to ask. It's better to know than keep agonizing about the possibility. Can I have the rest of the day off?"

"If you're going to see Regina, then I'll be happy to take over your appointments."

"Okay, then. I guess I should go." She gripped the chair arms but didn't move.

"Don't feel like I'm forcing you, but knowing the truth will make life easier."

Melanie stood. "I feel like a person walking the gangplank, but part of me is dying to know."

"You'll be fine. If you need to talk later, I'm here for you."

"Thanks." With slow steps, Melanie left my office, and I sank back into my chair. The idea of warning Regina flitted through my mind, but it didn't seem fair to Melanie.

No, I'd mind my own business and check my schedule for the rest of the day.

I lost myself in the joy of working with animals. I juggled my time between playing and grooming. Heinz was my last client of the day. He'd had his bath, nails clipped, and I was down to scissor-cutting the hair around his face. The little thing feared electric clippers near his face, and who could blame him?

Melanie appeared and plopped onto a stool. "Regina's never been pregnant. I'm not hers. I'm not really anybody's daughter."

I held out a treat to Heinz. "That doesn't mean there aren't people who care about you. My fiancé lost his parents when he was six. He bounced around from one foster home to the next. It wasn't easy for him, and I don't know your life story, but your past doesn't have to define your future."

"Easy for you to say."

I brushed Heinz, and Melanie approached and took the brush from my hand. "This is Heinz, right?"

"Yes, and I think you groomed his sister earlier this week. Chole."

"I remember her. Heinz probably weights four or five pounds more than she does. Do they ever get to play together?" Melanie checked his ears, reached for a cotton ball and rubbed them.

"Yeah, their owners are friends." I watched her gentle touch with the Westie. "Will you stay here now that you know Regina's not your mother?"

"She was my last lead, but I won't bore you with the details. Will you keep me on staff?"

"You're good with the animals, and I'd like for you to stay."

"Then that's what I'll do. Thanks, Andi Grace." She shooed me with her fingers. "I've got this."

"Peanut is napping in back. If you have time, he could use some loving. He had a rough night."

"Sure thing."

Time with pets could be the best therapy for Melanie, so I left her in charge. "Sunny, come with me." I opened the gate to the play area, and she met me. "Let's go see Marc and Chubb."

We walked the path along the Waccamaw River.

I heard Chubb's bark before I spotted the golden retriever.

Sunny barked a greeting, and the two dogs met in the field chasing after each other.

Marc and Lincoln appeared farther down the trail, and I joined them.

"Lincoln, it's good to see you."

He gave me a big bear hug. "Marc's been catching me up on you. Girl, you gotta be more careful."

My breathing hitched. Lincoln was right. This time Marc had gotten hurt. It could've been so much worse. "I'll be more careful next time."

Marc burst out laughing. "As much as I hope there's no next time, if Heyward Beach has another murder case, you'll probably be right in the middle of the investigation."

I shrugged. "Let's talk about you two. How's your case going, Lincoln?"

"Ongoing. I'm heading back to Georgia. My family needs me, and Marc can handle the tabloids from here."

"It sounds like things are better in your personal life. I'm happy for you, Lincoln."

"We're taking a step in the right direction. I'm cutting back on touring, to spend more time with the family. Hopefully that'll help."

Marc patted Lincoln's shoulder. "I'm sure it will."

The dogs ran a circle around us before heading to Marc's place.

Marc said, "Come back to the house with us, Andi Grace."

Lincoln walked between us on the way to his truck. "I'll be working on your wedding song. I took lots of notes. Can't wait for you to meet my wife, Andi Grace." He reached for the door handle of his blue truck.

Marc slapped his back. "You be careful."

He laughed. "You two are the ones who need to be careful. Love ya, man."

The men hugged, then Lincoln embraced me. "Take care of my friend."

I nodded. "You bet."

He hopped in the truck and took off, leaving a cloud of dust in his wake.

The dogs drank from a large water bowl on Marc's front porch.

"Are you going to miss your home?"

Marc shook his head. "You, Andi Grace, are my home. That's just a house."

"Aw, man, you're going to make me cry." I pressed my lips together for a moment. "Again."

"As long as they're happy tears, you can cry anytime."

I kissed him. "It's getting late. Would you like to join me for a little adventure? It'll be safe."

"Safe? You're talking my language."

Chapter Forty-seven

IT WAS DARK AND WINDY, and Marc and I were about the only people on the beach. We stood between the pier and Cutter's Landing. "This is Jeremiah's favorite spot for finding treasure."

Marc pulled two rolls of quarters from his khaki shorts. "One for each of us?"

"Yes. Jeremiah said he likes to stay above the towel line." I took one roll and opened it. "Let's try not to be too obvious. Spread them between here and the parking lot."

Marc tossed the coins up like a kid feeding seagulls. They fell to the beach in a haphazard pattern. "Do you want me to cover them with sand?"

"Sure, but let's not bury them too deep. I don't know how effective his machine is." It didn't take us long to accomplish our task, then we walked to my house.

"Do you want to meet at the pier for an early breakfast?"

"Yes, but I don't want Jeremiah to suspect we had anything to do with his treasure. So, no."

"It's always fun to share joy with others. We can be discreet." We turned onto my street. Juliet, Nate and Griffin were sitting in the chairs on my front porch. "Wonder what's going on? If it's not bad news, it could be a good opportunity to tell Juliet and Nate we're giving them the B and B."

"Good idea." I picked up my pace, and we joined the others. "What are y'all doing?"

Nate said, "Griffin's in town for a few days, and we got to talking about his future."

Griffin stood and motioned for me to sit in the black rocking chair he'd vacated. "I spoke to Ike, and we've come up with a plan for me to work on his cottage. I'm also considering applying to manage Piney Woods Apartment Complex, at least for a year. It'll give me time to oversee renovations. They need to be done right, and it's a project I'd love to tackle. Marc, I heard you're giving up your home. I can move into Chip's unit."

"Sounds good. I didn't want to leave you homeless."

I sat in the chair and rocked. "Dylan would like to work some projects with you."

Griffin nodded. "I'll be happy to have him on my payroll."

Marc leaned against a white column. "Nate and Juliet, have you two picked a wedding date?"

Juliet beamed. "October seventeenth."

I gasped. "We picked the same day."

Juliet clapped. "Double wedding? I won't take any reservations at the B and B that weekend, if it's okay with you."

"Now that you mention it, Marc and I have decided to give you the main house and some of the property. I want to keep the dog barn, but we can go into specifics later."

Nate dropped his head. "I don't know what to say."

I reached for his hand. "We've always looked out for each other. I don't need the land except for the barn."

Juliet said, "I thought you were considering some of the property for a dog shelter."

"Details can be worked out later. What do you say?"

Juliet and Nate looked at each other and broke out into big smiles.

I held my breath, hoping Nate's pride wouldn't hamper Juliet's dream. "Well?"

Nate turned to me. "Thanks, Andi Grace. We appreciate your generosity. You too, Marc."

"It's our pleasure." Marc winked at me.

I hopped up and wrapped my arms around Marc. He'd be busy taking care of Lincoln's legal battles and drawing up paperwork for gifting my siblings. His generosity never ceased to amaze me. Agreeing to marry Marc was the smartest decision I'd ever made. I knew he'd have my back whether it was in dealing with family, dogs, or solving murders. Not that I *planned* to stumble across another dead body. At least not anytime soon.

About the Author

Former Kentuckian Jackie Layton loves her new life in the Low Country. She enjoys time on the beach, despite one vacation that ended with cracked ribs from riding her boogie board with the kids and another trip that ended with a fish hook in her foot and a trip to the emergency room. There's nothing like time at the beach, although she tends to be a bit more cautious these days. Jackie is the author of four Low Country Dog Walker Mysteries, including *Bite the Dust*, *Dog-Gone Dead*, *Bag of Bones*, and *Caught and Collared*.

CPSIA information can be obtained
at www.ICGtesting.com
Printed in the USA
LVHW102026220223
740161LV00004B/396

9 781958 384565